Mirror, Mirror, Fatal Mirror

Mirror, Mirror, Fatal Mirror

AN
ANTHOLOGY OF MYSTERY STORIES
by the
MYSTERY WRITERS OF AMERICA

edited by HANS STEFAN SANTESSON

PUBLISHED FOR THE CRIME CLUB BY

DOUBLEDAY & COMPANY, INC.

GARDEN CITY, NEW YORK

1973

ISBN: 0-385-05073-9
Library of Congress Catalog Card Number 73–81986
Copyright © 1973 by Mystery Writers of America
All Rights Reserved
Printed in the United States of America
First Edition

ACKNOWLEDGMENTS

"The Gun Next Door" by Michael Avallone. Originally published in the September issue of MIKE SHAYNE MYSTERY MAGAZINE. Copyright © 1964 by Renown Publications, Inc. Reprinted by permission of the author and the author's agent, Jay Garon.

"Untouchable" by Robert Bloch. Originally published in the March 1962 issue of THE SAINT MYSTERY MAGAZINE. Copyright © 1962 by Fiction Publishing Company. Reprinted by permission of the author.

"Chinatown Evening" by Stephen Bond. Originally published in the September 1967 issue of THE SAINT MAGAZINE. Copyright © 1967 by Fiction Publishing Company. Reprinted by permission of the author.

"The Scar" by Wenzell Brown. Originally published in the April 1964 issue of THE SAINT MYSTERY MAGAZINE under the byline of Guy Tolman. Copyright © 1964 by Fiction Publishing Company. Reprinted by permission of the author.

"The Weaker Vessel" by James Cross. An original story. Published by permission of the author.

"Lost Generation" by Dorothy Salisbury Davis. Originally published in the September 1971 issue of ELLERY QUEEN'S MYSTERY MAGAZINE. Copyright © 1971 by Dorothy Salisbury Davis. Reprinted by permission of the author and by arrangement with EQMM.

"The Moment of Time" by Miriam Allen deFord. An original story. Published by permission of the author.

"Black Belt" by Richard Deming. Originally published in the November 1972 issue of ALFRED HITCHCOCK'S MYSTERY MAGAZINE. Copyright © 1972 by H.S.D. Publications, Inc. Reprinted by permission of the author and H.S.D. Publications, Inc.

"The Question" by Stanley Ellin. Originally published under the title, "The Question My Son Asked," in the November 1962 issue of ELLERY QUEEN'S MYSTERY MAGAZINE. Copyright © 1964 by Stanley Ellin in BLESSINGTON METHOD AND OTHER STRANGE TALES, published by Random House in 1964. Reprinted by permission of the author.

"Watch for It" by Joseph N. Gores. An original story. Published by permission of the author.

"Murder In Eden" by Morris Hershman. Originally published in ARGOSY for July 1971. Copyright © 1971 by Popular Publications, Inc. Reprinted by permission of the author.

CONTENTS

INTRODUCTION

The original call for stories for this anthology pointed out that much of the material in our field echoes the complexities of our times fully as much as the stories of the Victorian novelists, often written under similar stress conditions, likewise were mirrors of their complex times.

What we aimed for was an anthology which could be said to echo the passions and the problems, the fears and the hopes, the violence and the despair, which in part make up the fabric of our days. Without necessarily making the concessions to the voyeurism of these days which the so-called mainstream novel is so often guilty of, we have tried to bring you a group of stories reflecting both the fear in our streets and the breakdown in public and private morality which we all talk about, and the co-existent dreams and laughter and hope for the future found, not only among our young in heart but also among those who've not entirely withdrawn from the outside world.

While not forgetting the primary entertainment purpose of story telling we've therefore not been concerned with the never-never land of pure escapism, tenanted largely by yesterday's sexually indestructible private eyes, by now promoted to International Agent, with whom so many, withdrawing into their private dream worlds, can identify. We have instead brought you stories in these pages which their authors felt *could* be said to mirror our times.

These can, with some justice, be termed fatal mirrors, in keeping with these days in which it is at times difficult to be hopeful about the world we are leaving to our children. The seeds we've sown have already come to bloom, and in a generation that has yet to know lasting peace, it thus behooves us to take a long hard look at ourselves and to wonder what the world will be like in the days after Tomorrow.

I chaired a panel recently on what that world of the twenty-first century—and later—might be like. Perhaps a copy of this book will survive until then, for the edification of that generation's social historians who will want to know to what extent we had advanced since the days of Sue and Dickens.

And for that matter of Hogarth . . .

HANS STEFAN SANTESSON

THE GUN NEXT DOOR

by Michael Avallone

Suburbia lives with the knowledge that, to a split-level housewife, a prowler can be a nightmare kind of menace—or worse . . .

On that fatal day, Joan Wilkins had said: "I'm telling you, there's a prowler in the neighborhood and I aim to get me a gun."

I knew she wasn't kidding. She talked like that because she was from the far west, had three growing sons and her husband worked all day.

My wife looked at me across the breakfast table and winked. "Come on, now," Nan said. "It can't be that bad."

"It is," Joan said vehemently, pushing red curls away from her freckled face. "For two nights now I've been hearing rattling at the front door. I turn the lights on and the noise stops. And just last night, I saw this man running away."

I checked my watch, swallowing coffee in the process. I had just barely enough time to catch the bus into the city.

"Why don't you call the police, Joan?" I asked. "As small a community as Crestville is, there's a good chance they have at least a sheriff's office."

I didn't know for sure. Nan and I had just taken the gamble, buying a seven-room, split-level home in the wilds of New Jersey. "If you report the prowler, and there is one, and he sees policemen snooping around, it's bound to scare him off."

"You'll be late, Pete," Nan said, nodding her head at me to tell me she'd calm Joan down. Joan was noisy, outspoken and dropped in on us more than three times a day. But I was glad for Nan's sake, and we both liked her.

"All the same," I heard her say as I walked through the front door into a cold morning, "I'm going to ask Robert to buy me a gun. With him working overtime at the factory four nights a week and the boys sleeping, I just can't sit around with some strange man peeking into all of my windows."

Funny thing. That last line of hers stayed with me all the way along the long bus ride down the Turnpike into New York. It even kept me from concentrating on the *Times* crossword puzzle.

I got home at ten o'clock that night. Nan was waiting up for me, watching the Garry Moore show. The house was dark and peaceful, save for the glow and hum of the TV. I hung up my coat and Nan stirred, a smile creasing her lovely face.

"Liz sleeping?" I asked.

"Like a good girl. Your daughter gets better and better every day. Know what she said this morning? You'll never guess. She actually—"

Liz was barely two, but like all parents from Siam to Seattle we found a lot of wonder in her.

But before Nan could tell me what Liz had said I interposed another question. "What happened with Joan and her prowler?"

Nan sighed. "You'll laugh."

"Why?"

"She bought a gun today."

I shrugged. "Maybe it's not too bad an idea. But she should have called the cops."

"Try telling anybody from the cowboy belt what to do. Robert's working overtime again tonight. She's plenty scared. And that's all there is to it."

I blinked at the TV. Alan King was doing a stand-up monologue on homeowners again—his favorite specialty routine. But Nan never seems to tire of it.

"There must be some Calamity Jane in our red-headed neighbor," I said. "She's not too scared to make up her mind about protecting herself. A gun, huh? Did she show it to you?"

"She did."

"Well?"

Nan shuddered. "A forty-five Army gun. I never realized they were so big."

I laughed. "They are, honeybunch. Dangerous too. They can blow a hole as big as a barn in a man."

"Pete, stop."

"Well, they have been known to do just that."

"That's not the point," Nan said, "it isn't right for her to have a gun around the house with three growing boys all over the place. You know how wild those kids can be. They're regular *Indians*."

"It's none of our business," I said, which closed the discussion the easiest way. "Don't forget to turn the heat down. I'm going up to bed. It was a helluva day again. The usual."

But it was our business. And became such around a quarter to midnight.

The gunshot when it came jerked me upright in bed. The blast was still reverberating off the bedroom walls and I didn't need to be reminded that the Wilkins' house was just behind ours, a scant ten yards separating their carport from our southern wall. Nan moaned, startled wide awake.

"Oh, Pete, for the love of God—"

"Easy! I'll run out and—"

The next sound, the one that froze the words in my throat, was the most godawful scream I'd ever heard in my life.

"Oh, my lord!" Joan Wilkins' scream rose shrilly in the night. "*Robert*—"

CRESTVILLE had a police force all right. A half hour later our kitchen over-ran with them. Joan was on our living room sofa, hanging onto Nan for dear life, her eyes washed out with sorrow, her body shivering in a faded brown bathrobe. Her freckled hands were two knots of despair.

I made some coffee for the Crestville cops while lights blazed all over Farmdale Drive and the nosy neighbors peered from their curtained windows. The ambulance, with winking red light, had long since raced toward the Crestville Hospital. But it was too late. Much too late.

The details were simple and awful.

Joan had dreamed badly, propped up on the divan in the rumpus room and Robert had come home late, unfortunately a little tipsy from stopping to have a few with the boys. He'd had difficulty with the lock on the front door, and been too confused to recognize Joan's terrified voice. She had been too wrapped up in her nightmare about prowlers to think straight. I could still see the splintered panel of the front door, where Joan's one and only shot had shattered the wood, driving a forty-five calibre slug into Robert's chest.

I'd found him a good five feet from the door, flat on his back on the pathway, his eyes wide and glazed.

"Joan, please," Nan was saying. "You've got to pull yourself together."

"My boys, my boys—what am I going to tell my boys?" she moaned.

"They'll understand. It was an accident."

"Oh Nan. Do you really think they will?"

One of the Crestville cops motioned me into the kitchen. He was a tall, thin man with a florid face and understanding eyes.

"You know these people well, Mr. Slocum?"

"We've only been here two months, but they got along—if that's what you mean," I said.

He nodded. "No trouble at all?"

"Not as far as I could see. They came here to live, buy a house and raise a family."

"You know this Robert Wilkins?"

"Yes. He was always friendly. A good family man. He worked his head off, from what I could see."

"Hmmm." The tall man made a face. "Damn things. They happen too often. But they happen. People just don't know how to handle guns, do they?"

"I guess not," I said. "You taking her in?"

He frowned. "What for? No jail is ever going to make her feel worse than she does right now. But they'll be having an inquest, of course."

"Tough on her. There's the three kids—"

He scowled. "She had no call buying a gun, if she was going to be so careless with it."

Later, when they had gone, and Nan had done what she could to get Joan and the three kids settled down until morning, we talked about it in the bedroom. Sleep was out of the question for us. How can you readjust when the family next door has just disintegrated with one fatal shot?

"Pete?"

"Yeah."

"You think it was an accident, don't you?"

I looked at my wife. "That's a pretty crazy question, Nan."

"I know. I'm sorry. But—"

"But what?"

"Women talk a lot about things to each other and I never mentioned this to you. But Joan and Robert haven't been exactly lovey-dovey lately. Not according to her and there is a heavy life insurance policy—"

"Nan." I kissed her. "Go to sleep. You've seen too much bad TV lately. That hillbilly could no more plot a murder than the man in the moon. Go to sleep now. I'll go down and make sure everything is locked up."

"Well—"

"Sleep now. That's an order."

I padded downstairs to check the doors and windows. Darkness, undiminished by a full moon, covered the back yard. I could see the

Wilkins' house looming like a square monster in the gloom. I was surprised nearly out of my wits to see Joan motioning to me from the living room window. I found her waiting outside, shivering in her wrapper in the darkness.

"Pete," she cried. "Do you think they know—?"

"You go to bed," I whispered back fiercely. "We shouldn't be seen talking together."

UNTOUCHABLE

by Robert Bloch

There were several reactions to this story, within days of its appearance. Most people reacted to words—to a word, rather—and few saw it as a rather wicked portrait of a type known to all too many abroad, and the story of what happens to him . . .

Race was bored with India.

"Nothing moves here, you know?" he griped. "Where's all the action?"

He gave everybody a hard time on location, and finally Simon took him on. Simon had always been able to handle him, and maybe that's why he was directing the picture; a lot of people just wouldn't work on a Race Harmon production any more.

"Look, sweetheart," he said. "I know it's been a drag. First the heat, then the rains, and then everybody coming down with the trots. Miller called me last night about the budget figures—the way he screamed, I could have heard him loud and clear from Bel Air without a phone."

"Let him suffer," Race muttered, then took a gulp of his drink. "I should bleed for him, shacked up in that air-conditioned office with the blonde throw-rug and a chick to match? Why doesn't he get off his butt and fly over here? We'll see how he likes being cooped up with a bunch of dumb niggers—"

"Please!" Simon frowned. "That's one of the things I wanted to warn you about. They're *not* niggers. Why, some of those technical people we hired out of the studios down in Bombay could run rings around any crew in Hollywood. The trouble is, they hear you talking on the set and they resent your attitude. Just remember, you're not home now."

"You can say that again! Where I come from, we call a spade a spade, whether he wears shoes or not. And that's the way it's gonna be, so kindly lay off the jazz, huh?"

Race poured himself another drink.

"Another thing," Simon said. "Aren't you hitting the sauce a little hard lately?"

"Got to get my kicks somewhere, Pops. This is a nothing unit here, you know? When we came out, I thought I had it made with Gladys, only she's got eyes for that Method swish, that Parker. So I gave a little play to this script-girl of yours, Edna what's-her-name—"

"Messy." Simon sighed. "You didn't have to break into her trailer."

"All right, she made a federal case out of it." Race emptied his glass and thumped it down. "What am I supposed to do for some action? I'm hurting bad."

"Control yourself. We'll wrap up our location shots and be out of here in two weeks."

"Two weeks? Look, Dad, this is Race Harmon you're talking to, not Barry Fitzgerald. I may have to make the scene with some of that dark meat. Noticed all these chicks in the sarongs, or *saris*, whatever you call 'em, parading down by the river. Why I spotted one yesterday, she couldn't be a day over fifteen, but she had a pair of—"

"Race, that's murder!" Simon shook his head. "I saw you talking to that girl, and so did everyone else. You're lucky you left it at that —one false move and there'd have been a riot. I only hope they didn't hear about it up at the palace."

"So what?"

"Can't you understand? These people are *not* ignorant savages. You've met the Maharajah; he's an intelligent man. If you want me to lay it on the line, I think he's a damned sight more civilized than you are."

"He's a nigger."

"Well, you'd better not make any such statements tonight," Simon said. "Don't forget, we're invited to the palace for dinner."

"I'll eat here."

"You'll come to the palace." Simon's voice was firm. "It's important, Race. We're guests here in the Maharajah's territory. We've rented his land, hired his people. We can't afford to offend him. I want you to show up sober and on your best behavior. Is that clear?"

"I dig you, Pops." Race waved his glass. "Okle-dokle, it's a take. Who knows? Maybe he'll give us a little of that old Southern hospitality—"

His Highness' hospitality was lavish and unmistakable. There were twenty at table, including Race, Simon, and the principals of the cast. The only representative of the household was a bearded Sikh introduced as his major-domo.

"Actually, Singh commanded the palace guard," the ruler explained. "But since I am no longer the official ruler of this territory, he too has been deposed. We have bowed to progress, or at least, to governmental decree."

"They took away your title, huh?" Race paused and emptied his champagne-glass for the fourth time since starting dinner. "I suppose they got to your harem, too."

"Harem? But I am not a Moslem, my dear fellow."

The Maharajah was plump, middle-aged, bespectacled, and he wore a conservative grey tweed suit. But his complexion was unmistakably swarthy, and people with unmistakably swarthy complexions didn't go around calling Race Harmon "my dear fellow". Even if they *did* serve damned good champagne.

"Come off it!" he said, holding out his glass for a re-fill. "Everybody knows you rajahs have a ball. I'll bet the joint is full of—whaddya call 'em?—concubines. Yeah, concubines. That's the bit."

"Sorry. I'm afraid I can't oblige you, Mr. Harmon."

"Never mind the double-talk," Race told him. "Bring on the dancing-girls!"

"Devadasi? But they are confined to their temples."

"So take me to your temple!" Race laughed, then broke off as he realized none of the others were joining in.

Their host stared at an imaginary spot on the table-linen before him. "Perhaps it would be wise, Mr. Harmon, if I explained the customs of my country. Nonbelievers are not welcomed in our places of worship. There is a certain—prejudice, shall we say? You see, there is still ignorance amongst my people. They even resent the notion of a stranger making approaches to an untouchable such as the water-carriers in the village. It would be most embarrassing if an outsider were to exhibit any—any—"

"So you heard about that, eh?" Race waved his glass. "I get the message. Hands off, is that it? Yankee, go home!"

"Please, Mr. Harmon—"

"Never mind. You heard about old Race, huh? That's why you locked up the harem."

"I assure you, I have only one wife. At the moment she happens to be in Chandigarh."

Race grinned. "Sure, sure! Well let me tell you something. Nobody upstages me. And if I want a little poontang, I'm gonna get it, understand?"

"Poontang?"

"What's the matter, don't you niggers understand plain English?" Race stood up, ignoring Simon's frantic gestures. "Ah, forget it. Where's the head?"

The Maharajah glanced at his major-domo. Race watched them,

fuzzily alert for any indication of anger. That's what he was waiting for; just let the nigger blow his top and he'd *really* let him have
it.

But there was no anger, merely a quiet exchange of glances and a
nod. Then the bearded Sikh rose and gestured politely, and Race
followed him out of the room and down a long, dim corridor.

For a moment there was silence in the dining-hall behind; then
everybody started talking at the same time.

Covering up, Race thought. *The civilized bit*. Well, if they
wanted to be polite to niggers, that was their business. He knew what
he wanted to do. What had that snotty spade said about his wife?
She was in Chandigarh, whatever the hell that was. And damned
lucky, too, because right now, if he could find her—

"Here we are, sir." The bearded man bowed and stepped aside.
Race entered a modern bathroom.

Three minutes later he stood before the mirror, shaking the cold
water out of his eyes and towelling off his face. He'd sobered somewhat, just enough to feel a sneaking distaste about rejoining the
others in the banquet hall. Maybe the best idea was to just cut out of
here.

He stepped into the deserted hall, moving slowly past a row of
closed doors. That is, they had all been closed when he'd followed
the major-domo. Now one of them was slightly ajar. As he passed
he was aware of a heavy, musky scent drifting into the corridor.

Race halted and peered into a darkened room. Moonlight filtered
from barred windows. Beneath the windows was a couch. On the
couch was a girl. Her sole garment was a *sari* and she wore no orna-
ments, but such artifices were unnecessary. She was young and lovely,
and when she rose in wide-eyed wonder the *sari's* transparency dis-
closed an undulating outline in the moonlight.

"Hot damn!" Race muttered, as he stepped inside and closed the
door behind him.

"Sir—"

The girl moved back towards the couch.

"Sir—"

Race grinned and reached for her.

"Please, sir—it is not permitted. I am untouchable—"

Her knees pressed against the couch and she fell. Race held her
there, his hands ripping the soft silk, feeling the incredible warmth
of the body beneath. For a moment she writhed in resistance, until

his lips found the fiery crater of her mouth, its tongue erupting like molten lava.

"Untouchable, huh, baby?" Race whispered. "Well, we'll see about that—"

He left her sobbing, without a word. What the hell was there to say? He knew she wouldn't talk, and neither would he. If anybody back at the banquet hall asked where he'd been so long, he'd tell them he got sick, heaved his cookies. Nobody would ask any questions.

But sometime, just before they pulled out of here for good, he'd find a way of letting the big shot know what happened. That uppity nigger thought he was so damned smart, handing out a line of jazz about keeping his hands off all the chicks. It would be a real gasser to see his face when he found out somebody had scored with his wife.

Well, he'd played it cute, but Race had the last laugh. It was all he could do to keep from busting out right now when he walked back into the banquet scene.

He got a real break because nobody even seemed to notice when he came in. They were all standing around some guy in a white suit at the head of the table.

Then the Maharajah looked up and saw him.

"Feeling better, Mr. Harmon?" he asked.

Race nodded, trying to hold back the grin.

"That is good. But if you felt ill, you could consult with Dr. Ghopura here."

Race blinked. "You called a doctor for me?"

"No—it just so happened that he arrived a few moments ago. I asked him to fly in from Bombay."

"It is useless, of course," the little doctor said. "If what you told me is true, the patient will surely die. All I can hope to do is ease the suffering in the terminal phase. I only pray you have kept her isolated."

"Wait a minute!" Race's throat was dry. "Your wife—she's sick—?"

"My wife is in Chandigarh, Mr. Harmon. We are speaking about a poor untouchable from the village whom I discovered the other day. I brought her here immediately to avoid panic and the spread of contagion, for the disease is invariably fatal."

"What disease?"

"Cholera."

The other shrugged and turned away. "Doctor, if you will come with me, please? Her room is right down the hall—"

Everything started to whirl. Just before he fell, Race thought he saw the Maharajah exchange a smile with his major-domo, but he could not be sure. All he was sure of was the pain flooding his head and throat. It was a hot pain—hot and throbbing, like the mouth and tongue of the untouchable.

CHINATOWN EVENING

by Stephen Bond

This murder probably never did take place. But the meeting described at one stage of Jimmy Chen's investigation is part of the author's memories of a Chinatown the tourists never get to know.

She'd been dead for hours when the kids found her—dead, very very dead as she lay there staring up into the grey tenement-circled sky, eyes screaming the horror of those last minutes—those last seconds, a ragged bloody slash in her pitifully summer-like dress. She'd been there for hours and she might have been there for days if two kids hadn't chased each other into that corner of the weed-covered lot and stumbled over the limp body with the flies hovering over the clotted blood.

What hurt was that she was too young to die—too young and too pretty. She should have been down on Coney Island or over at the Park, eating spun candy and hot dogs and frozen delights and arguing about the latest records or that new step they were trying out on TV last night—instead she was lying there in this dirty lot, huddled as she'd fallen after the killer had struck, handbag—open—at her side, one high heeled shoe—fragile like she had been—just beyond the body. She must have twisted and fought with everything she had in her in those last minutes—but she hadn't been strong enough or lucky enough . . . I knew someone would remember afterwards that they'd heard a cry sometime earlier that night, but nobody had done anything about it naturally—people mind their own business in this part of town—and whoever had killed her had lost himself in the shadows and run—no, probably just walked—down the street and around the corner and into the void.

For the time being.

Something told me we would find him. What hurt was what I'd have to do now—go down the street and across Chatham Square and up Bayard Street and then stop before her father's shop. I'd have to walk in—and the bell would ring—and Ah Goy would come out and bow his happiness to see me and I would have to, in effect, slap him and I would have to beat him down and hurt him—hurt him bad—when I told him his daughter Lee was dead—murdered. . . .

Of course I didn't beat him—of course I didn't slap him—I'm talking nonsense I suppose—but he *looked* like I'd done that when I was through, staring at me with her eyes, waiting for me to go on. . . .

"Where is she now, Jimmy?"

"The Police are still there, Father of Lee. They—" I broke off—
he had motioned impatiently and turned, in the next minute, to
the cash register. He pulled at the bills that were there—unseeing
eyes staring straight ahead all the time—then he was switching off
the lights and standing there in the door, waiting for me to move.
Five minutes later and we were back at the lot—crowded now with
police and newspapermen and ghouls and the curious.

Ah Goy stood there by the body for a minute and we could see
him age right there in front of us—age and grow stern and straight
with something of the fighter he must have been reflected in him as
he turned to the lieutenant to ask where he could claim the body. I
knew what must be raging inside him. Lee—fragile, lovely Lee—had
been the widower's pride and joy—and torment as she had discovered dancing and the movies and the excitement of the social clubs
in the neighborhood, the more exciting because he'd forbidden her
to go to them.

I couldn't keep up with the old man—he walked as if he'd lost
twenty years suddenly, and was as young and allegedly active as I'm
supposed to be. And as tough. He had followed me when we
crossed the square—I was following now—and following as he walked
straight up Mott Street and stopping when he stopped in front of
the door with the sign scrawled in black on the door—a prosaic looking bell at the side.

He turned to me—and told me "Come!"—and I followed him up
the stairs, my hands in my pockets—one hand clutching my gun.

A door.

Two knocks.

And then one.

And a voice.

"Brother?"

And Ah Goy—"It is your humble brother who keeps the shop of
the jasmine flowers and his young friend, the son of the Venerable
Chen. We seek advice and guidance."

"Enter."

A narrow room—and a curtain in the middle.

And a guard behind us.

Ah Goy motioned reassuringly to me, and then began to speak—
not in our Cantonese but in some dialect I didn't recognize—soft,

liquid phrases that were suddenly harsh and insistent as he obviously was telling about the murder.

And then he was silent.

Dead silent.

I could hear the guard breathing behind us—and the rustle of papers and someone moving, perhaps more than one person, behind the curtain, and then an old voice was speaking—now in Cantonese, a very old voice by the sound of it and faintly familiar for a second. . . . "My son, our brother tells us you are a resourceful man—doing well in this work that you turned to in defiance of your venerable father's wishes. Perhaps this was destined that this should be so. We have ourselves been aware of this and of what you have been doing and happy that you were bringing credit to the men of our province —but now we ask you to serve your own and to join us in the search for this—this evil soul."

The muffled voice—still so familiar and still unrecognized—was silent.

I bowed.

"It is an honor to serve the Association—an honor and a responsibility—but I would anyway have done my best to find the man who did this. I have known the venerable Ah Goy for many years and watched his daughter grow to maidenhood. She was like my younger sister, oh venerable one, and I swore back there—by her body—that I would search for this evil one—before the venerable Ah Goy asked me to come before you."

The guard's breathing was stilled.

Ah Goy turned towards me as the old voice behind the curtain finally spoke softly.

"It is well, my son. We shall have need of you. But remember that we of the South avenge our own!"

The next hours—the next days—were crowded and anything but dull. I slept three hours the first night and two the next. I had reported ill that first morning and sent a messenger over with a note from Doctor Lee—but nobody had put two-and-two together apparently—there'd been a curt "O.K." and that'd been that—I was free to be ill or drop dead or do what I pleased, within reason of course.

Within reason?

The stumble bum I was slapping around thought there was no reason in me—but I was trying to get sense out of his mumbling about the "Chinky kid and the big guy." The sour old hag who was cashier at the movie had thought she'd seen Lee standing outside the movie that night—looking at the "Coming Attractions"—and talking to something tall and male in a sport shirt that shouted money who was standing there next to her—she'd thought Lee knew him. The old man had been sitting in the doorway next to the movie, that she knew—Lord Peter had staggered over to the two and tried to bum enough for a drink out of the man—she'd seen him search for a coin and give it to the old man—and then a customer had come up to the change booth and when she'd looked again, Lee and the man were gone.

The man had been only something tall and male in a sleek looking sport shirt to her—she'd never seen his face—but the old man had talked to them and the old man had seen his face and—damn it —why didn't he talk!

"Lord Peter! Wake up!"

"Wurra ye shay?"

"Wake up, man!"

"Wurra ye hittin' me fur? Ya bloody chink, WURRA YA 'ITTING ME FUR? I'll 'ave t' lar an ya, ah will—yah—yah—the lar on ya!"

"Wake up man! We've got to find out something—"

"Who ya cullin' man—am Lo Peetr ya kna—donsha firgit dat—hic!" The old man swayed—a little less than gracefully—bleary-eyed —stinking to high heaven—face flushed where I'd slapped him.

"What kind of man was Lee Goy with tonight, Lord Peter! What kind of guy"—I was speaking slowly and distinctly now—"What kind of guy was she with earlier tonight?"

"Washa talking abou'? Wa'guy?"

"The man with Lee outside the movie earlier tonight? You came over to them and bummed a cigarette off him and then he gave you some money and you went into the saloon next to the hotel—"

"He—*he*? Thash goo guy?"

"Listen, Lord Peter—listen, damn you! You know Ah Goy's daughter?"

"Yeh—"

"You saw her outside the movie tonight—"

"Yeh—"

"With a guy?"

"Yeh but—"

"What did he look like?"

"Dun kno'!"

"WHAT DID HE LOOK LIKE?"

"Dun kno—I tell you—ah dun know!"

"What's the matter—did you close your eyes when you went up to them?"

"Who them?"

"Lee Goy and the fellow she was with—"

"Oh!"

My patience was wearing thin—I spat out the words—"What *did* he look like?"

"'Im? Nice guy!"

"God damn it!", I grabbed the old man by his dirty shirt—"you BASTARD! WHAT DID HE LOOK LIKE?"

"Tak yer goddam hans offa me ya Chink—ya foget who-whom me!"

"The hell I do! Listen—Lord Peter! WHAT DID THAT SONOFABITCH LOOK LIKE? WAS HE YOUNG? OLD? BLACK HAIR? BLOND HAIR? WHAT DID HE LOOK LIKE? LEE GOY WAS MURDERED—"

The old man stared up at me—bloodshot eyes suddenly startled and quivering—"Lil Lee?"—and slowly, "Leetl Lee? Dead?"

I nodded—

Lord Peter was standing again—not too straight but with something of the dignity of the very drunk—but something was added—his voice was firmer and clearer. "Th' man wi' her? He was tall—most six feet tall—with a scar on his hand—with . . ." And the suddenly soberer Lord Peter proceeded to describe the man who had thrown him a quarter—describe him with a wealth of detail that made you wonder just what the old man had been before he'd ended up on the Bowery.

I turned away finally—only to have him call after me—"Hey Jimmy—look—I'm sorry I called you a Chink—I didn't know—I liked little Lee. . . ." His eyes filled as he stood there, leaning against the wall of the building—unshaven—dirty—sick bloodshot eyes staring at and through me . . .

Two telephone calls and an hour later I was through for the night—through for the morning, rather. Dawn was a matter of an hour or so away—dawn over the new Chatham Square and the rat traps and the tourist holes and the vinos sleeping in the doorways and the ones who wouldn't get up when you kicked them because they couldn't fight any more. Dawn was a matter of an hour or so away and the early delivery trucks were coming down the Bowery, fast—too fast—as they headed for the Row.

There are some advantages to being a Cantonese. I'd always known it—and I learned it again a couple of hours later, when I was down on the street again—my head splitting apart on me—my body yelling for more rest than the hours I'd had upstairs—cold hate driving me on, despite headache and tiredness, knowing I was hours behind this unknown man who had walked across the lot with little Lee and then—I was suddenly cold and very much awake. . . .

As I said, there are some advantages to being a Cantonese. I knew one of those advantages when I spoke at the Splendid Endeavour Benevolent Association's meeting that night—describing the man Lord Peter said had been with Lee—describing him the way Lord Peter had done—from the scar on his hand to the tic in his eye.

And I thought it again, later that evening, when I repeated the description at the Central Laundrymen's Association—three hundred men listening quietly as I described the shirt the man had worn the way Lord Peter had described it—and then the man himself—from the scar on his hand to the tic in his eye to the color of his hair —warning them, though, that Lord Peter might be wrong in some point and that we couldn't be certain that this *was* the killer. . . .

There *are* some advantages to being a Cantonese.

I knew it when an old man in the back of the room stood up and said he thought he knew the man—he had seen him once when he had come to his humble establishment, complaining that a shirt had been torn—usually the Filipino boy who did for him picked up the laundry but this time he'd come down himself—angry and blustering the way all these Americans blustered when they were uncertain. . . .

There was a murmur in the room. . . .

But he was right, the old man insisted. These people always blustered—they always behaved as if the laundrymen were coolies—shouting at them—complaining—arguing about this and arguing about that—yes—*this* man was known to him—he wore the kind of shirt that the English drunk had described. . . .

Juan Tarasey proved accommodating. Maybe because he was accommodating anyway. Maybe because Murray had a habit of shouting at him too—blustering—damning him for an ignorant sonofabitch—a Filipino sonofabitch—not understanding that this sort of thing is not always appreciated by our Filipino brothers.

I searched the man Murray's apartment, a matter of hours after we'd learned about him. I'd gone back to the narrow room with the curtain in the middle, and reported what we had learned—and then I'd gone up there in the sixties—found out where Murray lived—and gone on from there. Juan Tarasey proved accommodating—easy to convince—Tao held a twenty-dollar bill in one hand and a knife in the other, once we'd gotten in. Juan had promptly chosen the twenty dollars. . . .

I phoned downtown and had them bring up Lord Peter in a car —and then we sat there, outside the apartment house, waiting for Murray to come home—talking quietly among ourselves—Lord Peter, sober and grim, with eyes fixed on the front door.

Finally a man—a tall man—neared the building.

We tensed.

No—he was walking past us.

Another—no—he'd turned off before he reached this house.

But now—finally—it had to be *he!*

Lord Peter looked like he wanted to get out of the car—like he wanted to push his way through us. "That was him," he shouted— "that was him."

It *was* Murray. . . .

It was Murray—but we had no proof that he had killed the girl. What now?

He went out a while afterwards, and we went up to the apartment —Lord Peter had gone back to the Bowery but the others were with me—two able young men whom the Association had loaned me.

It *was* Murray—what now?

Juan Tarasey came up with a suggestion—with more than one suggestion, actually. He had wondered when things would get too difficult for Murray, and the very possibility that Murray might have murdered the girl made him doubly cooperative.

Very much so.

Juan went home at ten o'clock.

When Murray returned at two o'clock—he was startled to find the door to the apartment open—but nothing had apparently been disturbed. Nothing—he suddenly realized—except a portrait he'd never had—a portrait of that little Chinese girl.

He swept the picture off the table. Somehow it fell on a side—and there the girl was staring at him with those wide naive eyes of hers.

He went into the bedroom.

Another picture facing the bed this time—and now Murray was

scared. He'd wondered first if he was seeing things—if he was drunk—but these were no visions—this was real—and frightening.

The telephone rang and something told him he shouldn't answer it—he took the receiver off the hook quietly and started to listen—it was *her* voice—a young Chinese girl's voice anyway! He slammed down the receiver and started to sob with fright.

Out—he must get out.

Anywheres!

He couldn't stay there—not with these pictures and these calls and the knowledge that something had gone very very wrong—as wrong as anything could be!

The next thing we knew Murray was half-staggering, half-running out of the building. Coatless. Without a hat.

Wandering aimlessly down the avenue—saying something to himself that we couldn't catch as we followed in the car.

Until we got to the Aloha—the clipjoint up on the Boulevard with the darkened lights and fading beauties and watered whiskey. Fading but willing beauties, very willing. . . .

And now a murderer—or at the very least a man at the bar with a very guilty conscience—who didn't know anything until he felt Tao's knife in his back and the whispered warning, "Come quietly. We are armed!"

The four of us were lost in the crowd—some minutes later we were outside and sitting in Shen's car—Tao, next to Murray in the back, ostentatiously playing with his knife, each time whirling it closer to Murray's face.

Closer.

And closer.

And closer. . . .

There was blood on Murray's shirt when we were through—very little, really, but still his own blood—he was sobbing and swearing that he hadn't meant it—he hadn't meant it. . . .

And suddenly I was very sick of it all. Sick of the blood. Sick of the filth that was this man.

Sick enough to tell him that perhaps we would let him live after all—if he did one thing—walk into the police station across the way and confess to the murder of Lee Goy.

It's possible that we may have persuaded him a little more—a little more impatiently than was entirely proper. But all of us were tired—I had hardly slept for days—and there was something disgusting about this shaken hulk of a man who had been brave enough to kill little Lee but was so afraid, himself, of death. . . .

Oh yes—we won the argument.

We sat in the car—perhaps an hour later, probably much less—and watched him drag himself up the stairs and into the police station.

And we got the signal—I'd phoned a friend and arranged for it—we got the signal that he'd given himself up for the murder of Lee Goy.

We'd have waited for him outside there, otherwise. . . .

Even though we were all so tired.

We would have waited for him. . . .

THE SCAR

by Wenzell Brown

Men like Hugh Whitehead have been with us in every decadent society, but more so in ours, appealing to the shallow and the easily
bored—or should one say the easily stirred . . .

The bitter enmity that lay between the two men had always been one-sided. Or at least that was the way it had seemed to Lincoln.

Hugh Whitehead and Karl Dinze formed a study in contrasts. Whitehead was tall, blond and spare with a handsome, rather weak face. Dinze was short and swarthy with irregular features, piercing brown eyes and coarse black hair that grew low over a bulging forehead. His voice was a sharp staccato and his hands were never still.

Once Lincoln had shared a rat-infested studio in Greenwich Village with his two friends. They had been young then, and ambitious. Whitehead was an artist. He painted with hard, clear lines that had simplicity, clarity and sometimes a touch of humour. There was a spark of greatness in his work but he rarely sold a canvas.

Dinze was a composer. Beneath the strident, raging clash of chords which marked his compositions lay a whiplash beat that set the nerves to screaming. Critics recognized the surging power in the man and in his music but they said he lacked form and discipline. As for Lincoln, he was a dabbler, writing intermittently on a novel which was to grow yellow in his trunk. He was content to bask in the superior talents of his friends and to prevent their bickering from erupting into open quarrels.

Whitehead and Dinze each recognized the genius in the other and each, in his own way, spurred the other to greater effort. Whitehead through gentle raillery. Dinze through shouted diatribes. Neither bothered about Lincoln. He was not a rival. When he threw in the sponge to take a steady job they joined in congratulating him on the wisdom of his decision.

There was a second cause of rivalry between the two. Each was attracted to the same type of girl. Black-haired, with pallid skin, overly large eyes and fragile bodies. Again Lincoln had been no competitor. He favoured big, buxom blondes. Eventually he had married one and moved away from the Village. He only drifted back once in a while to visit his old friends.

Without Lincoln's calming influence, Whitehead and Dinze soon separated. Success came early to Whitehead although not in the pattern that he had planned. A chain of popular magazines picked him up to do illustrations. His portraits of languorous, long-legged girls and handsome young men with crew hair-cuts were in evidence on every news-stand. At thirty he wasn't as famous as Kent or Falter but he was well on his way.

He moved into a large, well-lit studio in Macdougal Alley. He asked Dinze to share his quarters but the invitation was caustically refused. Dinze might be a failure but he still had his pride. He wasn't accepting charity from Whitehead. Dinze found a basement room and worked at odd jobs to eat and pay the rent. The two men gravitated into different circles. Whitehead was constantly surrounded by a coterie of admirers. Dinze hung about the fringes of the artistic world, mingling with those who, like himself, were down and nearly out.

At first, when their paths crossed, Whitehead made friendly overtures. They were always rebuffed.

"Keep your hands off me," Dinze would snarl. "Maybe to your fancy friends you're a big shot. But to me you're a no-good bum who's sold his talent for a mess of pottage."

Whitehead would turn away, spreading his hands in resignation, a hurt look on his handsome face. "There's a man who's a great artist," he would say. "All he needs is one break to hit the top. Gee, I wish I could give it to him."

Soon Lincoln remained the only link between them. He still admired them both. Sometimes he'd sit in a dingy bar with Dinze, paying for the beers and listening to Dinze rant against Whitehead.

"He's a pretty boy, shallow and smug. But, believe it or not, he had the spark of genius in him. There was a time when he could paint. But not now. He's prostituted his art too long. Candy box stuff. That's all he's good for. Cheap tawdry trash."

"Some people think he's tops."

"You know better. He may be rolling in green but he's still a punk. Peddling his stuff around like a two-bit floozie. I hate his guts. I'd like to kill him."

Lincoln would study the bitter, brooding face, then surreptitiously slide ten or twenty dollars across the table. The money came from Whitehead but Lincoln never dared admit it. If he had, Dinze would have ripped up the bills.

Dinze would pocket the money and drink in angry silence. Lincoln knew that the jealousy was inflamed not only by his enemy's success but by the girls he'd lost to Whitehead. Jennie—Ellen—Sue. Half a dozen more whose names Lincoln couldn't remember. Dinze's defeat was all the more humiliating because Whitehead had made no apparent effort to attract the girls. Sometimes he'd even try to send them back to Dinze. But none of them wanted the squat, ugly, down-at-the-heels composer. Not after they'd met Whitehead.

Dinze would snap out of his reverie long enough to growl, "Go back to that pretty-faced punk and tell him to keep his nose out of my affairs. If he messes around with me again, by God, I swear I'll finish him."

On another evening, Lincoln sipped Martinis with Whitehead in the Jumble Shop. "What gives with you and Dinze?" he asked.

"There's a guy who'll never give himself a break. I sent word to him that Meredith needs some scores for a T.V. show I've got a hand in. Stuff that Dinze could knock off with both hands tied. You know what? Dinze wouldn't even go up and talk with Meredith. He says he's above cheap commercialism."

"Why don't you wash Dinze out of your hair? He hates you and he could be dangerous."

"Sure. I know. But all the same I admire the guy's integrity. In a way he's right too. Long after I'm forgotten, he'll live among the immortals. He's really got what it takes." He shrugged and gave a rueful grin. "As for myself, I want a little of my pie while I'm on earth to enjoy it."

Perhaps the violence would have lain dormant in Dinze if it hadn't been for Phoebe Crane. Lincoln never knew where Dinze found her. She was like his other girls. Dark hair. Deep sorrowing eyes. A wistful mouth. A soft rounded chin. She wasn't Lincoln's type but even he could feel her appeal and recognize her fragile beauty.

Lincoln was with Whitehead the night that Phoebe came to the studio door. Just a timid rap, so muted that at first both of them had thought it was the wind. Whitehead had gone to the door anyway and opened it. Phoebe slid into the room. Half-shy, half-frightened, her lips quivering.

"I had to come. Please let me stay."

"For Pete's sake, you're Dinze's girl. Go on back to him."

"I won't. I won't. I'd rather die."

"Don't talk nonsense, child."

"I mean it. I'll throw myself in front of a subway train."

"Oh, come off it. Dinze isn't that bad."

"All he thinks of is his piano. He sits there and pounds and pounds at the keys. The music's crazy, filled with hate. I'm afraid of him, Hugh. There's a demon in him."

Whitehead moved closer to her and suddenly she was in his arms, her face nestled against the lapel of his pale blue suit. He looked over her head at Lincoln and lifted a shoulder as though to say, "What can I do?"

Lincoln was embarrassed. He said, "I'll be shoving along."

"No. Stick around for a while."

But Lincoln had already picked up his hat and was at the door.

Lincoln was with Whitehead again the night that Dinze struck. They came out of the studio into the darkness of the alley. The gas lamp near the door had been extinguished and heavy shadows lay across the uneven roadway. Only a stippling of yellow light seeped through the curtained windows.

Dinze stepped out of a strip of blackness into the pale glow. There was something comic about the squat, arrogant figure in his shapeless clothes.

He twisted to face Whitehead. "You rotten lousy bum. I'm going to fix you this time. You're not going to get away."

Whitehead's voice was casual. "Cut it out, Dinze. Why can't we be friends?"

Dinze growled deep in his throat and his right arm swung back. It was then that Lincoln saw the steel chain looped about his fist, the end links honed to razor sharpness. He called a warning but Whitehead had caught the glint of steel, too.

"Drop it," Whitehead said softly.

Dinze bared his teeth in a grin and his arm raised high, the tail of the chain swirling.

Whitehead could have run but he stood still, balanced on the balls of his feet. The chain came whistling towards him. Whitehead jerked backward, twisting away from the blow. But he wasn't quite quick enough. The end link slashed across his cheek, slicing into the flesh, covering his face with blood.

Whitehead toppled to one side, scrabbled on his hands and knees, then slid slowly to the cobblestones and lay face down, motionless.

Dinze's shadow fell across him but he made no effort to strike again. He stood there, almost as though in meditation, looking down at his fallen enemy. The cop came out of nowhere, his feet pounding, his voice raised in a wordless yell.

The alley offered an escape route between two houses but Dinze didn't choose to take it. Instead he stood flat-footed until the cop was almost upon him, then raced forward as though to duck under the outflung arms.

The cop grabbed him and spun him around. The chain snaked out and slashed across the cop's throat. In the darkness, he probably never knew what struck him. He gave a strangled cry, broken off almost before it was started, and crashed downward in a broken heap.

Dinze fled then, his footsteps echoing frenziedly as he ran to the mouth of the alley and swung south towards the park.

They arrested Dinze an hour later. He had gone back to his basement room and was beating out a weird, dirge-like composition on his battered piano when the police broke in to charge him with murder.

They told him the cop had died, his jugular severed by the honed steel edge of the chain. Dinze appeared indifferent.

"What about Whitehead?" he asked.

"He'll live," he was told. "The side of his face was ripped open but it will heal."

"He'll have a scar," Dinze said. "He won't be a pretty boy any longer."

The officers exchanged glances but they didn't say anything. They were strangely gentle with Dinze. He was a cop killer and he was precious. They wanted to make sure that they delivered him safely to the electric chair.

Lincoln didn't see Dinze again until the trial. He was subpoenaed as a witness. Testifying against his old friend wasn't pleasant. He looked straight ahead while he answered the questions that were fired at him.

Whitehead followed Lincoln on the stand, the side of his face still swathed in a bandage. He was an unco-operative witness, stammering excuses for Dinze, trying to assume some of the prisoner's guilt. The reluctant evidence didn't help Dinze. Lincoln, watching the jury, could see their faces grow hard, could sense their growing determination that Dinze should die.

The verdict was guilty of murder in the first degree without a recommendation of mercy. Dinze's fate was sealed. He was smiling when he listened to the sentence of death. There were delays. An automatic appeal. A stay of execution. Nearly two years passed before the sentence was carried out.

Lincoln bought a fifth of gin that night and drank himself into a stupor. He couldn't bring himself to see Whitehead. Not until the mid-afternoon of the following day did he drop into the studio.

He had expected Whitehead to be broken up, probably nursing a hangover. Certainly he wasn't prepared for what he saw. Whitehead was in front of the big mirror in his bedroom, studying the slanting scar that crossed his cheek. He turned at Lincoln's approach.

"Dinze burned last night," Whitehead said tonelessly.

"Yeah. I know."

"Crazy, isn't it? The stupid jerk tries to kill me and all he does is grant me a favour."

"A favour."

"The scar. You know, I sort of like it. The girls all go for it too. They ask me if I got it in a duel."

"What do you tell them?"

"That a murderer gave it to me. It goes over big. The girls fall all over me."

Lincoln looked at Whitehead's face. The wound had healed but it had left a deep gash from the cheekbone to the corner of the mouth.

Dinze had been right. Whitehead wasn't a pretty boy any longer. The scar gave strength to the face, a vulpine quality that would arrest the attention of women. The weakness was gone and in its place was something reckless, dangerous and cruel.

"It's a pretty good scar," Whitehead said. His blue eyes were bland; his voice controlled.

Lincoln didn't answer. Suddenly a lot of things clicked into place and made a pattern he'd never recognized before. The hatred between the two men hadn't been one-sided. Whitehead had hated too.

But more than that he saw the evil, the inhuman quality in Whitehead that had enraged Dinze.

There was nothing he could say. He turned and walked to the door. At the sill, he stopped and looked back.

Whitehead had forgotten all about him and was staring into the mirror, his fingers gently caressing the scar. . . .

THE WEAKER VESSEL

by James Cross

Deputy Sheriff McCall is a type of investigator seldom met with in these more formulae-minded days. He functions in a world which most of us imagine peopled by craggy-faced men and wholesome and somewhat less than dangerous women. We forget that there are no frontiers in today's America, and that even the hills known to the People have changed.

Sunday I like to sleep late; so I was really burned up when John Two-Bear and Charlie White Elk drove in from the reservation in their World War II surplus jeep and woke me. I was pulling weekend duty on the folding cot in the sheriff's office, and I figured to sleep maybe till eight; and here it was six o'clock and just about dawn. In Mescalero County, outside of the tourist season, you don't figure to see much action on weekends. Maybe a few drunks in Mesa Verde; but Chief Wittenburg and the Hurley brothers, Gordon and McKinley, can handle it. Out in the county, we don't have the jurisdiction.

Maybe, as they say, at this point I should introduce myself. My name is Brian McCall. After my mother died when I was seven, my old man and I kept the ranch going together. I got through high school and college, working summers, thanks to my old man; and even a year of law school at the State University up North. When he died, I had to drop out a year and work the ranch and save enough for another year. That's the way it's been. I've got one more year for my law degree. Meanwhile I'm keeping an eye on the ranch and working as deputy for Sheriff Roy Larson. He was a friend of my old man, and anyhow, he figures my two years of law make up for my lack of experience. Next year I figure to finish up and then start my own law practice. I'll only be twenty-eight.

I was remembering all this as I rolled out of the cot and started the coffee going for my early-rising friends.

"You are up early, my brothers," I said in the language of the People. "Do you have something to tell me?"

"Hell with that noise, Bri," John Two-Bear said in English. (He had been graduated from the Agriculture School). "We've got a little business for you. Plane crash out by the reservation. Couple of hours ago, Charlie and I were rounding up a few ponies, we heard this plane flying very low. Then suddenly there was a big flash, we saw one wing blow off. Then it zigzagged around a bit and dropped at the edge of the mesa."

"We're up to date here," I said, "we've got phones and all that. Why didn't you call, you could have saved a couple of hours."

"Poor Indians don't have phones," Charlie White Elk said, "so we come fast in four-wheel magic car to bring news to Great White Chief."

"Get off it, Charlie," John Two-Bear said. "Fact of the matter, Bri, we were about halfway between the phone and your office; we figured it was easier to drive in."

"So we could see the Great White Father face to face," Charlie White Elk said, "look at him eye to eye, so that he could see that his Red Brother did not speak with a forked tongue, that his words were straight. I have spoken. Haugh!"

I was getting a little mad. Charlie White Elk spoke better English than I did, we'd played baseball together at college. If he hadn't been a friend, I'd have loosened a couple of his front teeth. I have a bad temper; the old man always told me so.

"Stop kidding the paleface," John Two-Bear said. "Look, Bri, you're the only law for fifty miles. Why don't you tell the sheriff and then come on out with us?"

That I'd figured out already, so I called Roy Larson and told him what had happened and where I was going.

"All right, Brian," he said sleepily, "go ahead and I'll join you later. Just don't mess anything up, boy, that's all."

That's the trouble with someone who's been "Uncle Roy" since you were in short pants, no confidence. I locked up the office and got in the jeep. "Let's go," I said.

When we got there it was a real mess. Bits of airplane smashed over a mile or so. I spotted one body at once, before I even started looking.

"John, Charlie," I said, "there'll be about ten thousand cops out here soon. Is there any way you can rope the area off, keep the people away?"

John Two-Bear rummaged in the back of the jeep and pulled out a couple of red blasting flags, began to slice them up with his sheath knife. Charlie White Elk started cutting mesquite branches. In a few minutes the whole area was surrounded with mesquite twigs, each bearing a strip of red cloth.

"This is the mark of the dead," John Two-Bear said, "the People will know it and respect it. Will the White-Eyes do as much?"

"I don't know," I said, thinking of the state police and the reporters, press, radio, and TV, who would gravitate to the scene. "I'll try to take care of them."

We started walking over the area. It was a mess. The first thing we spotted was the starboard wing of the plane, torn off and isolated, with a huge gash in its middle, the aluminum alloy spreading outward, charred and twisted from burning gasoline. Then the body of the plane, twisted and blackened, but less so than the broken wing. It was there that we found the bodies. There was a young woman. Her hair had been long and corn-yellow, but on one side it was burned away. Her face was almost calm as if she had very suddenly fallen asleep. In the blackened seat next to her, a young man hung, still suspended by the safety belt. The dark hair on his head was almost all scorched away. His face was twisted and ugly as if he had fought hard for an instant before death came.

The front of the plane had broken off where it hit, and the cockpit was a hundred yards or so away. It had burned very badly. Up against the instruments were a couple of dark, gloved hands. Then, if you looked carefully, you could see a kind of shriveled mummy that added up to the pilot. Whoever he was, he'd ridden the plane down all the way. I shook my head. I'm not really good for this work. Speeding tickets, picking up drunks and sobering them in the tank, delivering papers, that's okay; but I don't like corpses, not any kind. When you're dead, you're dead a long time.

"Not good, brother," Charlie White Elk said, "not good."

"Let's look around," I told him, "let's see what we can find. But don't move anything. Just stick a stake in the ground near whatever we find. Let the experts handle it later."

We didn't find very much, or at least not anything that meant much to me. We found a lot of pieces of airplane and cloth and luggage, and we staked them all out precisely. Then we sat and waited. Roy Larson was the first to arrive. He took one look around and then turned to us.

"Pretty good, boys. You've all done pretty good. All we have to do now is keep the place roped off till the experts"—there was the very faintest sneer—"till the experts arrive. John, Charlie, please, tell the People to stay away; Brian and I will handle the others."

"None of the People will pass the marks of the dead," John said, "but to be sure, Charlie and I will pass the word to them, and ask them to stand guard. We will keep them off, either the People or the White-Eyes."

"Well, not all of them," the sheriff said. "Some of the White-Eyes will have business here."

"Very well," Charlie White Elk said gravely—I could see he was trying not to laugh. "None of the People. And for the White-Eyes, we will tell them first they must speak to you."

"Good," Sheriff Larson said. A few minutes later when John and Charlie had ridden off in their jeep, he turned to me. "Brian," he said, "you know the People. I'm too old. I was born out here when it was still a Territory. My grandfather, the People skinned him alive during the last war. They still bother me."

"I guess we still bother them," I said, "but I like them; and I think they like me. Don't worry about the People. If John and Charlie tell you, you can believe it."

"All right," he said, "the expert stuff, like how did the plane crash —that we have to wait for till the FAA people arrive; but meanwhile, let's see if we can find out who the bodies are."

There were markings and numbers on the plane that we still could read, so we got on the radio-telephone in the sheriff's car to the capital and asked for identification. Meanwhile we wandered around the staked out area, finding nothing but pieces of airplane luggage and maybe human flesh, which we carefully marked and left alone. After a while, the radiophone on the car began to buzz. I picked up the receiver.

"A rental out of New York, eight days. Last check in at Las Cruces. Rented to Jeff Carter, husband of the former Lynda Allen, pilot and owner, Earl Torrey. You want a rundown, or do you read the papers?"

"Negative," I said, "I can read."

"What's the identification?" Sheriff Larson said, coming up on me suddenly.

"Lynda Allen," I said, "Jeff Carter. You remember the names, or maybe *you* don't read the papers. Forget the pilot, Earl Torrey; nobody's heard of him."

"Oh Christ," Roy said, "that tears it. We'll get them all—state police, people from the governor's office, FAA characters, lawyers, reporters—press, radio, TV—from all over the country. Why the hell didn't those dumb bastards crash in Jicarilla County; it's only ten miles away."

"Maybe they weren't given the choice."

"All right, Brian, you know how I meant it; don't get hardnosed."

"You know who these people are, Roy?"

"Not really. The names just sound important, that's all."

"Okay," I said, "I'll give you the word. This Lynda Allen to start. A few weeks ago she inherited either five or ten million, depending on what paper you read. She married a would-be pop singer named Jeff Carter and they honeymoon in the West Indies—just like you and me. One day they want to get back to New York, but the scheduled planes aren't running. So Lynda and Jeff they hire an airline plane for $10,000 and breeze into Kennedy where the press meets them. Then Lynda decides she wants to Do Good, so she starts giving the money away to anyone who asked—some of it cash; most of it checks. Most of the checks bounce; there's a little trouble with the trustees of the estate. But she does give a little cash away—like $500 to a heroin addict so he can stoke his fires for a few extra weeks, things like that."

"And no one to lock her up," Roy said, "that's what's wrong with this country."

"I don't like it any more than you do, but it's a free country, nuts and all. Well, the checks start bouncing all over, but meanwhile, some half-witted TV character's signed up Lynda and her husband Jeff to sing a duet on his program. It's not much of a program to begin with, but Jeff and Lynda bomb a little worse than usual, and there goes the career as a teen-age idol."

"Jesus Christ, Brian, you really get around. Where do you pick up this garbage."

"Sheriff, I keep in touch with mass communications: I read the news magazines garbage; I read the fan magazine garbage; we've got radio garbage in the car, and there's a TV set in the office. It's hard *not* to know what the creeps are doing all over the country."

"All right," the sheriff said, "so they flopped on TV. Then what happened."

"Then there were stories about most of the good-will checks bouncing, and then Lynda told the press she was unappreciated because she was fifty years ahead of the times. Then a couple of weeks of silence, and then a story the two of them were renting a small plane and setting out across the country from New York to Jicarilla County, next door, where Lynda owns a ranch, doing good wherever they landed. I guess the yucks were supposed to surround every remote county airport where they put down, but maybe they didn't get the word."

"Sometimes, Brian, I think you have a cynical streak in you."

"Not at all, Sheriff. Like Harry Mencken said, 'nobody ever went broke underestimating the intelligence of the American public.' I just figure Lynda and Jeff had wised up to that fact before their last flight."

"It's still a couple of dead bodies, plus the pilot," he said, "you don't seem to take it very hard."

"If they're just dead," I said slowly and carefully, "I sure don't take it hard; good riddance. On the other hand, if it's murder, that's another thing."

"I wish I could figure you out, Brian," he said.

"Plenty of time, Sheriff. I figure I'll be back a few more times before I get set up for myself. Right now, let's get some sleep. We'll have half the country on us tomorrow. But meanwhile, the People will keep the ground clear."

Next morning we were out at Mesa Verde at dawn, watching them all come in. The stakes were still up and John and Charlie had commissioned a dozen hard-looking friends to patrol the area and keep anyone out without a clearance from Sheriff Larson or me. The first arrivals were from the FAA; we let them through right away. Then there was some kind of executive assistant from the governor's office to remind me that the late Lynda Carter was, presumptively, a legal resident of our state and that the governor was taking an interest. Hell, this has been a one-party state for three generations—except for Mescalero County—but my family has always voted the wrong way. So I gave him a quick brush-off, he didn't have any authority. Then there was a lawyer from New York, representing the Allen Trust. I figured that Lynda was a resident of our state and died here; but, still he was with a pretty big New York outfit, and you never could tell where you might want to work, so I talked with him a bit; or actually I mainly listened: the way I figure, Mescalero County or New York, if you just listen, you pick up quite a lot. What I learned was that the way the Allen trust was provisionally set up was that if Lynda died without issue, it all went back to the only surviving relative of Grandpa Allen, some kid of seven living on the Riviera with his mother and her fourth husband, some kind of Romanian nobleman. Well, maybe that's New York state law, but Lynda was a resident of our state, and out here we have an odd mixture of English Common Law, and Code Napoleon, and Spanish Law, and a few special ordinances set up by the territorial governors. They still apply.

After a while, the FAA men came scurrying up in a hurry. Absolutely no doubt; the plane had been blown up. The outward-pointing position of the metal on the blown-off wing made it clear; big deal, I could have told them that yesterday. Meanwhile, the state police were checking back. The night before, the plane had run short of gas and put down in an emergency cow pasture in the eastern end of the state. They'd landed at dusk and slept in the plane all night. There'd been no one at the field, so the three had sacked down with a lot of grumbling, according to a witness who turned up later. In the morning, the wife stayed in the plane while the pilot checked it out. Meanwhile, the husband, poor old Jeff Carter, went roaming down the highway before dawn without even his electric guitar. He hitched a ride to the nearest town, paid a bonus to a trucker with a load of Avgas to make a special trip to the emergency field. Witness number one—the farmer who gave Jeff Carter the ride to town in his pickup—testified to the fact that the other two were in the plane, that no one else was around, that Jeff Carter was in a very bad humor. Witness number two—the driver of the Avgas truck—testified that Carter was a snotty son of a bitch, that the plane was still at the auxiliary field, with no one there but the pilot and Lynda Carter; that he had fueled the plane and been paid; that Jeff Carter and his wife Lynda had conducted a knock-down brawl for half an hour during the fueling; finally that the plane had taken off in the half-dark without difficulty. Half an hour later, in the Mesa Verde area, about fifty miles from the Allen Ranch where Lynda had planned to put down in a homemade airstrip, the plane had exploded in midair, on a calm, clear day without a cloud in the sky, and had been noted at the moment of explosion by John Two-Bear and Charlie White Elk, neither of whom had ever known any of the deceased.

After a little more of this, there didn't seem to be much doing, so I picked up John and Charlie and we started looking around in some of the areas the FAA and the state police had overlooked: some of the places where the going wasn't too good, gullies and dry washes and foothills full of rattlesnakes. It was about ten feet up the outcropping of a foothill where John Two-Bear found the thin fragments of rubber and the odd bits of clockwork. I picked the rubber fragments up and sniffed; they still smelled of gasoline.

"Many thanks, friends," I said. "I think I know how the plane was blown up."

When we got back to the state police, Sam Harkness, the lieutenant in charge, listened to me politely; then he shook his head in annoyance.

"All right," he said, "you've half convinced me. You put the clockwork time bomb in a rubber sack, then you drop it in one of the wing tanks. The rubber sack keeps the works dry; then the bomb goes, it blows off half the wing and ignites the gasoline at the same time.

Very smart, but what the hell does it tell us? Those damn things can be set for twelve hours, or you can get something a little more complicated that'll take a week or so to go off. So the bomb could have been set up any time between New York and last night. How don't matter so much; it's When and Who that interests me."

"Well, one thing it does mean, Sam, is someone who had access to the wing tank, not just an ordinary passenger leaving it off before the charter."

"I guess that's so, but I still want to know where and when and who."

I could see he was just repeating himself, so I wandered off back to the car and started thinking a little. Outside it was about 100° in the shade, so I started the car up, turned on the air-conditioner and drove around a little. Nobody missed me.

First of all, I thought, who, in the last few days could have planted the bomb? Unless someone had crawled up on the wing before the plane left New York opened up the wing tank and dropped the bomb in, the only people who could have done it were Lynda, her husband or the pilot. But whoever did it, it meant suicide. I don't discount the high proportion of paranoids in this great republic; but in practice, it's a million-to-one chance; and you don't get rich playing long shots. Okay, how about motive? Pilot had none; he just wanted his charter fee. Husband? Well maybe old Jeff Carter had hopes for a piece of Lynda's five or ten million; but he's not going to be dumb enough to blow himself up for it. Lynda herself? No point at all.

I drove back and found the lawyer for the Trust, fellow named Hathaway, and I talked with him a bit. Now, lawyers like that are usually pretty close-mouthed; but Hathaway had been on the scene for hours and, except for our conversation earlier, nobody was paying any heed to him. When I came up, he greeted me like a long-lost brother and let himself go. I picked up quite a lot of information. Normally, I suppose, he would have clammed up; but he was in a strange country; he was half dead of heat; nobody was giving him the consideration he was used to—he was like a patient warmed-up on a psychiatrist's couch. Once he got started, the trouble was cutting him off and moving on to the next subject. All kinds of bits and pieces. First of all, Jeff Carter, himself, had a pilot's license. Then, the plan was they were going to land at Lynda's ranch in Jicarilla County, and then by God, buy the plane outright, and send the pilot back to New York. Then about the pilot, this Earl Torrey; he was the one who'd approached Lynda with the idea of the cross-country flight; he'd seen the newspaper stories and figured there was some business there—almost like one of the characters coming around for a handout.

Sometimes, they say, a student still in law school knows more about certain things—because he's just been studying them—than an attorney with fifty years practice behind him. Anyhow, I got a hunch, so I thanked Hathaway and got hold of Roy and asked him to okay a flight to the state capital. Roy grumbled a bit but he finally agreed: nobody was making any headway so far, and whoever did was going to be the fair-haired boy. So he let me go.

First thing I did at the capital was check in with an old law school professor and make absolutely sure how the state law worked when husband and wife died apparently simultaneously in an accident. Then I wandered over to some of the bureaus. We don't get the publicity of Nevada, but actually our state is a quick-divorce state too. And when the divorce decree incorporates a financial settlement, that settlement has to be filed and is open to the public—or at least to a deputy sheriff. I checked out what I wanted to find, and then I made a couple of extra trips, and that was it. I was back to Mesa Verde, our county seat, by nightfall.

Roy met my plane.

"You have anything, Brian?"

"I don't know. Listen, Roy, give me a little time; maybe I can put something together."

He shook his head.

"Okay, you're the lawyer; but you better move fast. They're having the inquest tomorrow."

"Anything happened while I was away?"

"Not much. FAA people agreed with your idea about the time bomb in the rubber sack. That's about it. Oh, a couple of new people turned up. Carter's divorced wife showed a couple of hours after you left; she drove over with Billy Dorset; I guess you know what that means."

Billy Dorset was the local ambulance chaser and full-time shyster. I knew damn well what that meant: the grieving ex-wife had smelled money and also figured there might be a negligence suit somewhere, and Billy had obliged.

"I talked with them," Roy said, "nobody said much of anything; but they sure as hell want to talk with you, Brian. Want you to call them at the motel soon as you got back."

"Which one?" I asked. We have two tourist inns, complete with swimming pools, in town.

"Desert Flower."

"Okay, I'll look them up. It's a long drive back home and I don't know how long this will take. Do we have enough in the budget to put me up for one night in the Desert Flower?"

"Go ahead, I'm driving back right now. I'll drop you off on the way."

At the Desert Flower, I registered, got my room and took a quick shower. Then I put in a call to the room number I'd been given. Billy Dorset answered the phone.

"You wanted to talk with me, Billy," I said. I was very polite: as I said, Hathaway's New York firm, Billy Dorset's ambulance-chasing outfit; you never can tell where you'll be working.

"Sure thing, Brian. You eaten yet?"

"I ate on the plane."

"Well come on over to 127; we can have a drink and talk a bit."

Number 127 was over at the far end of the south wing, very quiet and very private. I knocked on the door and Billy Dorset opened it.

"Come on in, Brian. What can I pour for you?"

"Scotch," I said, "scotch and water." I guess I'm the only man in this state who drinks scotch and water, but I heard it's the class drink back East; and you never can tell.

The door to the bedroom opened and the girl walked out. I couldn't say a word; I just stood there and looked at her. She was short, almost tiny, with long straight blonde hair and deep violet eyes. She was tiny, I said, but everything was in proportion: long, straight legs below the miniskirt, long torso, high, perfect breast; maybe a little too big for her frame, but I wasn't measuring; I was just looking.

"You're the deputy," she said. It came out sort of double: on the one hand, "Oh, you're just the deputy"; on the other, "Oh, you're the man I've been waiting for."

I took it the good way.

"Nicole," Dorset said, "this is Deputy Brian McCall—an old friend."

"I'm glad to know you, Brian," she said. I've read the etiquette books—we have them out here—and I know it isn't incumbent on the woman to offer her hand; but she put out her hand and I took it and it was warm and alive, as if she'd been waiting for me all her life.

Dorset made the drinks and we sat down.

"The reason I called you, Brian," he said, "was that I am representing Nicole in whatever claims she has against the estate. Now, I know that you at the moment are deputy sheriff of the county, but actually you're almost an attorney, so I think we can speak the same language."

"I suppose you're talking about the 'weaker vessel' concept."

"Exactly. When a husband and wife die simultaneously, the wife is considered to be the 'weaker vessel' and to have died earlier than the husband. It doesn't matter how much earlier—a split second will do."

"You know, of course, that quite a few disaster studies—people in life boats, for example, have come up with the empirical findings that, physically, women are stronger, and usually live a short while more than men."

"That doesn't matter. In this state, the statutory assumption is that the wife expires first, leaving the husband."

"Billy," I said, "I spent the afternoon at the Capital. I am quite aware that Nicole is the former wife of Jeff Carter. They were divorced in this state, three years ago. I've even read the property settlement that was filed with the decree. You know, like Nicole gets the $12,000 Maserati free and clear. The interesting part is that Carter's property in his will was to go, one hundred per cent, to his infant son. And by our community property law, the son inherits half Carter's present wife's estate—quite a few millions."

"You know what that means?"

"It means your client's child has just inherited half of five or ten million dollars. And your client's got sole custody and the kid will be a minor for about sixteen more years. Good deal."

"That's fine," he said, "I just wanted to get it from an expert. Look," he went on, "I'm starving. How about some food."

"I told you I ate on the plane down."

Nicole looked at him very carefully.

"So did I," she said. "Why don't you get something, Billy; and I'll see you in the morning. I want to talk a little with Brian and find out more about what happened to Jeff."

Dorset looked at me carefully, but he went quietly. After he had gone, Nicole smiled.

"These lawyers," she said. "How about another drink."

"Fine; I'm not going anywhere. That Maserati," I went on, "a great car. You still have it?"

"You couldn't buy it from me. You know, when Jeff had it, he just ran it into the ground. When I got it, the first thing I did was to take a few lessons from a mechanic. Right now, I can tune it myself."

"Good," I said. "Take me out in it some time."

"Maybe I will if you're interested."

When I was almost sixteen I was in high school in Mesa Verde. It was too far to drive in from the ranch, so my father arranged for me to stay with the family of a friend of mine, Bob Bradley. There was a sister, Amy, about six or seven years older. She was engaged to an older man in California, a doctor, a very good match, her family were delighted; everyone in Mesa Verde thought it was just great. One evening, about a week before the marriage, Amy and I were alone in the house. She'd been something like an older sister to me. We were sort of clowning around, and the next thing I knew we were on the couch together, and that was it. I don't know whether she led me on and I did it to her, or whether it was her all the way. All I know was that we spent every night together for a week, and then the last morning she got up and got married. But what I'm getting at was that the very first time she had a kind of look in her eyes I can't describe but never have forgotten it. That's the way Nicole was looking at me now.

"God," she said, "that Billy Dorset. What a bore. He's trying to hold me up for twenty-five per cent, and then he seems to think he can get a little more in trade."

"Ma'am?" I said. I find this Gary Cooper approach very useful.

"Don't you know what I mean? Here I am all alone, and your friend Dorset, well, you know."

"Well, maybe his approach is a little rough; but I can hardly blame him."

"McCall, I don't know whether you're very smart or very dumb. Anyhow, let's have another drink." Then she reached over and put her arms around me.

"Jesus," she said, a little while later, looking up at me from the rumpled sheets on the Desert Flower, Free-Flo Mattress, "I don't know whether you just have natural talent, or whether you've got something that could be bottled or patented; either way, you could make a fortune out of it."

"Just so long as I own fifty-one per cent of the corporation."

"Come on, come on; protect your investment."

A long while later, Nicole asked me about myself, what I did, where I lived, what I was planning for my life, that kind of stuff. She was particularly interested in my relations with the People.

"You're almost a savage yourself," she said, "you talk the language; you live like them."

"I didn't say 'savages'; I said 'the People.' "

"What's the difference?"

"A very important difference. Today, I was talking with John Two-Bear and Charlie White Elk. They were the Indians who reported the plane crash. What they didn't report and what they told me later—tonight—was two of the People spotted the crash before they did. They went out to it and looked, but they were afraid of the White-Eyes law so they went quickly home."

"What difference does that make?"

"A lot. The two Indians who first saw the crash went right up to the plane. They saw the dead man and the dead woman in the body of the plane. And they told John Two-Bear that the man was dead, but that the woman was still half alive. She muttered a few words and then died."

"I don't believe it."

"This is what John Two-Bear says. Maybe the men will turn up at the inquest, maybe not. The People don't like the White-Eyes law, they don't want to have anything to do with it. So maybe they just won't show—not unless we bring them in."

"Oh Christ, Brian, what's the point! It won't catch the murderer. All it means is, if Jeff died first, everything goes to that dumb kid on the Riviera. Don't I have a right?"

"I don't know."

"Look, you have me; you can have what ever you want. Just leave it alone. Your job is to catch the murderer, not to take my share away from me."

"I don't know," I said, "I don't know what's going to happen."

"When this is all over, Brian," she said very carefully, "I'm going to be in charge of an awful lot of money. I'm going to need someone to help me take care of it—not an average ambulance-chaser like Billy Dorset, but someone who has an interest in me as well as the money."

"That sounds great," I said leaning over toward her and bending her back. "I could finish law school easily."

That night I figured it was smart to stay in my own room in case Roy called, so I left her about 2:30, left her lying back on the bed like a well-fed, satisfied cat, smiling happily. But I came around early next day and drove her over to the grammar school where the inquest was being held. I got her a good seat and waited around for Billy Dorset to take over for her. Then I took off for a while. I had a couple of things to do. Anyhow, the early part of the inquest was going to be pretty cut and dried. Doc Higgins, our coroner, would talk a bit about causes of death and time of death. Then a little from John Two-Bear and Charlie White Elk; then a break for lunch and they'd ask me to say what I'd seen. A few more witnesses and they could wrap it up—murder by person or persons unknown—and continue the investigations. Then the part about the will would move into probate up at the capital; after a while Nicole could get control of her half and that would be it. We'd work on the murder part of it down here, with a certain amount of help, and maybe Nicole would get in touch with me and maybe not. That's the way I guessed she had it figured.

My testimony took about fifteen minutes; about three questions and that was it. I could see the coroner getting ready for the cut-and-dried verdict. Then I moved out into the aisle and got his attention.

"Doc," I said. "You've asked me about what I saw and I told you. There's just a couple of more items I'd like to wrap up before the verdict."

"Wait a minute," Billy Dorset said, "he's finished his testimony. What's all this about?"

"As you should know, Counsellor," Doc Higgins replied, "I have pretty broad latitude in this inquest. If Brian has anything else to say, I'm willing to listen."

"I want it in the record that I protest this proceeding."

"Put it in," Higgins said to the court stenographer. "All right, Brian, you've already been sworn; don't need to repeat it; just sit down and continue."

"Well, the first thing," I said, "is in my earlier testimony I didn't get around to my investigations up at the capital. Nobody asked me; so I figured I better tell you about them before the verdict."

"Mr. Coroner," Billy Dorset broke in. "If you mean that business about the divorce settlement, we're just wasting time. That's already in the record here; and it comes from the original papers—not the notes of some college-boy deputy sheriff."

"Well, not just that," I said, "I agree with you there. But while I was up north I poked around a bit in some other offices. Mr. Coroner," I said, looking at Doc Higgins, "I have here a photostatic copy of the marriage of the former Nicole Carter, two days after the final divorce decree."

"Objection," Billy Dorset shouted. "It's no crime to get married a second time. Hell, this state makes almost as much money out of marriages as divorces."

Nicole was staring at me; I turned away from her eyes and looked at the coroner.

"Go ahead, Brian," he said.

"This is the marriage of the former Nicole Carter to Earl Torrey." I took the photostat from my pocket and handed it up. Doc Higgins read it quickly.

"You lousy pig," Nicole shouted. "So what if I did marry Earl Torrey; we broke up in a few weeks; I haven't seen him since then."

Billy Dorset grabbed her quickly and silenced her.

"Mr. Coroner," he said, "this has nothing to do with the case."

"Maybe not, Counsellor; but as you know we have a lot of discretion in an inquest. I'm going to ask Deputy McCall here to continue. You can object when he's finished, and meanwhile, you're instructed to keep your client quiet. Go ahead, Brian."

"Well, sir," I said, "one of my problems was to figure out who had the best motive to blow up the plane. We've established that, in this State, the wife is supposed to die first. It's community property, so the husband inherits half, even if he lives only a split second longer. Then there's the divorce agreement—a minor child inherits from the husband, and the ex-wife is the guardian: she's controlling quite a few million dollars until the boy is twenty-one or even older. So the motive here is pretty clear. What bothered me is how. But when I read about the marriage to Earl Torrey, it made pretty good sense. Torrey maybe wasn't living with his wife Nicole, but they were still legally married. He was supposed to sell the plane to Lynda Allen the day after the explosion and then go back East on his own. He could easily have dropped the time bomb in the tank, either in New York, or when they landed in the small private airstrip the day before the explosion. It would be set to go off well after he'd left. All he'd have to do was join Nicole and then help her live off the income of several million dollars."

"Earl Torrey, that is the late Earl Torrey, is not my client," Billy Dorset said, rising to his feet, "but I should bring up the point that the average layman is not competent to construct a time bomb of this sort."

"Earl Torrey was a pilot, but before that he'd been a mechanic; he was a racing car fan, did his own work. To someone like that, wiring a simple timer mechanism to a blasting cap and a few sticks of dynamite and enclosing them in a moistureproof sack would be child's play. And his wife, Nicole, she was another racing car fan. Probably knew as much as he did. Either could have done it."

"Mr. Coroner," Billy said, "this is really too much. Why would Earl Torrey have blown himself up?"

"He's right, Brian. It don't make sense."

"That's the way I figured," I said. "No sense. So I tried it out that Earl Torrey was the fall guy all the way. With all that money coming in, Nicole didn't want to be burdened by a second husband. Maybe she set up the timer a day early; maybe Earl set it up first and she reset it. That I don't know for sure. What I do know is that Nicole arranged it to go off while Earl Torrey was still in the plane. She'd get rid of an inconvenient second husband; she'd silence a witness against her; she'd cut the trail to her; she'd . . ."

"You filthy liar," Nicole screamed, "I loved him; I didn't want him killed; the damn thing went off too soon . . ."

"Shut up," Billy Dorset shouted. Then he recovered and turned to Doc Higgins.

"My client is not herself. I move her remarks be stricken."

Doc Higgins looked at him coldly.

"Has the stenographer recorded all of the last remarks?" he asked. "In the meanwhile, no one is to leave the courtroom until the verdict is handed down."

I looked at him for a moment.

"Except, that is, the sheriff and his deputy," he added.

I walked out of the court. It seemed a very long way to go. Nicole was staring fixedly at me; and this much, I'll give her: she didn't weep. That would have torn me up; as I said, maybe I'm not right for this business, maybe I should be for the defense. But she didn't weep; she just looked at me hard and cold; if she'd had anything to do it with, she'd have cut my throat right at the inquest. I was grateful; she made it easy.

Out in the dusty street I met John Two-Bear. He'd been outside but he'd heard it all through an open window.

"It is not pleasant, brother," he said in the tongue of the People, "but sometimes it must be done. What will you do?"

"I'm going up North," I said, "and finish school. Maybe I'll get the answer there."

"Go with the Sky-Father," he said.

LOST GENERATION

by Dorothy Salisbury Davis

There is no "sheer entertainment" and no "escape fiction" in the next pages. There is instead, in this story of a crime, for it is indeed a crime, a glimpse into that dark side of the nature of the race which, understandably, we tend to minimize, ignoring realities.

The school board had sustained the teacher. The vote was four to three, but the majority made it clear they were not voting for the man. They voted the way they had because otherwise the state would have stepped in and settled the appeal, ruling against the town . . .

Tom and Andy, coming from the west of town, waited for the others at the War Memorial. The October frost had silvered the cannon, and the moonlight was so clear you could read the words FOR GOD AND COUNTRY on the monument. The slack in the flagpole cord allowed the metal clips to clank against the pole. That and the wind made the only sounds.

Then Andy said, "His wife's all right. She came up to Mary after it was over and said she wished he'd teach like other teachers and leave politics alone."

"Politics," Tom said. "Is that what she calls it?"

"She's okay just the same. I don't want anything happening to her—or to their kid."

"Nothing's going to happen to them," Tom said.

"The kid's a funny little guy. He don't say much, but then he don't miss much either," Andy said.

Tom said nothing. He knocked one foot against the other.

"It's funny, ain't it, how one man—you know?" Andy said.

"One rotten apple in the barrel," Tom said. "Damn, it's getting cold. I put anti-freeze in half the cars in town today, but not my own. In his even."

"The kid—he's just a kid, you know," Andy said.

Tom wiped the moisture from beneath his nose. "I told you nothing's going to happen to him."

"I know, I know, but sometimes things go wrong."

The others came, Frankie and Murph, walking along the railroad tracks that weren't used any more except by the children taking a short cut on their way to and from school. You could smell the creosote in the smoke from the chimneys of the houses alongside the tracks. One by one the railroad ties were coming loose and disappearing.

The four men climbed the road in back of what had once been the Schroeders' chicken coops. The Schroeders had sold their chickens and moved down the hill when the new people took over, house by house, that part of town. One of the men remarked you could still smell the chicken droppings.

"That ain't what you smell," Tom said. "That coop's been integrated."

Frankie gave a bark of laughter that ricocheted along the empty street.

"Watch it, will you?" Tom said.

"What's the matter? They ain't coming out this time of night."

"They can look out windows, can't they? It's full moon."

"I'd like to see it. I'd like to see just one head pop out a window." Frankie whistled the sound of speed and patted the pocket of his jacket.

"I should've picked the men I wanted," Tom said, meaning only Andy to hear. "This drawing lots is for the birds."

"You could've said so on the range." The town's ten policemen met for target practice once a week. They had met that afternoon. After practice they had talked about the schoolboard meeting they expected to attend that night. They joked about it, only Andy among them having ever attended such a meeting before.

"I'd still've picked you, Andy," Tom said.

"Thanks."

Frankie said, "I heard what you said, Tom. I'm going to remember it too."

Andy said, "You might know he'd live in this part of town. It all adds up, don't it?"

No one answered him. No one spoke until at the top of the street Murph said, "There's a light on in the hallway. What does that mean?"

"It means we're lucky. We can see him coming to the door."

Tom gave the signal and they broke formation, each man moving into the shadow of a tree, except Tom who went up to the house.

The child was looking out the window. It was what his father made him do when he'd wake up from having a bad dream. The trouble was, he sometimes dreamed awake and couldn't go back to sleep because there were a lot of people in his room, all whispering. What kind of people, his father wanted to know. Men or women? Old people or young? And was there anyone he knew?

Funny-looking people. They didn't have any faces. Only eyes—which of course was why they whispered.

His father told him, Next time you tell them if they don't go away you'll call your dad. Or better still, look out the window for a while and think of all the things you did outdoors today. Then see if the funny people aren't gone when you look around the room again.

So at night he often did get up. The window was near his bed and the people never tried to stop him. Looking out, he would think about the places he could hide and how easy it would be to climb out from the bottom of his bed. He had a dugout under the mock-orange bushes, and under the old cellar doors propped together like a pup tent in the back of the garage; down the street were the sewer pipes they hadn't used yet, and what used to be the pumphouse next to Mrs. Malcolm's well, which was the best hiding place of all; the big boys sometimes played there.

Tom passed so close that the boy could have reached out and touched him.

The doorbell rang once, twice, three times.

The man, awakened from his sleep, came pulling on his bathrobe. He flung open the door at the same time he switched on the porch light.

A fusillade of shots rang out. The man seemed frozen like a picture of himself, his hand stretched out and so much light around him. Then he crumpled up and fell.

Twenty minutes later Andy was sitting on his bed at home when the ambulance siren sounded somewhere up the hill. His wife put out her hand to see if he was there. "Andy?"

"Yes?"

She went back to sleep until the town alarm sounded, four long blasts for a police emergency.

Andy dressed again and once more took his revolver from the bureau drawer.

"What time is it?" His wife turned over at the clicking sound as he refilled the chamber of the gun.

"Almost half-past three."

"It isn't right, a man your age."

"Somebody has to go." In the hall he phoned the police station for instructions.

This time Andy drove, as did the other deputies. Cars clogged the street where lights were on in all the houses, and people stood outdoors, their coats over their nightclothes, and watched the ambulance drive off. They told one another of the shots they took for granted to have been the backfires of a car.

Doc Harrington drove up. Black bag in hand, he went into the house. Andy followed on his heels. Both men stepped carefully around the bloodstains in the front hall.

The woman was hysterical. "They took our little boy. They killed his father and they took our little boy." She kept crying out for someone to help her; anyone. The Chief of Police and Tom, who was in the room with them, tried to calm her down. She couldn't say who "they" were.

When Doc appeared and commanded that someone get a neighbor woman in to help him, Tom started to leave. Andy caught his arm.

"I don't know what she's talking about," Tom said. "She says the boy's been kidnaped. More like a neighbor's got him, but I'm going to organize a search. If we don't find him it'll be the State Police, and after that the F.B.I."

"The kid's not here?"

"Maybe you can find him. I've been from basement to roof."

Room by room Andy searched the house. The child's bed had not been slept in much that night. You couldn't really tell, the things a youngster took in bed with him. The window was open just a little and it was hard to raise it higher. The back door to the house was open and Andy would have said the kid had gone that way because on the back steps was a woolen monkey, its ears still frosty damp with spittle.

Andy got a flashlight from the car and joined the other deputies, Tom, Murph, and Frankie among them. They went from house to house to ask if anyone had seen the child. No one had and the mother's cry of kidnaping had gone the rounds.

They searched till dawn. By then the State Police were in the town; the Chief cordoned off the house and set a guard. The house was quite empty. Doc Harrington had given the woman an injection and driven her himself the eight miles to the hospital.

The men, chilled to the bone, were having coffee at the station house when old Mrs. Malcolm, on her way to early Mass, stopped by to say she'd heard a noise that sounded like a kitten's mew at the bottom of her well. The well had long been dry and she'd had it boarded up after the Russo dog had fallen in and died there. But the kids kept coming back. They pried loose the boards and played at flushing "Charlie" from his underground hideout.

Tom and Andy were already in the Malcolm yard when the fire truck arrived. With their own hands they tore away the boards that weren't already loose at the well's mouth. The shaft was dark, but there were steps at least halfway down the shoring. It was decided, however, to put a ladder down.

Tom, again making himself the boss, said *he* was going down. The others linked themselves together, a human chain, to keep the ladder from striking bottom. The depth was about thirty feet. Andy was the signalman. He reported every step Tom took, and he cried out the moment Tom's flashlight discovered the child on the rocks heaped at the bottom of the dry well.

"He's sleeping," Tom shouted up. "He's sleeping like a little baby."

"He can't be, falling that far down. Be careful how you lift him," Andy said.

Tom steadied the ladder among the rocks, draped the limp child over his shoulder, and started up. The firemen went back to the truck for their emergency equipment. Andy kept up a singsong cautioning: a kid was just a little thing, it got hurt real easy. Tom was too large a man for such a job, and he ought to have more patience.

"Will you shut your damned mouth up there?" Tom shouted. "I'm coming up the best I can."

He'd got past halfway when the boy recovered consciousness. At first he squirmed and cried. The men crowded in to watch. Andy begged them not to block the light.

"Just keep coming easy," Andy crooned, and to the child, "There's nothing you should be a-scared of, little fella. You're going to come out fine."

Then—it was at the moment Tom's face moved into the light—the child began to scream and beat at him with fists and feet, and a rhythm of words came out of him, over and over again, until no one who wasn't deaf could mistake what he was saying: "My dad, my dad, you shot my dad!"

Tom tried to get a better hold of him, or so he claimed when he got up, but the child fought out of his grasp. Tom caught him by the leg; then the ladder jolted—a rock displaced below. The child slipped away and plummeted silently out of sight. That was what was so strange, the way he fell, not making any cry at all.

Tom lumbered down again. He brought the child up and laid him on the ground. Everyone could see that he was dead, the skull crushed in on top.

Andy searched the wrists anyway and then the chest where the pajamas had been ripped, but he found no heartbeat, and the mouth was full of blood. He looked up at Tom who stood, dirty and sullen, watching him.

"I didn't want to let go of him. I swear it, Andy."

Andy's eyes never left his face. "You killed him. You killed this baby boy."

"I didn't, Andy."

"I saw it with my own eyes." Andy drew his gun.

"For God's sake, man. Murph, Frankie, you saw what happened!"

They too had drawn their guns. The Chief of Police and the State Troopers were coming up the hill, a minute or two away. The two firemen coming with the resuscitator were unarmed.

Tom backed off a step, but when he saw Andy release the safety catch he turned and ran. That's when they brought him down, making sure he was immediately dead.

THE MOMENT OF TIME

by Miriam Allen deFord

This is possibly a "mirror of all times" for, as long as there has been an organized society there have been the Larissas of their day, in Ur in Abraham's time, in Florence of the Medecis, in the London Dickens knew.

It was a moment of the world, like any other. All over the earth people were being born and dying, working and playing, murdering and robbing and doing deeds of mercy and justice, sleeping and eating and undergoing operations and taking baths and reading books and making love.

The place was not like any other. It announced its era. It gleamed with chromium. Its stark furniture gave forth the faint flavor of something out of Ray Bradbury by Anais Nin. Its occupants wore clothes accustomed because they were fashionable, doomed to the ridicule of a quarter-century later. The hostess made conversation, wondering why the guests had come.

"Everything of importance in my life," Larissa Farnsworth was saying, "I can trace back to having borrowed a pair of white kid gloves when I was seventeen." But even this did not warn her that twenty years hence she could be saying to some other auditor, "Everything of importance since I was thirty I can trace to a day when Hugo Dean and Gail Preston dropped in unexpectedly." (Not that she would say it. Not ever.)

She glanced around her white-and-chartreuse living room, and she was well pleased with herself. Without her environment, she would not have known how to live.

Hugo Dean prepared to pour the cocktails. The crystal glasses were banded with black spirals.

"I brought this poor child here," he announced abruptly, "because she has a confession to make to you."

Larissa looked speculatively at him without speaking. Hugo Dean was a curious creature. He was a savage and relentless critic, because he was honest and possessed standards. If his dearest friend wrote a book he did not like, he would flay it cruelly and bitterly. Then he would go out and walk for miles, or stint himself of his small luxuries, to do that same friend a kindness. Larissa had cried for two hours over his review of her first novel. Soon after, he spent a weekend with old Bascome, and bullied the publisher into giving her a much better contract for her second. His review of that was almost as rancorous.

Gail Preston she scarcely knew. She had met the girl half a dozen times at literary parties, and had not been attracted by her taciturn angularity. She must, Larissa reflected, be really older than she was herself, and yet there was a specious look of childishness about her, in her sullen mouth and her thin arms. She made her living, people said, in the lesser forms of journalistic scavenging—ghost-writing and that sort of thing. One never saw Gail's name in print. One of Hugo's unexpected tender spots, undoubtedly; but what confession could she possibly have to make, one would have said, that would be of any interest to Larissa Farnsworth? Larissa suppressed a foolish shiver of apprehension: nonsense!

As if to answer the unworded question, Gail Preston stared gloomily into her cocktail and blurted out, in her husky voice:

"I don't know why you should care, or why I should tell you. But it slipped out when I was talking to Hugo, and he made me promise . . . I'm Harry's first wife."

Larissa gasped. The chromium and the black-banded glasses and all her beautiful concord with a highly polished machine civilization did not come as rewards from her writing. Her novels were precious, witty, advanced, the delight of a few but neglected by the many, of more interest to collectors of first editions than to the buying public. Her livelihood was in alimony from Harry Farnsworth.

"You're talking nonsense," she said harshly. "Harry never was married before. I would have known."

"We were married in Peoria, Illinois, on August 12, 1960," retorted Gail Preston bluntly.

This was a nuisance, and she didn't thank Hugo.

She calculated swiftly. She had met Harry in 1962, married him in 1963, divorced him in 1967. The dates fitted. But this wasn't at all the way one should be finding out a thing like that. It was ridiculous—Hugo putting his foot in it as usual, trying to compensate for his public severity by his private sentimentality. She laughed.

"What is this, Miss Preston, blackmail? If you'd ever been married to Harry, you'd be drawing alimony just as I am. He has plenty of money, you know. It's his only virtue."

Gail's face set in stubborn lines.

"I don't believe in alimony," she muttered. "I can earn my own living, under my own name. I married Harry for love, not for his money.

"Besides," she added with the effect of casualness, "we never were divorced."

There was a complete silence. Gail Preston stared at her cocktail, raised it slowly to her lips, and gulped it down. The tinkle as she set her glass on the crystal coaster broke the spell.

"But—" Larissa's voice was strictly under control. Her mind was racing. "But then Harry and I weren't legally married."

"Yes. I mean no," said Gail gauchely.

"Have you—can you prove any of this?"

"Of course. I have the certificate."

Silently Hugo refilled both their glasses. Larissa drank her own Martini fast.

"But that's outrageous!" she said icily. She clasped her hands tightly. "Not that I care about the conventional aspect, of course. But—why, even my name!" She laughed, a little shrilly. "I've always written—both my books, and the new one coming out, under the name of Larissa Farnsworth. I can't change it now, when my reputation is established. I can't build up another reputation on a scandal."

Hugo Dean turned away to smile. Larissa Tubbs hadn't been a very pretty name.

"And then there's the alimony," he remarked smoothly. "If you were never married, Larissa, of course you've never been divorced, either."

"I wouldn't have interfered," Gail muttered. "Hugo insisted."

Larissa turned on him fiercely.

"What business was it of yours? I suppose you want me to be noble and relinquish my income. Is that it? So you can say 'poor Larissa' and scramble about to find me a way to get by? *I* can't ghost-write the memoirs of prizefighters and beauty specialists, you know, like your friend Miss Preston," she added brutally.

"You could have Harry Farnsworth up for bigamy," Hugo suggested mildly.

"Very likely! I can see the headlines—NOVELIST SUES MILLIONAIRE EX-HUBBY. That would be grand publicity, with *Extrinsic Eros* coming out next month."

"I thought you ought to know." Hugo was quite unperturbed. "You need a little moral conflict, Larissa. It might make your books a bit more human."

"Thank you," replied Larissa bitterly. "Just a literary evangelist, aren't you? Well, I don't want my soul saved this afternoon, thank you. Take your mourner's bench away. You're like every critic, Hugo

—a frustrated writer. So, since you can't create, you take it out by injecting melodrama into the lives of your acquaintances."

"Your cliché is quite mistaken, my dear," Hugo answered calmly. "My interest is rather of a purely scientific nature. I was curious to see how you would react."

"Well, now that you have the butterfly safely in the cyanide jar, would you and your collaborator mind leaving it there? The laboratory is closed for the day. I don't know *what* I'm going to do—probably nothing. Does that satisfy your scientific curiosity, or shall I report on the experiment later, so that you can close your files?"

Larissa rose, and Gail immediately jerked to her feet. But Hugo remained comfortably seated—in fact, he crossed his legs and carefully selected a caviare on toast from the plate of canapes.

"I'd rather watch the experiment a bit longer, if you don't mind," he said serenely.

"But I do—" Larissa began. Gail interrupted her.

"Come on, Hugo," she said brusquely. "This is enough." She drew on her gloves with nervous fingers.

For the first time Larissa looked at her objectively. A swift cinema sequence passed before her memory—Harry in the little restaurant on Waverly Place; Harry and she at the license bureau; Harry and that filthy little blonde; Harry explaining the stock market; Harry the morning she had told him she was done with him.

She had thought then that she knew Harry through and through; from sheer boredom she had turned aside a hundred of his recollections. Yet now she knew that all the time he had been concealing—this!

Another thought came to her. Harry must have known *this* woman through and through, to have taken such a chance, living in the same city with her. He must have trusted her implicitly, relied in absolute conviction on her loyal silence, whatever he might do. No matter what had separated them, Gail had loved Harry Farnsworth fundamentally, as Larissa had never been able to love anyone; and Harry knew it. She gazed at Gail with a mixture of pity, respect, and scorn.

"You still love him, don't you?" she said slowly. Gail simply nodded.

The doglike love, Larissa thought contemptuously: fawning, patient, persisting through abuse. Harry was even more of a cad than she had believed—he deserved no mercy. I suppose she wouldn't divorce him because she kept on hoping to get him back. She'd take him back even now, if it were possible. I wonder how she ever brought herself to leave him. But of course, she didn't—he left her, that's obvious.

What was behind all this, in Gail's and Hugo's minds? Did they imagine Gail had a chance to capture him again? Was this inverse blackmail—no fuss from Larissa, and the alimony would be continued? How very funny. How little either of them understood her—or knew everything she knew!

"There's no chance we'll ever be reunited," Gail said as if against her will. "If we'd had a quarrel, it might have been different. But he just got tired of me."

Imagine confessing such a thing of oneself! Larissa's cold pity froze to disdain.

"A nice ethical problem, isn't it, Larissa?" remarked Hugo Dean coolly.

Larissa hated him with a cold hatred. She did not even answer him. But she could not stop her ears against his ruminating voice.

"Legally you haven't the right to a cent of Harry Farnsworth's money. You know damned well he'd never have given it to you voluntarily. He'd have fought the settlement hard if he hadn't been afraid you'd find out about Gail. But I'm not one to talk, and you can see that Gail isn't the sort that talks, either. You're perfectly safe, aren't you? We three are the only ones who know."

"And Harry," said Gail.

"And Harry, of course. Now that you know, Larissa, you could go to court and ask for a reversal of the settlement—say you can manage without it now. That would be pretty quixotic, I suppose. Or you could turn a substantial slice of it over to the person who is actually entitled to it."

"I wouldn't take it," Gail interposed quickly.

"No, I didn't suppose you would. But I thought maybe Larissa might offer it."

"I'm not such a fool," Larissa snapped.

"No, I guess you're not."

He rose slowly, setting down his glass.

"Where is Harry now, do you know, Larissa?"

She shrugged her shoulders.

"Heaven knows—somewhere in Africa, hunting, the last I heard. I don't hear from him directly—just through Collingson and Brock. They're his lawyers."

"Yes, I know Stu Collingson. We were classmates at Yale. In fact—" Hugo was staring at the glass-topped table, tracing its enameled design with a studious fingernail. "In fact, I saw Stu only today. Had lunch with him."

"Yes?" Manners forbade her opening the door for them, but she could not refrain from glancing at it.

"Yes. He told me a piece of news he'd just received."

There was a pause. Unostentatiously he moved nearer to Gail Preston. Then he went on evenly.

"Harry's dead. He died of fever, somewhere in the interior, almost a month ago. They've just got word out to Stu."

"Oh, no!" The strangled cry burst from Gail. Larissa sank back into her chair. Her cold lips scarcely moved.

"You're not being funny, Hugo."

"I'm not trying to be. It's true."

He put an arm around Gail's shoulders; she was sobbing, long, hard sobs that shook her body, but her eyes were dry.

"And Stu told me something else, Larissa. Harry left a will. A holographic will, with no witnesses, but that's legal in this state. Stu's had it in his office, but he never read it till today."

Larissa looked at him, unable to speak.

"He left everything to his wife, Gail Preston Farnsworth. Stu was puzzled—he didn't know Harry had ever been married, except to you. That's why he told me about it."

"I don't want it! I won't take it!" Gail cried hoarsely. Larissa shut her eyes; she felt dizzy.

"You'll have to, child. Of course, if you want to turn the money over to Larissa here—I suppose she'd accept it, even after the scandal."

Larissa jumped to her feet. Her fists were clenched. Her face was white under the make-up and her eyes spat sparks.

"Get out!" she whispered. "Get out—both of you—at once! You came here, Hugo Dean, knowing that—"

"I thought I'd give you a chance, Larissa," Hugo Dean said softly. "I've always liked you. I'm not a very good judge of character, I guess. I thought when you learned about Gail, you'd do the—shall we say the gentlemanly thing? As Gail would have done in your place."

His voice turned metallic.

"And in that case, I could have made it easier for you. You could have been the innocent victim—Collingson would take my word for it, wouldn't he? And Gail's soft—too soft: I know her. She would have forced some of the money on you—she'd do it even now, I'll wager, if I'd let her.

"But I shan't. Stu Collingson is going to know the whole truth—that before you knew Harry was dead, you were aware that you had never been legally married to him, knew you were taking alimony from him under false pretences, and had every intention of keeping on doing so."

"You make me sick!" he snarled suddenly and savagely.

Then his tone warmed. "Come along, Gail," he said tenderly. "We're going somewhere together—I'm not going to let you be alone just now. I'm sticking to you till you get over this. You can't get rid of me—"

He was still talking, like a mother to her infant, as he led the un-resisting figure to the door, opened it, and shut it softly behind him. Gail would have stumbled but for his arm.

Larissa stood for a full minute staring at the closed door. Then deliberately, with the slow gesture of a somnambulist, she picked out the glasses they had drunk from and dropped them hard on the black-and-chartreuse tiles of the unnecessary fireplace. With a frozen hand she reached for the telephone and dialed a number.

When she got it, she rasped: "Mr. Collingson, please." Her voice grew brittle. "All right, Stu: explain," she commanded. "What possessed you? If it was because of that whey-faced, sniveling little nincompoop—

"Are you completely out of your senses? No, I *won't* be careful; why should I be careful now?

"We had everything planned, everything arranged. You *promised* me. You told me yourself we'd better wait a month or two more—You told me Gail would never talk—

"And to Hugo Dean, of all people! Now you listen to me, Stu Collingson, and don't utter another word till I've finished. The arrangement is off. Naturally. How do you figure on getting half of a non-existent inheritance? The whole thing depended on your disposing of that imbecilic will, and *then* revealing the news about Harry's death.

"What are you *laughing* about, you idiot? What's so funny? Who made the first suggestion, you or I? And then to tell Hugo you *just* got word about Harry—and that you didn't know what was in that will! You told me yourself how Harry read it to you when he left it with you before he went to Africa.

"So I had to sit here, right in the presence of the *real* Mrs. Farns-

worth, and listen to Hugo telling me as a great piece of news that
Harry'd been married to that nonentity all along! It was all I could
do to keep from screaming at him that I'd known it a lot longer than
he had, that I learned it two weeks ago from *you*. And then inform-
ing us that Harry had died—for Heaven's sake, Stu, did you and he
stage that scene just so I could witness the poor fool's collapse? She
was the only one to whom it was news.

". . . Oh, oh—I'm beginning to understand! This whole thing
was a put-on, wasn't it? You *never* meant to destroy the will, did
you—and violate your sacred lawyer's trust? You *never* meant to
share Harry's money with me!

"What? You hoped what? What integrity? What are you talking
about?" She laughed. "Who's going to look after Larissa Farnsworth
but herself? I simply can't believe two grown men like you and Hugo
could be so stupid. Can't you just see me, falling all to pieces: *so*
sorry, I never dreamt, no, of course I can't make any claim now to
Harry's name, or his fortune either— Does that sound like me, Stu
Collingson, or like that mush of a Preston woman?

"All right, now you've had your fun, you and Hugo both. But I'm
not through. I'll sue you for extortion—I'll tell the whole story in
court. I'll tell how you tried to trap me into—

"Oh." Her voice grew dreary. "I see. I suppose with your snide
lawyer's tricks you've got me coming or going. If I say I accepted
the offer, then I suppose I could be accused of fraud. And if I say
I didn't know about Gail, you'll get Hugo to swear he was listening
in when we had that conversation on the phone two weeks ago, and
that I only pretended to be surprised when he put on his little show
today for Gail's benefit—and then if I'd testified otherwise I could
be accused of perjury. I might have known that you were both
Harry's friends, not mine.

"Damn you both, Stu. I never want to see either of you again as
long as I live. And to hell with your concern—what I'm going to do
next is my own business. So good of you to promise to keep quiet
now and let me go on using Harry's name! Where's Harry's money?
Don't I get any damages for what he did to me in the first place?
Don't I—"

She hung up abruptly. Nobody on earth would ever hear Larissa
Farnsworth weep.

BLACK BELT

by Richard Deming

As we have already seen, there are many drives which impel a man to what seems senseless behavior. One reason is that society bestows a certain glamour upon the man who can legally function beyond the law.

Deputy Inspector Maurice Ireland was thumbtacking a new duty roster to the bulletin board when the well-dressed man walked into the station house. The man's dapper appearance, combined with his cultured tone when he spoke to the desk sergeant, caused the precinct commander to turn and examine him. Neither dapperness nor culture were often encountered in the 41st Precinct.

"I wish to report a crime," the man said.

"All right," Sergeant Block said agreeably.

The complainant was somewhere in his mid-thirties, rather slight of build and with delicate, almost effeminate features. It crossed Ireland's mind that he must have driven to the station house, because he couldn't have walked through Hunts Point from a subway stop without being mugged.

When the man spoke again, Ireland realized he had been.

"It happened on 163rd Street, in front of St. Athanasius Church. This Puerto Rican chap exhibited a switchblade knife and demanded my money. In broad daylight, mind you, within sight of several pedestrians."

Sergeant Block showed no astonishment. The 41st Precinct received between ninety and a hundred assault and robbery complaints a month, and a good number of them occurred in broad daylight before witnesses. The only thing that could have astonished the sergeant would have been for one of the witnesses to accompany the complainant to the station house. Hunts Point residents never admitted witnessing crimes.

Poising a ballpoint pen over a squeal form, the desk sergeant asked, "Can you describe this man?"

"Oh, that won't be necessary. You may just send someone over to look at him. He's lying on the sidewalk."

Sergeant Block stared at the dapper little man without understanding.

"I'm afraid I killed him," the man said apologetically. "In disarming him I flipped him over my shoulder and his head hit the sidewalk. It rather thoroughly dashed his brains out."

Sergeant Block continued to stare up at him, his pen still poised over the complaint form. Ireland walked over to the desk.

"I'm Inspector Ireland, the precinct commander," he announced.

The smaller man thrust out his hand and the inspector found himself accepting a cordial handshake. "How do you do, Inspector? My name is Rollin Singer."

The desk sergeant recovered enough to lay down his pen, pick up the dispatch mike and order a radio car to the intersection of 163rd and Tiffany. Then he picked up the pen again and entered the name Rollin Singer on the complaint form.

"Address?" he asked.

"One-thousand-nine-and-a-half Simpson."

The sergeant stared up at him again. "You live there?"

"That's correct."

Sergeant Block's expression approached disbelief, but he wrote the address down. Ireland asked, "How long have you lived there, Mr. Singer?"

"I just moved in last evening. I was on my way to work when this Puerto Rican chap accosted me."

"You work around here?"

"Oh, no. I operate Rollin's Beauty Salon on Fifth Avenue in Manhattan. When I say I was on my way to work, I mean I was en route to the subway station at 163rd Street and Westchester Avenue."

This time both Sergeant Block and Ireland stared. Finally the inspector asked, "How did you happen to settle in this particular section of the Bronx, Mr. Singer?"

The dapper little man raised his eyebrows. "I'm afraid I don't understand the question. Or your disapproving tone."

"I didn't mean to sound disapproving, Mr. Singer. I am merely curious. You look and act like a man of some affluence. And the 1000 block of Simpson is hardly one of Hunts Point's better neighborhoods."

Rollin Singer shrugged. "I find the area quaint. And the rent is certainly reasonable."

Sergeant Block said sourly, "You won't find it so reasonable after you've been mugged a few times. We estimate that nine out of ten kids in that block are on smack, which makes it a pretty dangerous place to live. During the past three weeks the block you live in has had eighteen assaults and robberies, one rape, one murder, three overdose deaths and a baby suffocation."

"My, my," Singer clucked. "So short a distance from the station house too, and on the same street."

Ireland felt himself flushing. "The high crime rate in Hunts Point stems from drug abuse and substandard living conditions, Mr. Singer, not from inadequate policing. We make plenty of arrests."

"Oh, I'm sure you people do all you can," Singer said with an indulgent smile. "But you really don't have to worry about me. I'm quite adept at self-defense. I hold a black belt in jujitsu. From Japan, not one of the meaningless black belts handed out like popcorn by American schools. And in *real* jujitsu, not the adulterated version taught here. Do you know the difference?"

"No," Ireland admitted.

"What is taught as jujitsu in America is merely another simple variety of self-defense similar to judo, karate and aikado. But in its original form, as devised by the *samurai* and secretly handed down from generation to generation, it is a whole way of life. It involves rigid mental and emotional training as well as physical skills. And it encompasses *all* the techniques of unarmed combat. Judo, karate and aikado are all merely simple segments of jujitsu as taught by the samurai. I could easily tie in knots any American trained wearer of a so-called black belt in any of those three techniques."

Inspector Ireland looked him up and down with what started out as skepticism but turned to belief when he remembered the dead mugger lying in front of St. Athanasius Church. He said, "That still doesn't explain why you choose to live in the heart of a high crime area."

The smaller man looked Ireland up and down too. It took him longer because the inspector stood six feet four.

Eventually he said, "Are you implying that police permission is required to live in this neighborhood?"

Ireland felt himself flush again. "Of course not," he said shortly. Then, because the little man kept putting him on the defensive, he took it out on Sergeant Block. Glaring down at the desk sergeant, he snapped, "Make sure this matter is thoroughly investigated before you release Mr. Singer, Sergeant."

Sergeant Block gazed up at him quizzically, his expression suggesting wonder at why the precinct commander felt it necessary to instruct him that a man who had just confessed to homicide had to be held for investigation, even though presumably it was justifiable homicide. Doing an about-face, Ireland stalked into his office.

This occurred Wednesday morning. On Wednesday afternoon Sergeant Block informed Ireland that the medical examiner and the homicide team that had investigated the death of the would-be mugger in front of St. Athanasius Church had agreed it was justifiable homicide and that the circumstances didn't merit a formal inquest. The dead man had been a twenty-five-year-old drug addict named Edwin Garth with a long record of arrests for assaults and robberies.

Both muggings and homicides were too common in Hunts Point for the incident to interest the news media. It wasn't even reported in the newspapers.

Inspector Ireland took Saturdays and Sundays as his days off. When he logged in Monday morning the desk sergeant informed him that Rollin Singer had killed another mugger Saturday night, this time in the first-floor corridor of his apartment building. Again the M.E. and the investigating homicide officers had agreed it was so clearly justifiable homicide that no inquest was called for. This time the assailant had been a thirty-year-old man named Harry Purvis with three convictions for robbery with violent assault.

"Purvis was waiting under the stairs when Singer arrived home from having dinner out," the sergeant reported. "He jumped out and tried to brain Singer with a lead pipe. Singer gave him a karate chop between the eyes and it killed him."

Ireland sat at his desk and thought about this for nearly an hour. Finally he got up and went out to the squeal desk.

"Did this make the papers?" he asked Sergeant Block.

Since their conversation the sergeant had recorded complaints of five muggings, two rapes, seven burglaries, and a homicide. "Did what make the papers, Inspector?" he asked.

"This Singer fellow killing another mugger," Ireland said edgily.

"Oh. I don't think so. Why should it?"

"No particular reason, I guess," the inspector said in a glum voice. "Get in touch with Singer and ask him to drop by to see me."

"He'll be at his beauty salon in Manhattan now, Inspector."

"Well, phone him there and find out when he can get here. If he can't make it until evening, schedule an appointment anyway, and I'll either stay over or come back after dinner."

"Yes, sir," the sergeant said.

A little later he stuck his head in Ireland's office to report that Rollin Singer said he customarily got off the subway at 163rd and Westchester about a quarter to six, and he would come straight from there to the precinct house. The inspector decided to stay over to wait for him instead of leaving at five and coming back.

The man showed up at five minutes to six. Ireland asked him to be seated and got right to the point.

He said, "Although you've resided in this neighborhood less than a week, Mr. Singer, already you have been forced to kill two assailants in self-defense. Aren't you by now convinced that Hunts Point is a pretty precarious place to live?"

"Thousands live in Hunts Point, Inspector. Do you give them all that advice?"

Ireland made an impatient gesture. "Your appearance is an invitation to attack, Mr. Singer. You look prosperous and you look easy. It's inevitable that you'll be subject to more attacks if you stay here."

"I can defend myself, I assure you."

"What if the next mugger has a gun?"

Rollin Singer smiled. "I'm not foolhardy, Inspector. Unless he made the mistake of getting too close, I would never offer resistance to a robber with a gun. Since I seldom carry more than a few dollars, it wouldn't be worth it."

After gazing at him in silence for a time, Ireland said, "Even if you survive all future attacks, the police are going to look with a jaundiced eye at any more dead muggers. Are you aware that self-defense is a legally acceptable plea only when no more force than necessary is used to repel attack?"

"Oh, yes. You don't for a moment believe I deliberately killed either mugger, do you? Both deaths were quite accidental, because my intention was merely to protect myself."

The inspector said bluntly, "If you protect yourself so thoroughly a third time, you may find yourself on trial for murder."

The smaller man hiked his eyebrows. "Do you really think any jury would convict me, Inspector?"

"I think one might, if we established that you were deliberately inciting these attacks."

Rollin Singer looked astonished. "You know perfectly well I have done no such thing, Inspector. If I had been walking around deliberately flashing a roll of money, you might have some justification for such a charge. But both attacks on me occurred with absolutely no provocation on my part and in places where it seems to me I should have the right to feel safe from such attack. The first was in front of a church, in broad daylight, before witnesses, the second in a corridor of my own apartment building. I suspect that if a jury were called upon to consider the matter, it would conclude that the real culprit is the 41st Precinct, for failure to keep residents safe from such attacks."

Inspector Ireland examined the dapper little man sourly for a long time before heaving a resigned sigh. "All right, Mr. Singer. Just remember what I said about using only enough force to repel attack."

When the week passed with no further word of Rollin Singer, Inspector Ireland almost forgot him, but on Monday morning the inspector learned that a third would-be mugger had died and a fourth had been seriously injured during another attempt to rob Rollin Singer. The attempt had been made in midafternoon on Sunday at the intersection of Simpson and Westchester Avenue, a scant half block south of the police station, by two eighteen-year-old addicts, one armed with a hatchet and the other armed with a machete. Singer had spun the hatchet carrier in front of his accomplice's descending machete with the result that the youth had been nearly decapitated and had died instantly. The jujitsu expert had then flipped the machete wielder into the path of a passing truck, putting the second teen-ager in the hospital with a number of broken bones and internal injuries.

The dead youth had been named Felipe Lopez. The one whose machete had killed him was Jesus Flores. He had been charged with homicide. Rollin Singer had not been held.

"At least he didn't kill anyone this time," Sergeant Block said. "It was the guy's own buddy who did the killing."

But it was Singer's expertise that had placed the dead boy in precisely the right spot to get his head chopped nearly off, Ireland thought. It also was a matter of pure chance that the second youth wasn't also dead. The possibility that the truck might kill him must have occurred to the little man as he threw the boy in front of it.

"This one make the papers?" the inspector asked.

"Naw. The papers are so bored with Hunts Point violence that police reporters seldom drop in to check the blotter any more. They just phone to ask if anything newsworthy has happened. I thought you might not care to have this one mentioned, so I didn't."

"Good," Ireland said approvingly. "I don't want any crime news deliberately suppressed, but I'd just as soon Mr. Singer's exploits not be mentioned unless some reporter specifically asks about him."

The homicide team investigating Rollin Singer's first kill had run a check on him through the Bureau of Criminal Identification. There was no local package on him. Ireland decided it was time to be a little more thorough. He got off a wire to FBI headquarters in Washington, D.C., and the answer came back early in the afternoon. The little man had no criminal record.

The inspector decided the situation had reached the point where higher authority should be informed of it. He phoned Assistant Chief Inspector Horace Fitzer, police commander for all of the Bronx, and told him all about it. Fitzer said he would consult with the D.A. and call back.

Instead it was Bronx District Attorney Lyle Corrigan who phoned Ireland about a half hour later. He asked the precinct commander for a detailed report on all three cases involving Rollin Singer. Ireland not only gave him that, but described his meeting with the man in his office following the second mugger kill.

When he finished, Corrigan said, "This man is deliberately killing these muggers, Inspector. I know something of jujitsu in its ancient form, because I had some YMCA training in both judo and karate while I was in college. If he's as expert as he claims, he could have subdued his attackers without killing them."

"Maybe," Ireland agreed. "But it would take more than a personal opinion to convince a jury he used more force than necessary to repel attack. Even if they suspected he had, can you visualize them convicting a respectable businessman for murder when all of his victims were dope-addict muggers who died in the act of attacking him with weapons when he was unarmed?"

After a period of silence the D.A. emitted a reluctant, "No." Then he added, "You know this character is going to continue to kill muggers, don't you?"

"I suspect it."

"You also know some reporter is bound eventually to learn what's going on and make a sensational story out of it."

"Uh-huh. Which is the main reason I called Inspector Fitzer."

"It's going to put the 41st Precinct in a pretty poor light to have it publicized that police protection is so poor down there, a resident's only chance of survival is to become a jujitsu expert."

"It's going to put the whole Bronx in a poor light," Ireland told him. "You know how these things go. The minute interest is stirred up about the crime rate here, reporters will start gathering statistics to compare Hunts Point with other areas. And we're not the only section of the Bronx with a crime problem."

There was another period of silence before the D.A. said slowly, "It's also going to present me with a choice of the frying pan or the fire. If I don't try Singer for murder, my opponent in the next election can charge me with coddling a psychopathic killer. If I do, he can hit me for persecuting an innocent man whose only crime was defending himself against criminals who never should have been on the street in the first place if I had properly done my job of prosecuting *them* for previous crimes."

"What do you suggest?" Ireland asked.

"I want to talk to this Singer man. When can you get him to my office? On second thought, too many reporters drop in here at unexpected times, and one just might get curious about who he was. When can you get him to your office?"

"He made it at five of six last time. I can phone him at his beauty salon and ask him to drop by again this evening."

"All right. Inspector Fitzer and I will be there a few minutes before six, unless you call me back that you can't arrange it."

Ireland didn't have to call back, because Rollin Singer readily agreed to make the meeting.

Assistant Chief Deputy Inspector Horace Fitzer, a burly man of sixty, arrived at the precinct house at a quarter to six. District Attorney Lyle Corrigan came in five minutes later. He was a tall, slightly stooped man who wore horn-rimmed glasses and somewhat resembled Henry Kissinger. Rollin Singer showed up five minutes after the Bronx D.A.

After introductions and after everyone was seated, Lyle Corrigan said, "I'm not going to beat about the bush, Mr. Singer. I'm familiar enough with the original art of jujitsu as you practice it to know you wouldn't have had to kill any of your attackers in order to subdue them. Or at least not three of them. I'm convinced you are deliberately killing."

Singer examined him quizzically and quite calmly. "I think you would have considerable difficulty establishing that in court, Mr. Corrigan. I will go on record right now, under oath if you desire, that my sole intent was to protect myself against attack in all three instances. I assure you all three deaths were quite accidental."

Burly Horace Fitzer said in a surly voice, "You're wasting your time, Lyle. This guy is obviously a psychopathic killer who thinks he has cleverly figured out a legal way to get his kicks. You ought to disabuse him of that notion fast by dragging him before a grand jury."

The little man gazed at the Bronx police commander without resentment. In a pleasant tone he said, "Mr. Corrigan knows he could never get an indictment, let alone a conviction, Inspector."

The district attorney said, "Let's try a little reason in place of name calling. If you do not enjoy killing, Mr. Singer, may I assume you prefer to avoid any more of it?"

"Of course."

"Well, as long as you continue to reside in Hunts Point, it is probably inevitable that you will be subject to further attacks. It would solve the whole problem if you simply moved elsewhere."

Rollin Singer gave him a disapproving look. "I understand that in Moscow you have to live where you are told. I wasn't aware that as yet we had such police-state restrictions in the United States."

"I'm not *telling* you where to live," the district attorney said with patience. "I am merely asking your co-operation."

"Don't you think a fairer solution would be for the police to make the streets of Hunts Point safe to walk upon, at least during daylight hours? A couple of years back one of your medical examiners issued a report you may be familiar with based on an evaluation of the nearly forty deaths that had occurred in my immediate neighborhood over a ten-month period. Only two of the deaths were from natural causes, which means the residents of that section have only a one-in-twenty chance of dying a natural death. I consider that a disgrace to the police department."

"They weren't all violent deaths," Inspector Ireland growled. "I read that report. Over half were from alcoholism and drug overdoses."

"True," the little man agreed. "But fifteen were violent deaths, which amounts to one-out-of-four. That compares to a figure of ninety-three percent of all deaths throughout New York City being from natural causes. There is no way you can make Hunts Point sound as though it were adequately policed, Inspector."

With a touch of exasperation the D.A. said, "Then why do you persist in living here, Mr. Singer? You know you are going to continue to be attacked."

"Quite possibly."

"You also must know that eventually some reporter is going to stumble on the story and blow it wide open."

"The thought has occurred to me," Singer admitted.

"What do you think will happen then?" the D.A. asked sharply.

"Two things," the little man said promptly. "First, I imagine the publicity will bring an abrupt end to attacks on me, because word will circulate among the local addicts that I am not very safe prey."

Corrigan grunted. "What's the second thing?"

The little man smiled at him. "Why I think my beauty salon will become the most popular in Manhattan. Women will fall all over themselves to have their hair dressed by a genuine certified killer."

Silence in the room grew to a crescendo. The dapper little man rose to his feet.

"Is that all you wanted with me, gentlemen?" he asked politely.

Neither police officer made any answer, merely continuing to gaze at the man in silence. District Attorney Corrigan didn't say anything either, but he finally gave a bare nod.

Singer walked out of the room. Silence continued for some time. Presently Corrigan emitted a deep sigh and got out of his chair and strode to the door.

"I've been considering retiring to private practice for some time anyway," he commented, and walked out also.

The assistant chief inspector and the deputy inspector looked at each other. Horace Fitzer stood up.

"I could have retired six months ago if I had wanted to," he remarked en route to the door.

Ireland sat at his desk for a while before rising heavily and plodding over to look out at the complaint desk. Sergeant Block was no longer on duty, of course, having been relieved by the night-duty man some time ago.

The man on duty, a Sergeant Smithers, was a recent transferee about whom the inspector knew very little. Ireland knew he wouldn't really be able to put his heart into blasting out an inferior he knew so casually. To bring about a real emotional catharsis it had to be an underling of long and close association.

He decided he would just have to wait until morning to vent his feelings.

THE QUESTION

by Stanley Ellin

Professionals not only take pride in their work—they also enjoy it. As is only right and proper . . .

I am an electrocutioner . . . I prefer this word to executioner; I think words make a difference. When I was a boy, people who buried the dead were undertakers, and then somewhere along the way they became morticians and are better off for it.

Take the one who used to be the undertaker in my town. He was a decent, respectable man very friendly if you'd let him be, but hardly anybody would let him be. Today, his son—who now runs the business—is not an undertaker but a mortician, and is welcome everywhere. As a matter of fact, he's an officer in my Lodge and is one of the most popular members we have. And all it took to do that was changing one word to another. The job's the same but the word is different, and people somehow will always go by words rather than meanings.

So, as I said, I am an electrocutioner—which is the proper professional word for it in my state where the electric chair is the means of execution.

Not that this is my profession. Actually, it's a sideline, as it is for most of us who perform executions. My real business is running an electrical supply and repair shop just as my father did before me. When he died I inherited not only the business from him, but also the position of state's electrocutioner.

We established a tradition, my father and I. He was running the shop profitably even before the turn of the century when electricity was a comparatively new thing, and he was the first man to perform a successful electrocution for the state. It was not the state's first electrocution, however. That one was an experiment and was badly bungled by the engineer who installed the chair in the state prison. My father, who had helped install the chair, was the assistant at the electrocution, and he told me that everything that could go wrong that day did go wrong. The current was eccentric, his boss froze on the switch, and the man in the chair was alive and kicking at the same time he was being burned to a crisp. The next time, my father offered to do the job himself, rewired the chair, and handled the switch so well that he was offered the job of official electrocutioner.

I followed in his footsteps, which is how a tradition is made, but I am afraid this one ends with me. I have a son, and what I said to him and what he said to me is the crux of the matter. He asked me a question—well, in my opinion, it was the kind of question that's at the bottom of most of the world's troubles today. There are some sleeping dogs that should be left to lie; there are some questions that should not be asked.

To understand all this, I think you have to understand me, and nothing could be easier. I'm sixty, just beginning to look my age, a little overweight, suffer sometimes from arthritis when the weather is damp. I'm a good citizen, complain about my taxes but pay them on schedule, vote for the right party, and run my business well enough to make a comfortable living from it.

I've been married thirty-five years and never looked at another woman in all that time. Well, looked maybe, but no more than that. I have a married daughter and a granddaughter almost a year old, and the prettiest, smilingest baby in town. I spoil her and don't apologize for it, because in my opinion that is what grandfathers were made for—to spoil their grandchildren. Let mama and papa attend to the business; grandpa is there for the fun.

And beyond all that I have a son who asks questions. The kind that shouldn't be asked.

Put the picture together, and what you get is someone like yourself. I might be your next-door neighbor, I might be your old friend, I might be the uncle you meet whenever the family gets together at a wedding or a funeral. I'm like you.

Naturally, we all look different on the outside but we can still recognize each other on sight as the same kind of people. Deep down inside where it matters we have the same feelings, and we know that without any questions being asked about them.

"But," you might say, "there is a difference between us. You're the one who performs the executions, and I'm the one who reads about them in the papers, and that's a big difference, no matter how you look at it."

Is it? Well, look at it without prejudice, look at it with absolute honesty, and you'll have to admit that you're being unfair.

Let's face the facts, we're all in this together. If an old friend of yours happens to serve on a jury that finds a murderer guilty, you don't lock the door against him, do you? More than that: if you could get an introduction to the judge who sentences that murderer to the electric chair, you'd be proud of it, wouldn't you? You'd be honored to have him sit at your table, and you'd be quick enough to let the world know about it.

And since you're so willing to be friendly with the jury that convicts and the judge that sentences, what about the man who has to pull the switch? He's finished the job you wanted done, he's made the world a better place for it. Why must he go hide away in a dark corner until the next time he's needed?

There's no use denying that nearly everybody feels he should, and there's less use denying that it's a cruel thing for anyone in my position to face. If you don't mind some strong language, it's a damned outrage to hire a man for an unpleasant job, and then despise him for it. Sometimes it's hard to abide such righteousness.

How do I get along in the face of it? The only way possible—by keeping my secret locked up tight and never being tempted to give it away. I don't like it that way, but I'm no fool about it.

The trouble is that I'm naturally easygoing and friendly. I'm the sociable kind. I like people, and I want them to like me. At Lodge meetings or in the clubhouse down at the golf course I'm always the center of the crowd. And I know what would happen if at any such time I ever opened my mouth and let that secret out. A five minute sensation, and after that the slow chill setting in. It would mean the end of my whole life then and there, the kind of life I want to live, and no man in his right mind throws away sixty years of his life for a five minute sensation.

You can see I've given the matter a lot of thought. More than that, it hasn't been idle thought. I don't pretend to be an educated man, but I'm willing to read books on any subject that interests me, and execution has been one of my main interests ever since I got into the line. I have the books sent to the shop where nobody takes notice of another piece of mail, and I keep them locked in a bin in my office so that I can read them in private.

There's a nasty smell about having to do it this way—at my age you hate to feel like a kid hiding himself away to read a dirty magazine —but I have no choice. There isn't a soul on earth outside of the warden at state's prison and a couple of picked guards there who know I'm the one pulling the switch at an execution, and I intend it to remain that way.

Oh, yes, my son knows now. Well, he's difficult in some ways, but he's no fool. If I wasn't sure he would keep his mouth shut about what I told him, I wouldn't have told it to him in the first place.

Have I learned anything from those books? At least enough to take a pride in what I'm doing for the state and the way I do it. As far back in history as you want to go there have always been executioners. The day that men first made laws to help keep peace among themselves was the day the first executioner was born. There have always been lawbreakers; there must always be a way of punishing them. It's as simple as that.

The trouble is that nowadays there are too many people who don't want it to be as simple as that. I'm no hypocrite, I'm not one of those narrow-minded fools who thinks that every time a man comes up with a generous impulse he's some kind of crackpot. But he can be mistaken. I'd put most of the people who are against capital punishment in that class. They are fine, high-minded citizens who've never in their lives been close enough to a murderer or rapist to smell the evil in him. In fact, they're so fine and high-minded that they can't imagine anyone in the world not being like themselves. In that case, they say anybody who commits murder or rape is just a plain, ordinary human being who's had a bad spell. He's no criminal, they say, he's just sick. He doesn't need the electric chair; all he needs is a kindly old doctor to examine his head and straighten out the kinks in his brain.

In fact, they say there is no such thing as a criminal at all. There are only well people and sick people, and the ones who deserve all your worry and consideration are the sick ones. If they happen to murder or rape a few of the well ones now and then, why, just run for the doctor.

This is the argument from beginning to end, and I'd be the last one to deny that it's built on honest charity and good intentions. But it's a mistaken argument. It omits the one fact that matters. When anyone commits murder or rape he is no longer in the human race. A man has a human brain and a God-given soul to control his animal nature. When the animal in him takes control he's not a human being any more. Then he has to be exterminated the way any animal must be if it goes wild in the middle of helpless people. And my duty is to be the exterminator.

It could be that people just don't understand the meaning of the word *duty* any more. I don't want to sound old-fashioned, God forbid, but when I was a boy things were more straightforward and clear-cut. You learned to tell right from wrong, you learned to do what had to be done, and you didn't ask questions every step of the way. Or if you had to ask any questions, the ones that mattered were *how* and *when*.

Then along came psychology, along came the professors, and the main question was always *why*. Ask yourself *why*, *why*, *why* about everything you do, and you'll end up doing nothing. Let a couple of generations go along that way, and you'll finally have a breed of people who sit around in trees like monkeys, scratching their heads.

Does this sound far-fetched? Well, it isn't. Life is a complicated thing to live. All his life a man finds himself facing one situation after another, and the way to handle them is to live by the rules. Ask yourself *why* once too often, and you can find yourself so tangled up that you go under. The show must go on. Why? Women and children first. Why? My country, right or wrong. Why? Never mind your duty. Just keep asking *why* until it's too late to do anything about it.

Around the time I first started going to school my father gave me a dog, a collie pup named Rex. A few years after Rex suddenly became unfriendly, the way a dog will sometimes, and then vicious, and then one day he bit my mother when she reached down to pat him.

The day after that I saw my father leaving the house with his hunting rifle under his arm and with Rex on a leash. It wasn't the hunting season, so I knew what was going to happen to Rex and I knew why. But it's forgivable in a boy to ask things that a man should be smart enough not to ask.

"Where are you taking Rex?" I asked my father. "What are you going to do with him?"

"I'm taking him out back of town," my father said. "I'm going to shoot him."

"But why?" I said, and that was when my father let me see that there is only one answer to such a question.

"Because it has to be done," he said.

I never forgot that lesson. It came hard; for a while I hated my father for it, but as I grew up I came to see how right he was. We both knew why the dog had to be killed. Beyond that, all questions would lead nowhere. Why the dog had become vicious, why God had put a dog on earth to be killed this way—these are the questions that you can talk out to the end of time, and while you're talking about them you still have a vicious dog on your hands.

It is strange to look back and realize now that when the business of the dog happened, and long before it and long after it, my father was an electrocutioner, and I never knew it. Nobody knew it, not even my mother. A few times a year my father would pack his bag and a few tools and go away for a couple of days, but that was all any of us knew. If you asked him where he was going he would simply

say he had a job to do out of town. He was not a man you'd ever suspect of philandering or going off on a solitary drunk, so nobody
gave it a second thought.

It worked the same way in my case. I found out how well it worked
when I finally told my son what I had been doing on those jobs out
of town, and that I had gotten the warden's permission to take him
on as an assistant and train him to handle the chair himself when I
retired. I could tell from the way he took it that he was as thunder-
struck at this as I had been thirty years before when my father had
taken me into his confidence.

"Electrocutioner?" said my son. "An *electrocutioner?*"

"Well, there's no disgrace to it," I said. "And since it's got to be
done, and somebody has to do it, why not keep it in the family? If
you knew anything about it, you'd know it's a profession that's often
passed down in a family from generation to generation. What's
wrong with a good, sound tradition? If more people believed in tradition you wouldn't have so many troubles in the world today."

It was the kind of argument that would have been more than
enough to convince me when I was his age. What I hadn't taken into
account was that my son wasn't like me, much as I wanted him to
be. He was a grown man in his own right, but a grown man who had
never settled down to his responsibilities. I had always kept closing
my eyes to that, I had always seen him the way I wanted to and not
the way he was.

When he left college after a year, I said, all right, there are some
people who aren't made for college, I never went there, so what difference does it make. When he went out with one girl after another
and could never make up his mind to marrying any of them, I said,
well, he's young, he's sowing his wild oats, the time will come soon
enough when he's ready to take care of a home and family. When he
sat daydreaming in the shop instead of tending to business I never
made a fuss about it. I knew when he put his mind to it he was as
good an electrician as you could ask for, and in these soft times
people are allowed to do a lot more dreaming and a lot less working
than they used to.

The truth was that the only thing that mattered to me was being
his friend. For all his faults he was a fine-looking boy with a good
mind. He wasn't much for mixing with people, but if he wanted to
he could win anyone over. And in the back of my mind all the while
he was growing up was the thought that he was the only one who
would learn my secret some day, and would share it with me, and

make it easier to bear. I'm not secretive by nature. A man like me needs a thought like that to sustain him.

So when the time came to tell him he shook his head and said no. I felt that my legs had been kicked out from under me. I argued with him and he still said no, and I lost my temper.

"Are you against capital punishment?" I asked him. "You don't have to apologize if you are. I'd think all the more of you, if that's your only reason."

"I don't know if it is," he said.

"Well, you ought to make up your mind one way or the other," I told him. "I'd hate to think you were like every other hypocrite around who says it's all right to condemn a man to the electric chair and all wrong to pull the switch."

"Do I have to be the one to pull it?" he said. "Do you?"

"Somebody has to do it. Somebody always has to do the dirty work for the rest of us. It's not like the Old Testament days when everybody did it for himself. Do you know how they executed a man in those days? They laid him on the ground tied hand and foot, and everybody around had to heave rocks on him until he was crushed to death. They didn't invite anybody to stand around and watch. You wouldn't have had much choice then, would you?"

"I don't know," he said. And then because he was as smart as they come and knew how to turn your words against you, he said, "After all, I'm not without sin."

"Don't talk like a child," I said. "You're without the sin of murder on you or any kind of sin that calls for execution. And if you're so sure the Bible has all the answers, you might remember that you're supposed to render unto Caesar the things that are Caesar's."

"Well," he said, "in this case I'll let you do the rendering."

I knew then and there from the way he said it and the way he looked at me that it was no use trying to argue with him. The worst of it was knowing that we had somehow moved far apart from each other and would never really be close again. I should have had sense enough to let it go at that. I should have just told him to forget the whole thing and keep his mouth shut about it.

Maybe if I had ever considered the possibility of his saying no, I would have done it. But because I hadn't considered any such possibility I was caught off balance, I was too much upset to think straight. I will admit it now. It was my own fault that I made an issue of things and led him to ask the one question he should never have asked.

"I see," I told him. "It's the same old story, isn't it? Let somebody else do it. But if they pull your number out of a hat and you have to serve on a jury and send a man to the chair, that's all right with you. At least, it's all right as long as there's somebody else to do the job that you and the judge and every decent citizen wants done. Let's face the facts, boy, you don't have the guts. I'd hate to think of you even walking by the death house. The shop is where you belong. You can be nice and cozy there, wiring up fixtures and ringing the cash register. I can handle my duties without your help."

It hurt me to say it. I had never talked like that to him before, and it hurt. The strange thing was that he didn't seem angry about it; he only looked at me puzzled.

"Is that all it is to you?" he said. "A duty?"

"Yes."

"But you get paid for it, don't you?"

"I get paid little enough for it."

He kept looking at me that way. "Only a duty?" he said, and never took his eyes off me. "But you enjoy it, don't you?"

That was the question he asked.

You enjoy it, don't you? You stand there looking through a peephole in the wall at the chair. In thirty years I have stood there more than a hundred times looking at that chair. The guards bring somebody in. Usually he is in a daze; sometimes he screams, throws himself around and fights. Sometimes it is a woman, and a woman can be as hard to handle as a man when she is led to the chair. Sooner or later, whoever it is is strapped down and the black hood is dropped over his head. Now your hand is on the switch.

The warden signals, and you pull the switch. The current hits the body like a tremendous rush of air suddenly filling it. The body leaps out of the chair with only the straps holding it back. The head jerks, and a curl of smoke comes from it. You release the switch and the body falls back again.

You do it once more, do it a third time to make sure. And whenever your hand presses the switch you can see in your mind what the current is doing to that body and what the face under the hood must look like.

Enjoy it?

That was the question my son asked me. That was what he said to me, as if I didn't have the same feelings deep down in me that we all have.

Enjoy it?

But, my God, how could anyone *not* enjoy it!

WATCH FOR IT

by Joseph N. Gores

Because we are by now in danger of becoming a fragmented nation, a loose confederation of subcultures speaking essentially the same language, with little intercommunication and less understanding of one another's drives, we ignore the reality that Ross speaks for a school of thought which many of our young, and still others, see as that of latter-day Zorros, working for that illusory Tomorrow—dreamed of since Time began . . .

Eric's first one. The very first.

And it went up early.

If I'd been in my apartment on Durant, with the window open, I probably would have heard it. And probably, at 4:30 in the morning, would have thought like any straight that it had been a truck back-fire. But I'd spent the night balling Elizabeth over in San Francisco while Eric was placing the bomb in Berkeley. With her every minute, I'd made sure, because whatever else you can say about the federal pigs, they're thorough. I'd known that if anything went wrong, they'd be around looking.

Liz and I heard it together on the noon news, when we were having breakfast before her afternoon classes. She teaches freshman English at SF State.

Eric Whitlach, outspoken student radical on the Berkeley campus, was injured early this morning when a bomb he allegedly was placing under a table in the Student Union detonated prematurely. Police said the explosive device was fastened to a clock mechanism set for 9:30, when the area would have been packed with students. The extent of the young activist's injuries is not known, but

"God, that's terrible," Liz said with a shudder. She'd been in a number of upper-level courses with both Eric and me. "What could have happened to him, Ross, to make him do . . . something like that?"

"I guess . . . Well, I haven't seen much of him since graduation last June . . ." I gestured above the remains of our eggs and bacon. " 'Student revolutionary'—it's hard to think of Eric that way." Then I came up with a nice touch. "Maybe he shouldn't have gone beyond his M.A. Maybe he should have stopped when we did—before he lost touch."

When I'd recruited Eric without appearing to, it had seemed a very heavy idea. I mean, nobody actually expects his vocal, kinky, Rubin-type radical to go out and set bombs; because they don't. We usually avoid Eric's sort ourselves: they have no sense of history, no discipline. They're as bad as the Communists on the other side of the street, with their excessive regimentation, their endless orders from somewhere else.

I stood up. "Well, baby, I'd better get back across the Bay . . ."

"Ross, aren't you . . . I mean, can't you . . ."

She stopped there, coloring; still a lot of that corrupting Middle America in her. She was ready to try anything at all in bed, but to say right out in daylight that she wanted me to ball her again after class—that still sort of blew her mind.

"I can't, Liz," I said all aw-shucksy, laughing down inside at how *straight* she was. "I *was* his roommate until four months ago, and the police or somebody might want to ask me questions about him."

I actually thought that they might, and nothing brings out pig paranoia quicker than somebody not available for harassment when they want him. But nobody showed up. I guess they knew that as long as they had Eric they could get whatever they wanted out of him just by shooting electricity into his balls or something, like the French pigs in Algeria. I know how the fascists operate.

Beyond possible questions by the pigs, however, I knew there'd be a strategy session that night in Berkeley. After dark at Zeta Books, on Telegraph south of the campus, is the usual time and place for a meet. Armand Marsh let me in and locked the door behind me; he runs the store for the Student Socialist Alliance as a cover. He's a long skinny redheaded cat with ascetic features and quick nervous mannerisms, and is cell-leader for our three-man focal.

I saw that Danzer was in the mailing room when I got there, as was Benny. I didn't like Danzer being there. Sure, he acted as liaison with other Bay Area focals, but he never went out on operations and so he was an outsider. No outsider can be trusted.

"Benny," said Armand, "how badly is Whitlach really hurt?"

Benny Leland is night administrator for Alta Monte Hospital. With his close-trimmed hair and conservative clothes he looks like the ultimate straight.

"He took a big splinter off the table right through his shoulder. Damned lucky that he had already set it and was on his way out when it blew. Otherwise they'd have just found a few teeth and toes."

"So he'd be able to move around?"

"Oh, sure. The injury caused severe shock, but he's out of that now; and the wound itself is not critical." He paused to look pointedly at me. "What I don't understand is how the damned thing went off prematurely."

Meaning I was somehow to blame, since I had supplied Eric with the matériel for the bomb. Armand looked over at me too.

"Ross? What sort of device was it?"

"Standard," I said. "Two sticks of dynamite liberated from that P.G. and E. site four months ago. An electric blasting cap with a small battery to detonate it. Alarm clock timer. He was going to carry the whole thing in a gift-wrapped shoe box to make it less conspicuous. There are several ways that detonation could—"

"None of that is pertinent now," interrupted Danzer. His voice was cold and heavy, like his face. He even looked like a younger Raymond Burr. "Our first concern is this: Will the focal be compromised if they break him down and he starts talking?"

"Eric was my best friend before I joined the focal," I said, "and he was my roommate for four years. But once we had determined it was better to use someone still a student than to set this one ourselves, I observed the standard security procedures in recruiting him. He believes the bombing was totally his own idea."

"He isn't even aware of the *existence* of the focal, let alone who's in it," Armand explained. "There's no way that he could hurt us."

Danzer's face was still cold when he looked over at me, but I had realized he *always* looked cold. "Then it seems that Ross is the one to go in after him."

"If there's any need to go at all," said Benny quickly. I knew what he was thinking. Any operation would entail the hospital, which meant he would be involved. He didn't like that. "After all, if he can't hurt us, why not just . . ." He shrugged.

"Just leave him there? Mmmph." Danzer publishes a couple of underground radical newspapers even though he's only twenty-seven, and also uses his presses to run off porn novels for some outfit in L.A. I think he nets some heavy bread. "I believe I can convince you of the desirability of going in after him. If Ross is willing . . ."

"Absolutely." I kept the excitement from my voice. Cold. Controlled. That's the image I like to project. A desperate man, reckless, careless of self. "If anyone else came through that door, Eric would be convinced he was an undercover pig. As soon as he sees me, he'll know that I've come to get him away."

"Why couldn't Ross just walk in off the street as a normal visitor?" asked Danzer.

"There's a twenty-four-hour police guard on Whitlach's door."

Benny was still fighting the idea of a rescue operation. "Only the doctors and one authorized nurse per shift get in."

"All right. And Ross *must not* be compromised. If he is, the whole attempt would be negated, worse than useless." Which at the moment I didn't understand. "Now let's get down to it."

As Danzer talked, I began to comprehend why he had been chosen to coordinate the activities of the focals. His mind was cold and logical and precise, as was his plan. What bothered me was my role in that plan. But I soon saw the error in my objections. I was Eric's friend, the only one he knew he could trust—and I had brought him into it in the first place. There was danger, of course, but that only made me feel better the more I thought of it. You have to take risks if you are to destroy a corrupt society, because like a snake with a broken back it still has venom on its fangs.

It took three hours to work out the operational scheme.

Alta Monte Hospital is set in the center of a quiet residential area off Ashby Avenue. It used to be easy to approach after dark; just walk to the side entrance across the broad blacktop parking lot. But so many doctors going out to their cars have been mugged by heads looking for narcotics that the lot is patrolled now.

I parked on Benvenue, got the hypo kit and the cherry bombs from the glove box, and slid them into my pocket. The thin strong nylon rope was wound around my waist under my dark blue windbreaker. My breath went up in gray wisps on the chilly wet night air. After I'd locked the car, I held out my hand to look at it by the pale illumination of the nearest street lamp. No tremors. The nerves were cool, man. *I* was cool.

3:23 A.M. by my watch.

In seven minutes, Benny Leland would unlock the small access door on the kitchen loading dock. He would relock it three minutes later, while going back to the staff coffee room from the men's lavatory. I had to get inside during those three minutes or not at all.

3:27.

I hunkered down in the thick hedge rimming the lot. My palms were getting sweaty. Everything hinged on a nurse who came off work in midshift because her old man worked screwy hours and she had to be home to baby-sit her kid. If she was late . . .

The guard's voice carried clearly on black misty air. "All finished, Mrs. Adamson?"

"Thank God, Danny. It's been a rough night. We lost one in post-op that I was sure would make it."

"Too bad. See you tomorrow, Mrs. Adamson."

I had a cherry bomb in my rubber-gloved hand now. I couldn't hear her soft-soled nurse's shoes on the blacktop, but I could see her long thin shadow come bouncing up the side of her car ten yards away. I came erect, threw, stepped back into shadow.

It was beautiful, man; like a sawed-off shotgun in the silent lot. She gave a wonderful scream, full-throated, and the guard yelled. I could hear his heavy feet thudding to her aid as he ran past my section of hedge.

I was sprinting across the blacktop behind his back on silent garage attendant's shoes, hunched as low as possible between the parked cars in case anyone had been brought to a window by the commotion. Without checking my pace, I ran down the kitchen delivery ramp to crouch in the deep shadow under the edge of the loading platform.

Nothing. No pursuit. My breath ragged in my chest, more from excitement than my dash. The watch said 3:31. Beautiful.

I threw a leg up, rolled onto my belly on the platform. Across to the access port in the big overhead accordion steel loading door. It opened easily under my careful fingertips. Benny was being cool, too, producing on schedule for a change. I don't entirely trust Benny.

Hallway deserted, as per the plan. That unmistakable hospital smell. Across the hall, one of those wheeled carts holding empty food trays ready for the morning's breakfasts. Right where it was supposed to be. I put the two cherry bombs on the front left corner of the second tray down, turned, went nine quick paces to the fire-door.

My shoes made slight scuffing noises on the metal runners. By law, hospital firedoors cannot be locked. I checked my watch: in nineteen seconds, Benny Leland would emerge from the men's room and, as he walked back to the staff coffee room, would relock the access door and casually hook the cherry bombs from the tray. I then would have three minutes to be in position.

It had been 150 seconds when I pulled the third-floor firedoor a quarter-inch ajar. No need to risk looking out: I could visualize everything from Benny's briefing earlier.

"Whitlach's room is the last one on the corridor, right next to the fire stairs," he'd said. "I arranged that as part of my administrative duties—actually, of course, in case we *would* want to get to

him. The floor desk with the night duty nurse is around an ell and
at the far end of the corridor. She's well out of the way. The policeman will be sitting beside Whitlach's door on a metal folding chair.
He'll be alone in the hall at that time of night."

Ten seconds. I held out my hand. No discernible tremor.

Benny Leland, riding alone in the elevator from the basement to
the fourth floor administrative offices, would just be stopping here
at the third floor. As the doors opened, he would punch *four* again;
as they started to close, he would hurl his two cherry bombs down
the main stairwell, and within seconds would be off the elevator
and into his office on the floor above. The pig could only think it
had been someone on the stairs.

Whoomp! Whump!

Fantastic, man! Muffled, so the duty nurse far down the corridor
and around a corner wouldn't even hear them; but loud enough so
the pig, mildly alert for a possible attempt to free Whitlach, would
have to check . . .

I counted ten, pulled open the firedoor, went the six paces
to Eric's now unguarded door. Thirty feet away, the pig's beefy blue-
clad back was just going through the access doors to the elevator
shaft and the main stairwell.

A moment of absolute panic when Eric's door stuck. Then it
pulled free and I was inside. Sweat on my hands under the thin rubber gloves. Cool it now, baby.

I could see the pale blur of Eric's face as he started up from his
medicated doze. His little night light cast harsh, antiseptic shadows
across his lean face. Narrow stubborn jaw, very bright blue eyes,
short nose, wiry, tight-curled brown hair. I felt a tug of compassion:
he was very pale and drawn.

But then a broad grin lit up his features. "*Ross!*" he whispered.
"How in the hell—"

"No time, baby." My own voice was low, too. I already had the
syringe out, was stabbing it into the rubber top of the little phial.
"The pig will be back from checking out my diversion in just a minute. We have to be ready for him. Can you move?"

"Sure. What do you want me to—"

"Gimme your arm, baby." I jammed the needle into his flesh, depressed the plunger as I talked. "Pain-killer. In case we bump that
shoulder getting you out of here, you won't feel anything."

Eric squeezed my arm with his left hand; there were tears in his eyes. How scared that poor cat must have been when he woke up in the hands of the fascist pigs!

"Christ, Ross, I can't believe . . ." He shook his head. "Oh, Jesus, right out from under their snouts! You're beautiful, man!"

I got an arm around his shoulders, as the little clock in my mind ticked off the seconds, weighing, measuring the pig's native stupidity against his duty at the door. They have that sense of duty, all right, the pigs: but no smarts. We had them by the shorts now.

"Gotta get you to the window, cat," I breathed. Eric obediently swung his legs over the edge of the bed.

"Why . . . window . . ." His head was lolling.

I unzipped my jacket to show him the rope wound around my waist. "I'm lowering you down to the ground. Help will be waiting there."

I slid up the aluminum sash, let in the night through the screen. Groovy. Like velvet. No noise.

"Perch there, baby," I whispered. "I want the pig to come in and see you silhouetted, so I can take him from behind, dig?"

He nodded slowly. The injection was starting to take effect. It was my turn to squeeze his arm.

"Hang in there, baby."

I'd just gotten the night light switched off, had gotten behind the door, when I heard the pig's belatedly hurrying steps coming up the hall. Too late, you stupid fascist bastard, much too late.

A narrow blade of light stabbed at the room, widened to a rectangle. He didn't even come in fast, gun in hand, moving down and to the side as he should have. Just trotted in, a fat old porker to the slaughter. I heard his sharp intake of breath as he saw Eric.

"Hey! You! Get away from—"

I was on him from behind. Right arm around the throat, forearm grip, pull back hard while the left pushes on the back of the head . . .

They go out easily with that grip, any of them. Good for disarming a sentry without using a knife, I had been taught. I hadn't wasted my Cuban sojourn chopping sugar cane like those student straights on the junkets from Canada. I feel nothing but contempt for *those* cats: they have not yet realized that destroying the fabric of society is the only thing left for us.

I dragged the unconscious pig quickly out the door, lowered his fat butt into his chair and stretched his legs out convincingly. Steady pulse. He'd come around in a few minutes; meanwhile, it actually would have been possible to just walk Eric down the fire stairs and out of the building.

For a moment I was tempted; but doing it that way wasn't in the plan. The plan called for the maximum effect possible, and merely walking Eric out would minimize it. Danzer's plan was everything.

Eric was slumped sideways against the window frame, mumbling sleepily. I pulled him forward, letting his head loll on my shoulder while I unhooked the screen and sent it sailing down into the darkness of the bushes flanking the concrete walk below. I could feel the coils of thin nylon around my waist, strong enough in their synthetic strength to lower him safely to the ground.

Jesus, he was one sweet guy. I paused momentarily to run my hand through his coarse, curly hair. There was sweat on his forehead. Last year he took my French exam for me so I could get my graduate degree. We'd met in old Prof Cecil's Western Civ course our junior year, and had been roomies until the end of grad school.

"I'm sorry, baby," I told his semiconscious, sweat-dampened face. Then I let go and nudged, so his limp form flopped backward through the open window and he was gone, gone instantly, just like that. Three stories, head-first, to the concrete sidewalk. He hit with a sound like an egg dropped on the kitchen floor. A bad sound, man. One I won't soon forget.

The hall was dark and deserted as I stepped over the pig's outstretched legs. He'd be raising the alarm soon, but nobody except the other pigs would believe him. Not after the autopsy.

The first sound of sirens came just after I had stuffed the thin surgical gloves down a sewer and was back in my car, pulling decorously away from the curb. The nylon rope, taken along only to convince Eric that I meant to lower him from the window, had been slashed into useless lengths and deposited in a curb-side trash barrel awaiting early morning collection.

On University Avenue, I turned toward an all-night hamburger joint that had a pay phone in the parking lot. I was, can you believe it, ravenous; but more than that, I was horny. I thought about that for a second, knowing I should feel sort of sick and ashamed at having a sexual reaction to the execution. But instead I felt . . . *transfigured.* Eric had been a political prisoner anyway; the pigs would have made sure he wouldn't have lived to come to trial. By his necessary death, *I* would be changing the entire history of human existence. *Me.* Alone.

And there was Liz over in the city, always eager, a receptacle in which I could spend my sexual excitement before she went off to teach. But first, Armand. So he could tell Danzer it was all right to print what we had discussed the night before.

Just thinking of that made me feel elated, because the autopsy would reveal the presence of that massive dose of truth serum I had needled into Eric before his death. And the Establishment news media would do the rest, hinting and probing and suggesting before our underground weeklies even hit the street with our charge against the fascists.

Waiting for Armand to pick up his phone, I composed our headline in my mind:

PIGS PUMP REVOLUTIONARY HERO FULL
OF SCOPOLAMINE; HE DIVES FROM WINDOW
RATHER THAN FINK ON THE MOVEMENT

Oh yes, man. Beautiful. Just beautiful. Watch for it.

MURDER IN EDEN

by Morris Hershman

What precisely is meant by those words, *Can* murder happen, in the accepted sense of the word, in a society which has withdrawn from the outside as fully as has Isham Valley?

Sam Dunn got out of the bright red Chrysler, dust-caked from city traffic, and walked over to the wooden cabin. He could smell greenery and animal droppings as he moved in the Isham Valley, but didn't look to his right or left.

He reached into a pocket for a silver key on a white string and tried to unlock the cabin door. The lock wouldn't move. He had been told that nobody locked his door in the Isham Valley, but not until that moment was he able to believe it.

He walked into a big room. The furniture didn't look like much, but it was exactly what a man alone would want; two walls were jammed with fishing rods and the other two looked as if they had been stuffed with hunting rifles.

Sam Dunn took a heavy step toward the nearest wall and was glaring at a gun in its silver rack when he heard a girl's voice say softly, "All the guns are in good condition."

"I suppose they are, but I didn't come up here for the sake of sports."

He had turned swiftly and found himself facing a small, wiry brunette in loose-fitting jeans and a soft blouse that looked as if it had been made by hand. She was wearing gray suspenders, and a cowboy hat was on the floor by the couch. She was barefoot.

"I don't even want to look at those things," he said, and gestured behind him toward the silver rack. "Will you please get the hunting and fishing stuff out of here. I'd do it myself but—well, I've never been handy."

The girl shrugged, not caring that he had hit the last word heavily. It meant nothing to her then.

"Every house in the Valley has some fishing rods, at least," the girl said in that pleasant voice. "You never entered the Isham Valley before?"

"No, I rented this place by mail." He glanced at his watch, wordlessly and with city-bred efficiency dismissing the young girl he now knew wasn't likely to be of much help to him. "I'll pay you for this little trouble with the guns and the fishing rods, of course."

Dunn went out to park his car on the premises, then drew out his suitcases and his clothes hangers. It took him three trips back and forth. The air was almost fresh enough to knock him down, without a trace of acrid smoke.

He unpacked roughly, wishing he hadn't just thrown clothes into the places picked out for them, and was tucking pajamas under the pillow when he heard barefoot steps pad-padding on boards. He took two singles out of his cowhide wallet and went out to the living room.

The girl shook her head at his offer.

"No, thanks." She smiled attractively. "You'll need other chores done and there would be no end of your paying out."

"No, I'm planning to be alone here for a while and get some rest."

"Food has to be prepared for you."

"As long as there are cans, I'll do it myself."

"Oh, you'll just eat any mess of slops to keep you alive." At her next smile, Sam Dunn asked himself whether or not she had seen her twentieth birthday. "Besides, somebody has to be here who knows about the electric light, you see."

"What about it?"

"The light comes from a diesel caterpillar in the shed. Most of the time, it runs pretty good, but if it don't keep up, you might be needing help and not finding it."

"You can't sleep in."

"There's a little spare room," the girl said, and pointed. "No trouble. My name is Nina, by the way."

Dunn glanced at the walls, which were bare now except for steel pegs that had held rifles and rods against patches of wall that were only a little brighter than the rest. He left the money on a table and told her she couldn't stay, then walked back into his bedroom.

He was too tired for a meal. At seven in the evening, he stripped and put on pajamas and a bathrobe. He locked the door, but couldn't do anything about the windows because there weren't any catches on the wooden ledges. There wasn't a thought in Sam Dunn's head except to do the next chore and the next and the one after that; but it needed an hour of restless tossing later on before he could sleep.

The padding of bare feet woke him, and he saw Nina come out of the side room. Her dark hair was held in place by a rubber band at the back and she looked as fresh as the new day itself. He was always expecting the wiry girl to be scruffy and unkempt, but she kept herself spotless. Her bare feet, for instance, left no tracks.

"How did you get in?" he asked, startled.

"One of the windows." Nina smiled. "Not hard for me."

Dunn started to ask if she didn't know when she wasn't wanted, but she had turned away, moving gracefully. Nothing in this girl's life had bent her back or put any dent into her zest for living.

He had expected to make breakfast for himself, but it was waiting for him. He hesitated, then ate two eggs sunny-side-up, and warm, rich toast. Nina didn't make strong coffee of the sort where he could taste the grounds at the bottom of the percolator, but Sam Dunn did drink half a cup of the stuff, then spilled the rest of the percolator's insides into the earth and covered them over thoroughly. He guessed he'd be doing that every morning as long as he stayed in the Isham Valley.

After reading a few sheafs of reports from his briefcase, Dunn locked the case and put it away, then got into the Chrysler and started out to see the Valley. He got out of the car a few hundred feet before his first sight of the two stores that made up the only street.

It took a few steps, smiling at people he passed and being stared at by an old man, a middle-aged woman in a white apron and a toothless child, before he realized what mistake he had made. He should never have dressed in his sports outfit of gray shorts and a purple shirt with green lightning streaks.

He walked past Harry's Tavern and the General Store and Gas Station. It was possible to look in at the window and see a middle-aged fellow behind the counter, as well as wall pictures of Teddy Roosevelt and some tablecloths and made-to-order clothes for sale. The fellow behind the counter stared at Dunn, and Dunn walked over to his fire-red Chrysler and drove back to the cabin.

Nina was bustling around when he arrived. Her eyes fixed firmly on him as soon as he walked inside. He fairly ran into his room and didn't come out again until he was dressed in comfortable slacks and a neutral blue sports shirt.

"I'd like to see some of the grounds out there," he said, and surprised her by adding, "if you want to be my guide. I don't think I'd be so handy out there, either, if you want to know something."

She nodded, but didn't give any response to his second use of a word that would have been meaningful if she had known about the person Sam Dunn had come here to locate.

Twenty minutes afterward, they were walking in what Dunn would certainly have considered a wilderness.

"Them are moose," Nina said at one point after he had shied in fright. "Leave them alone and they'll not bother you."

"Are they *deer* over there? The gray-looking animals, I mean."

"Elk is what those are. They graze on such slopes as they can find in the Isham."

"I never knew that."

"*Those* are deer." There was grass under her bare right foot, and she raised the foot gently. "Give a deer bottom land for *his* grazing, and you make him happy."

"Did you just hear a noise?" Dunn asked suddenly, whirling around to see gleaming water. "Something was dropped in there, I think, but I'm not sure."

"I saw a rainbow trout stick himself a little above the creek water and then drop back inside," Nina said easily. "That's as must be it."

"At least it wasn't anything really danger—Great heavens!"

"Only a bear," Nina said pleasantly. "He comes over sometimes to root for grubs."

"He won't maul anybody?"

"Not as you don't make sudden moves or look as if you lost two year's growing."

Dunn drew a deep, thoughtful breath. "I can understand taking a vacation up here, but not living in this place all year long."

"There are fine points to it for us."

"Is it so good to be primitive?"

"The Emersons are here in the Isham, for instance, because they think so," she said suddenly, tossing her hair. "They built their own cabin and furniture, and nowadays they grow vegetables for themselves. Maryann Garry, now—Mrs. Garry—still makes her own soap after all these years. She loses herself in work for essential things, like all the people here."

"Do they have to make their own electricity, too?" he asked a little maliciously, remembering the setup in the shed of his rented cabin. "That's a lot of trouble."

She shook her head. "Only your cabin has the side shed. None of the others."

Sam Dunn's jaw dropped. "Do you mean that the people out here are still using kerosene?"

"Oh, yes. They draw their own water, so why not use kerosene, too? Does a people have to be living as if they were cripples and could do nothing for their own selves? And would we have the hemlock and silver aspen on the grow if—"

Sam Dunn refused to let himself be distracted. "But how do you get your clothes ironed, for instance, without electricity?"

"It is possible to use flatirons and a gasoline iron," Nina said almost brusquely, as if she was hoping he would talk about something else.

"What about storing meats?" Sam Dunn asked with a stubborn tilt to his jaw. "How can you do that without a refrigerator?"

"Food can keep just as ripe in a fridge as runs on the propane gas," Nina said spiritedly. "Now, can't we talk about some different thing?"

Fresh questions rose to his lips, but all of them could be answered with the truisms of past generations. It was hard, though, to keep from asking.

He had cleared his throat just as they passed a group of sharp-edged trees that he could now identify as whispering pine. Nina turned to her left and ran ahead. Sam Dunn followed at a slower pace. The cabin was in sight and she was leading him toward it, if only to stop the flow of questions about electric power.

He sat in the rocking chair for a while, looking at the scenery that took his breath away, then went into the bedroom to examine a few more of the reports he had brought with him, and walked out to the big but primitive living room. Nina was in the kitchen, working deftly with shiny pots and chicken wings and breasts.

"And what about the young people, Nina?" he asked softly. "The late teens and twenties and thirty-year-olds don't stay in the Isham Valley."

She shrugged warily. "Who would want to stay if she's young and can marry rich or learn to operate a riggymajig machine?"

"You do, apparently," he said. "What makes you stay here? What is there for you in the Isham Valley?"

"I was born here and here is where I mean to stay."

"Do your parents approve?"

"They're gone, Mr. Dunn." A cloud scurried across the youthful face. "They went out to Cincinnati, and me with them. Then some people made a riot and my folks were in a car that was turned over. They burned to death. I hurried back to the Isham before any adoption homes could find me."

"People who stay in this valley die, too, I'm sure."

"The parents of my mother are still here in the Valley, as for many more years—God be willing."

"And so you stay to be near them?" He was beginning to talk in a slightly old-fashioned way himself, and in him it was put on. He swore silently.

She must have misunderstood him because she said, "I stay to help them."

"Help them with chores?"

"Protect them," she said firmly. "Them and the others."

He couldn't help sounding amused. "You're the sheriff, you mean?"

"There is no sheriff. There are no police here."

It was on the tip of his tongue to say that he had probably found the only known commune for older hippies, but the words wouldn't come. He was glad about that later.

He turned away and took dinner by himself. Washing up afterward took longer than he had expected, what with having to use a water pump, but he spent the time deep in thought.

A preoccupied Sam Dunn smoked a last pipe and stayed up late reading reports that suddenly had lost interest for him. He fell asleep with some reports in his hand, then put them away when he woke a little later, and locked the suitcase. It made no sense, but he locked the door before going back to sleep.

He went into town again next morning, having been careful to dress in long pants and a quiet gray shirt. The same middle-aged man he had seen in the general store yesterday waited on him today.

While Dunn's few impromptu purchases were being wrapped in coarse brown paper and rope to match, he asked, as if idly, "Have you lived here all your life?"

"No, sir." The man smiled. "I only came to the Isham 'bout seven years ago."

"And you've stayed ever since?" Dunn asked, even though he realized that the man's accent wasn't much different from Nina's. "Do you have children?"

"Two." The storekeeper smiled ruefully. "Probably they're going to leave when they become older."

"Do you think the Valley is the right place to prepare them for what lies outside?"

"I have the feeling that after a few years out of the Isham, they'll come back with a wife and a husband. Many of our kids do."

Dunn hesitated. "And you expect that you and your people will be here forever?"

"Oh, yes. And if Mr. Flenders is still on his pins, he can help tuck me away when my time should come."

"The funeral director, I suppose." Dunn pursed his lips. "I think I'd like to see the cemetery. There must be plenty of old graves out here."

The cemetery was a long walk from the General Store, in a north-westerly direction. Mr. Flenders, who farmed the land nearby and also "steered people into the beyond," as he apparently liked to say, was smoking meditatively while Dunn talked to him, and answering back in half- or quarter-sentences. He must have been in the seventies.

"The dead out here go back to the nineteenth century," he said when Dunn asked. "You can look around if you like."

"Thanks very much."

"Some of them was my friends," Mr. Flenders added in an endless monologue as he followed the visitor. "Not a fellow like Joseph Minafer, whoever he might be, as died in the year eighteen-oh-eight, according to the stone. Oh-oh," he put in, apologetic as any housewife, "I guess a drift of wind came up and blew earth across the stone. It does happen sometimes, but I generally clear it away."

Dunn was close to smiling at the idea of wind in the valley but he remembered the turned-over earth with which he had tried to wipe away the signs of having purposely spilled Nina's coffee after his first breakfast in the Valley.

With a subdued thanks, he said good-bye to Mr. Flenders, walked back to his car and then to the cabin. His business had taken a shorter time than he could have expected, considering the size of the Valley and the number of people who lived in it. He put his bags flat open on the bed and started to pack swiftly.

Nina came in while he was working. Her eyes rested on the suitcases.

"What *did* you want in the Valley?" she asked softly. "A man who pries around a day or so is not a man on the vacation."

Sam Dunn didn't hesitate. "Yes, you've got every right to know. You're the one who protects the people of the Valley. Do you know of a man named Harold Handy? He was a tall man with graying hair, long sideburns—"

"I've seen him, but not to know his name." The girl didn't seem surprised at Sam Dunn's first direct reference to it. Her head was cocked alertly.

"Two days ago, Mr. Handy left the town of Pitchford for the Valley. Mr. Handy was a reliable man on a business trip, but he hasn't been heard from since then."

The girl's eyes widened slightly. "And you have come here to find out why not?"

"I've already found out." Sam Dunn's voice rose harshly. "I want to know why you say that you live in a peaceful place and yet you murdered a man. You killed a respectable, hard-working executive—and we both know it now."

Her hands were opening and closing, but the small lips remained drum-taut.

"Harold Handy is in the coffin of Joseph Minafer, isn't he?" Dunn continued, but not as if he needed the answer any longer. "You put him there, probably with the knowledge and even the help of Mr. Flenders. But you're the one who did it. I want to know why you killed a man."

Nina picked words carefully. "You called that man reliable and respectable, but he wasn't either of those things when he came to the Valley for his abominable business. He was suspicious and contemptible. He felt while he was here, that a young girl in the Valley could be made to do what he wanted. He was wicked, and were he not dead I would be truly disgraced."

Sam Dunn drew a deep breath.

"Let one more such man arrive with a horrid business mission," Nina added before Sam Dunn could put in another word, "and it will happen to that person as well. The Valley folk will see that it's done, by me or by another. Remember what I say."

Nina turned around and walked out the door. Sam Dunn watched the door close gently and knew that he'd never be able to write a report telling what had taken place in the Isham Valley; something had happened to him as well as to the late Harold Handy.

So he packed his things and put them into the Chrysler and drove along the Valley for one more look at it. He had never thought of himself as not being happy with his own day and age, but he couldn't help driving past cabins without imagining television antennas scarring their roofs, and thinking about kids who would hang around in front of the sets for hours and hours when they could have been exploring the Valley instead, with all its God-given wonders.

Over here, in the ample area he was passing, somebody might put up a drive-in, and over there might rise a whole series of stores with automatic equipment of all sorts for sale. Thousands of new people could come to the Valley and every one of them would be able to spend considerable money on items that were sure to break down quickly. It would all have changed for the worse; it would all be cheaper—and very little of it would be worth while.

He drove past the cemetery, dozing in warm sunlight, and tried to make out the gravestone under which was resting the body of Harold Handy, that utilities executive who had come out to the Valley to make plans for the first link-in of the area's electric power line.

He drove out of the Valley without looking back. Traffic grew thick and the freeway was smoke-clogged, it seemed, by the time he was only fifty miles from Pitchford. He sighed and then gritted his teeth. At his first distant sight of a factory smokestack, he swore and then cut himself off in mid-oath. Carefully, making sure that the change wouldn't disturb some other drivers, Sam Dunn turned the car around.

THE OBLONG ROOM

by Edward D. Hoch

This MWA Edgar Award-winning story has to do with two young men whose search for what they feel must be The Truth can be said to reflect the restlessness, the hopelessness, you might almost add the sense of betrayal, which is making so many of our young likewise deny our mores and our Gods. They say the world we are leaving them is a shambles, morally and politically, destroying itself before its time. So they take refuge in its shadows . . .

It was Fletcher's case from the beginning, but Captain Leopold rode along with him when the original call came in. The thing seemed open and shut, with the only suspect found literally standing over his victim, and on a dull day Leopold thought that a ride out to the University might be pleasant.

Here, along the river, the October color was already in the trees, and through the park a slight haze of burning leaves clouded the road in spots. It was a warm day for autumn, a sunny day. Not really a day for murder.

"The University hasn't changed much," Leopold commented, as they turned into the narrow street that led past the fraternity houses to the library tower. "A few new dorms, and a new stadium. That's about all."

"We haven't had a case here since that bombing four or five years back." Fletcher said, "This one looks to be a lot easier, though. They've got the guy already. Stabbed his roommate and then stayed right there with the body."

Leopold was silent. They'd pulled up before one of the big new dormitories that towered toward the sky like some middle-income housing project, all brick and concrete and right now surrounded by milling students. Leopold pinned on his badge and led the way.

The room was on the fourth floor, facing the river. It seemed to be identical to all the others—A depressing oblong with bunk beds, twin study desks, wardrobes, and a large picture window opposite the door. The Medical Examiner was already there, and he looked up as Leopold and Fletcher entered. "We're ready to move him. All right with you, Captain?"

"The boys get their pictures? Then it's fine with me. Fletcher, find out what you can." Then, to the Medical Examiner, "What killed him?"

"A couple of stab wounds. I'll do an autopsy, but there's not much doubt."

"How long dead?"

"A day or so."

"A day!"

Fletcher had been making notes as he questioned the others. "The precinct men have it pretty well wrapped up for us, Captain. The dead boy is Ralph Rollings, a sophomore. His roommate admits to being here with the body for maybe twenty hours before they were discovered. Roommate's name is Tom McBern. They've got him in the next room."

Leopold nodded and went through the connecting door. Tom McBern was tall and slender, and handsome in a dark, collegiate sort of way. "Have you warned him of his rights?" Leopold asked a patrolman.

"Yes sir."

"All right." Leopold sat down on the bed opposite McBern. "What have you got to say, son?"

The deep brown eyes came up to meet Leopold's. "Nothing, sir. I think I want a lawyer."

"That's your privilege, of course. You don't wish to make any statement about how your roommate met his death, or why you remained in the room with him for several hours without reporting it?"

"No, sir." He turned away and stared out the window.

"You understand we'll have to book you on suspicion of homicide."

The boy said nothing more, and after a few moments Leopold left him alone with the officer. He went back to Fletcher and watched while the body was covered and carried away. "He's not talking. Wants a lawyer. Where are we?"

Sergeant Fletcher shrugged. "All we need is motive. They probably had the same girl or something."

"Find out."

They went to talk with the boy who occupied the adjoining room, the one who'd found the body. He was sandy-haired and handsome, with the look of an athlete, and his name was Bill Smith.

"Tell us how it was, Bill," Leopold said.

"There's not much to tell. I knew Ralph and Tom slightly during my freshman year, but never really well. They stuck pretty much together. This year I got the room next to them, but the connecting door was always locked. Anyway, yesterday neither one of them showed up at class. When I came back yesterday afternoon I knocked at the door and asked if anything was wrong. Tom called out that they were sick. He wouldn't open the door. I went into my own room and didn't think much about it. Then, this morning, I knocked to see how they were. Tom's voice sounded so . . . strange."

"Where was your own roommate all this time?"

"He's away. His father died and he went home for the funeral." Smith's hands were nervous, busy with a shredded piece of paper. Leopold offered him a cigarette and he took it. "Anyway, when he wouldn't open the door I became quite concerned and told him I was going for help. He opened it then—and I saw Ralph stretched out on the bed, all bloody and . . . dead."

Leopold nodded and went to stand by the window. From here he could see the trees down along the river, blazing gold and amber and scarlet as the October sun passed across them. "Had you heard any sounds the previous day? Any argument?"

"No. Nothing. Nothing at all."

"Had they disagreed in the past about anything?"

"Not that I knew of. If they didn't get along, they hardly would have asked to room together again this year."

"How about girls?" Leopold asked.

"They both dated occasionally, I think."

"No special one? One they both liked?"

Bill Smith was silent for a fraction too long. "No."

"You're sure?"

"I told you I didn't know them very well."

"This is murder, Bill. It's not a sophomore dance or class day games."

"Tom killed him. What more do you need?"

"What's her name, Bill?"

He stubbed out the cigarette and looked away. Then finally he answered. "Stella Banting. She's a junior."

"Which one did she go with?"

"I don't know. She was friendly with both of them. I think she went out with Ralph a few times around last Christmas, but I'd seen her with Tom lately."

"She's older than them?"

"No. They're all twenty. She's just a year ahead."

"All right," Leopold said. "Sergeant Fletcher will want to question you further."

He left Smith's room and went out in the hall with Fletcher. "It's your case, Sergeant. About time I gave it to you."

"Thanks for the help, Captain."

"Let him talk to a lawyer and then see if he has a story. If he still won't make a statement, book him on suspicion. I don't think there's any doubt we can get an indictment."

"You going to talk to that girl?"

Leopold smiled. "I just might. Smith seemed a bit shy about her. Might be a motive there. Let me know as soon as the medical examiner has something more definite about the time of death."

"Right, Captain."

Leopold went downstairs, pushing his way through the students and faculty members still crowding the halls and stairways. Outside he unpinned the badge and put it away. The air was fresh and crisp as he strolled across the campus to the administration building.

Stella Banting lived in the largest sorority house on campus, a great columned building of ivy and red brick. But when Captain Leopold found her she was on her way back from the drug store, carrying a carton of cigarettes and a bottle of shampoo. Stella was a tall girl with firm, angular lines and a face that might have been beautiful if she ever smiled.

"Stella Banting?"

"Yes?"

"I'm Captain Leopold. I wanted to talk to you about the tragedy over at the men's dorm. I trust you've heard about it?"

She blinked her eyes and said, "Yes. I've heard."

"Could we go somewhere and talk?"

"I'll drop these at the house and we can walk if you'd like. I don't want to talk there."

She was wearing faded bermuda shorts and a bulky sweatshirt, and walking with her made Leopold feel young again. If only she smiled occasionally—but perhaps this was not a day for smiling. They headed away from the main campus, out toward the silent oval of the athletic field and sports stadium. "You didn't come over to the dorm," he said to her finally, breaking the silence of their walk.

"Should I have?"

"I understood you were friendly with them—that you dated the dead boy last Christmas and Tom McBern more recently."

"A few times. Ralph wasn't the sort anyone ever got to know very well."

"And what about Tom?"

"He was a nice fellow."

"*Was?*"

"It's hard to explain. Ralph did things to people, to everyone around him. When I felt it happening to me, I broke away."

"What sort of things?"

"He had a power—a power you wouldn't believe any twenty-year-old capable of."

"You sound as if you've known a lot of them."

"I have. This is my third year at the University. I've grown up a lot in that time. I think I have, anyway."

"And what about Tom McBern?"

"I dated him a few times recently just to confirm for myself how bad things were. He was completely under Ralph's thumb. He lived for no one but Ralph."

"Homosexual?" Leopold asked.

"No, I don't think it was anything as blatant as that. It was more the relationship of teacher and pupil, leader and follower."

"Master and slave?"

She turned to smile at him. "You do seem intent on midnight orgies, don't you?"

"The boy is dead, after all."

"Yes. Yes, he is." She stared down at the ground, kicking randomly at the little clusters of fallen leaves. "But you see what I mean? Ralph was always the leader, the teacher—for Tom, almost the messiah."

"Then why would he have killed him?" Leopold asked.

"That's just it—he wouldn't! Whatever happened in that room, I can't imagine Tom McBern ever bringing himself to kill Ralph."

"There is one possibility, Miss Banting. Could Ralph Rollings have made a disparaging remark about you? Something about when he was dating you?"

"I never slept with Ralph, if that's what you're trying to ask me. With either of them, for that matter."

"I didn't mean it that way."

"It happened just the way I've told you. If anything, I was afraid of Ralph. I didn't want him getting that sort of hold over me."

Somehow he knew they'd reached the end of their stroll, even though they were still in the middle of the campus quadrangle, some distance from the sports arena. "Thank you for your help, Miss Banting. I may want to call on you again."

He left her there and headed back toward the men's dorm, knowing that she would watch him until he was out of sight.

Sergeant Fletcher found Leopold in his office early the following morning, reading the daily reports of the night's activities. "Don't you ever sleep, Captain?" he asked, pulling up the faded leather chair that served for infrequent visitors.

"I'll have enough time for sleeping when I'm dead. What have you got on McBern?"

"His lawyer says he refuses to make a statement, but I gather they'd like to plead him not guilty by reason of insanity."

"What's the medical examiner say?"

Fletcher read from a typed sheet. "Two stab wounds, both in the area of the heart. He apparently was stretched out on the bed when he got it."

"How long before they found him?"

"He'd eaten breakfast maybe an hour or so before he died, and from our questioning that places the time of death at about ten o'clock. Bill Smith went to the door and got McBern to open it at about eight the following morning. Since we know McBern was in the room the previous evening when Smith spoke to him through the door, we can assume he was alone with the body for approximately twenty-two hours."

Leopold was staring out the window, mentally comparing the city's autumn gloom with the colors of the countryside that he'd witnessed the previous day. Everything dies, only it dies a little sooner, a bit more drably, in the city. "What else?" he asked Fletcher, because there obviously was something else.

"In one of the desk drawers," Fletcher said, producing a little evidence envelope. "Six sugar cubes, saturated with LSD."

"All right." Leopold stared down at them. "I guess that's not too unusual on campuses these days. Has there ever been a murder committed by anyone under the influence of LSD?"

"A case out west somewhere. And I think another one over in England."

"Can we get a conviction, or is this the basis of the insanity plea?"

"I'll check on it, Captain."

"And one more thing—get that fellow Smith in here. I want to talk with him again."

Later, alone, Leopold felt profoundly depressed. The case bothered him. McBern had stayed with Rollings' body for twenty-two hours.

Anybody that could last that long would have to be crazy. He was crazy and he was a killer and that was all there was to it.

When Fletcher ushered Bill Smith into the office an hour later, Leopold was staring out the window. He turned and motioned the young man to a chair. "I have some further questions, Bill."

"Yes?"

"Tell me about the LSD."

"What?"

Leopold walked over and sat on the edge of the desk. "Don't pretend you never heard of it. Rollings and McBern had some in their room."

Bill Smith looked away. "I didn't know. There were rumors."

"Nothing else? No noise through that connecting door?"

"Noise, yes. Sometimes it was. . . ."

Leopold waited for him to continue, and when he did not, said, "This is a murder investigation, Bill."

"Rollings . . . he deserved to die, that's all. He was the most completely evil person I ever knew. The things he did to poor Tom . . ."

"Stella Banting says Tom almost worshipped him."

"He did, and that's what made it all the more terrible."

Leopold leaned back and lit a cigarette. "If they were both high on LSD, almost anyone could have entered that room and stabbed Ralph."

But Bill Smith shook his head. "I doubt it. They wouldn't have dared unlock the door while they were turned on. Besides, Tom would have protected him with his own life."

"And yet we're to believe that Tom killed him? That he stabbed him to death and then spent a day and a night alone with the body? Doing what, Bill? Doing what?"

"I don't know."

"Do you think Tom McBern is insane?"

"No, not really. Not legally." He glanced away. "But on the subject of Rollings, he was pretty far gone. Once, when we were still friendly, he told me he'd do anything for Rollings—even trust him with his life. And he did, one time. It was during the spring weekend and everybody had been drinking a lot. Tom hung upside down out of the dorm window with Rollings holding his ankles. That's how much he trusted him."

"I think I'll have to talk with Tom McBern again," Leopold said. "At the scene of the crime."

Fletcher brought Tom McBern out to the campus in handcuffs,

and Captain Leopold was waiting for them in the oblong room on the fourth floor. "All right, Fletcher," Leopold said. "You can leave us alone. Wait outside."

McBern had lost a good deal of his previous composure, and now he faced Leopold with red-ringed eyes and a lip that trembled when he spoke. "What . . . what did you want to ask me?"

"A great many things, son. All the questions in the world." Leopold sighed and offered the boy a cigarette. "You and Rollings were taking LSD, weren't you?"

"We took it, yes."

"Why? For kicks?"

"Not for kicks. You don't understand about Ralph."

"I understand that you killed him. What more is there to understand? You stabbed him to death right over there on that bed."

Tom McBern took a deep breath. "We didn't take LSD for kicks," he repeated. "It was more to heighten the sense of religious experience—a sort of mystical involvement that is the whole meaning of life."

Leopold frowned down at the boy. "I'm only a detective, son. You and Rollings were strangers to me until yesterday, and I guess now he'll always be a stranger to me. That's one of the troubles with my job. I don't get to meet people until it's too late, until the damage," he gestured toward the empty bed, "is already done. But I want to know what happened in this room, between you two. I don't want to hear about mysticism or religious experience. I want to hear what happened—why you killed him and why you sat here with the body for twenty-two hours."

Tom McBern looked up at the walls, seeing them perhaps for the first and thousandth time. "Did you ever think about this room? About the shape of it? Ralph used to say it reminded him of a story by Poe, *The Oblong Box*. Remember that story? The box was on board a ship, and of course it contained a body. Like Queequeg's coffin which rose from the sea to rescue Ishmael."

"And this room was Ralph's coffin?" Leopold asked quietly.

"Yes." McBern stared down at his handcuffed wrists. "His tomb."

"You killed him, didn't you?"

"Yes."

Leopold looked away. "Do you want your lawyer?"

"No. Nothing."

"My God! Twenty-two hours!"

"I was . . ."

"I know what you were doing. But I don't think you'll ever tell it to a judge and jury."

"I'll tell you, because maybe you can understand." And he began to talk in a slow, quiet voice, and Leopold listened because that was his job.

Toward evening, when Tom McBern had been returned to his cell and Fletcher sat alone with Leopold, he said, "I've called the District Attorney, Captain. What are you going to tell him?"

"The facts, I suppose. McBern will sign a confession of just how it happened. The rest is out of our hands."

"Do you want to tell me about it, Captain?"

"I don't think I want to tell anyone about it. But I suppose I have to. I guess it was all that talk of religious experience and coffins rising from the ocean that tipped me off. You know, that Rollings pictured their room as a sort of tomb."

"For him it was."

"I wish I'd known him, Fletcher. I only wish I'd known him in time."

"What would you have done?"

"Perhaps only listened and tried to understand him."

"McBern admitted killing him?"

Leopold nodded. "It seems that Rollings asked him to, and Tom McBern trusted him more than life itself."

"Rollings asked to be stabbed through the heart?"

"Yes."

"Then why did McBern stay with the body so long? For a whole day and night?"

"He was waiting," Leopold said quietly, looking at nothing at all. "He was waiting for Rollings to rise from the dead."

JUSTICE HAS A HIGH PRICE

by Pat McGerr

The case against Charles Selden was admittedly a case in which everything had gone wrong. As a thousand men before him, and a thousand afterwards, he had dreamed—and hated—and cheated—only to, in his moment of need, come to depend on the wrong kind of witness . . .

Charles Selden was dreaming—one of those oppressive, frustrating nightmares that had lately become so frequent for him—and the scream at first seemed part of the pattern. Then he was awake and realized it was his wife's voice, high-pitched and ear-shattering.

He opened his eyes to see her sitting upright in the adjoining bed, one arm pointing toward the bureau. In the same instant there was an explosion and a flash of fire, and the scream was cut off and she slumped down in the bed.

Moving by instinct, without time for thought or fear, he threw aside the covers and leaped toward the shadowy figure across the room. The gun spoke again. He didn't count the shots, hardly felt the bullet that seared his left shoulder. In seconds he was on the intruder with an impact that knocked the gun from his hand and made it skim across the slick bedroom floor.

There was no contest. The stranger, slightly built and now weaponless, wanted only to escape. Twisting from Selden's grasp, he hurled himself through the ground-floor window by which he had entered. Racing after him, Selden's bare foot collided with the dropped pistol. He picked it up and carried it to the window, but the intruder had vanished into the trees behind the cabin. Clearly visible in the moonlight, the man's footprints marked the light coating of fresh snow.

Snow, Charles noted with a rush of familiar irritation. I told Helen we were due for bad weather. It was sheer stubborn nonsense to stay on in a summer cottage until snow falls. Then the thought struck him that they would not argue about this, or anything else, again. Helen's been killed and I— His hand went to his shoulder, felt the blood sticky on his pajama collar, and he knew a sudden faintness. Must get help. A doctor. Police. He started for the telephone between the two beds . . .

"Then I must have blacked out." Again and again he was to tell his story—first to the police, later to his lawyer, finally at the trial. "The next thing I remember, I was lying on the floor with my head feeling very fuzzy. I pulled myself up, got to Helen, and she—she wasn't breathing. There was no pulse, and I knew she was dead. I dialed the operator—I guess I couldn't have been very coherent, but she got word to the right people—and then there was nothing to do but wait."

The first policeman listened with a sort of stolid sympathy, asking few questions, making many notes. The only hint of skepticism came when Selden, striving for a description of the man he had grappled so briefly, suggested, "There are footprints in the snow outside. Won't they give you some idea of his size and help in identification?"

"Not now, there aren't," the officer answered. "It started snowing again about the time your call came through. That's what slowed us getting here. So if there were any prints, they're all filled in."

"Bad luck." Following another thought, Charles missed the significance of the policeman's *if*. "That road up the mountain's hard going when it's wet and slippery."

"And even worse when it's icy, like tonight. We don't usually have summer people here after the end of September. Yours is the only cabin still open."

"I know," Charles said. "The Davises, next door, went home ten days ago. I suppose that prowler, whoever he was, thought the whole area was deserted. A good time to pick up anything valuable that might have been left behind."

"Yeah, I guess that's what he thought," the officer said absently. He looked up as the medical examiner came out of the bedroom. "You finished in there, Doc?"

"All finished. No use trying to get an ambulance up here till daylight."

"I'll leave Murph on duty," the police captain said. "You be all right here, Mr. Selden? Or would you like to ride into town with us?"

"I'll stay here," Charles answered. "Unless there's some way I can help find the man who did it."

"Leave that to us. If he's still in the woods, we'll have him before morning. If he's gotten farther away—well, it'll take a little longer. Ready to go, Doc?"

"Ready. Don't worry about that shoulder, Mr. Selden." He glanced with professional satisfaction at the dressing he'd applied. "The bullet just grazed the flesh. Lucky for you it wasn't a couple of inches to the right."

Lucky. The word rang strangely in Charles's ears as he watched their car head down the narrow road. Very lucky. Deliberately he kept his thoughts away from the bedroom where a young police sergeant kept watch over Helen's body.

When the captain returned the next day, his inquiry veered quickly away from the subject of the prowler and went on to other matters.

"This is the fourth year you've come here, right, Mr. Selden? Do you always stay on into October?"

"No, we usually leave much earlier. But my wife loves—loved the outdoors. She never got tired of tramping over the hills or fishing the streams. So she was set on staying as long as the good weather lasted." More set on it, he added mentally, because she knew I was dying to get back to the city. Knew that and probably guessed why.

"And you didn't have to hurry back to a job?"

"My job can always wait." Bitterness edged Charles's voice. "It's with the family firm."

"Your family's?"

"No, my wife's."

The questions then grew more pressing, more personal—till Selden finally exploded.

"What the devil are you driving at? My wife's been killed, her murderer's on the loose, and you sit here prying into our private life! Sure, we had arguments. Show me any couple married five years who doesn't. But that's not going to help you find the man who shot her."

"We'll find him," the captain said, "if you'll just be patient. I know this is a bad time for you, Mr. Selden, but we have to cover all the angles."

So Charles went on answering questions whose relevance he didn't understand until the interview was interrupted by the arrival of Helen's brother. They exchanged awkward condolences, discussed the necessary funeral arrangements. Charles had never been at ease with Arthur and if there was now an additional restraint, it seemed sufficiently explained by the circumstances.

But Charles still had no sense of his own jeopardy. Awareness began only when he read the evening paper. His story of the prowler with a gun was hedged throughout with doubting phrases—"Selden said," "Selden claimed," "according to Selden."

"My God!" He spoke aloud to the empty room. "They make it sound as if I'd invented the whole thing, as if there were no burglar, as if—oh, my God!"

But his panic quickly faded, snuffed out by his knowledge that there had indeed been a burglar. They'll find him, he thought, and that will be the end of it. Or even if the search fails, there must be plenty of evidence that the man was here. They have his gun—it can surely be traced. He probably left fingerprints. One way or another, there will be a dozen proofs of his existence.

Charles's confidence held through more interrogations and up to the time, right after Helen's burial, when he was arrested. He sat, stunned with disbelief, in a sparsely furnished jail cell, charged with the murder of his wife.

It was impossible, incredible, a new nightmare from which he must soon awaken. But it did not take on full reality until he sat across a table from the lawyer sent by his brother-in-law. From him came a crushing bit of news. The gun dropped by the intruder had been checked: it belonged to the owner of the cabin next door.

"Len Davis?" Charles asked, puzzled. "That doesn't make sense."

"The lock on the Davis' back door was broken. The rooms were disordered. Mr. Davis says he kept the gun in a desk drawer."

"Then the fellow must have gone in there before he came to our place." Charles's spirits lifted. "That adds up, doesn't it? Proves there was a stranger in the area, even if the police haven't been able to round him up. So why are they holding me?"

"They have a different theory," the lawyer answered. "Davis told them you knew about the gun."

"Sure I knew about it. Most of the summer he was only able to get out of town on week-ends and his wife was a little nervous about being up there alone. He got the gun for her protection. He even set up a target on one of the trees where she could practice. But what's that got to do with— No! Are they saying I broke into the Davis place and stole his gun and tried to make it look like— But that's crazy!"

"We have to face facts," the lawyer said. "The Davises left two weeks ago. That left you alone on the hilltop, free to plan and do whatever you chose in complete privacy. That's how it looks to the police."

"Facts, hell! I'll tell you how it looks to the police. They've a killing to solve and the killer's disappeared. What they want is a sitting duck—a nice neat solution worked out without leaving their armchairs. They've called off the hunt now, haven't they? They can save themselves a lot of trouble by simply pinning it on me."

"I'm sure the search is still on. But the chances of finding the man get less with each day that passes."

"No fingerprints, I suppose?"

"No. Presumably he wore gloves."

"One bad break after another! No prints—a gun from next door —snow covering his tracks. What else have they got against me?"

"The police have your pajama top with powder burns around the bullet hole. That's a clear indication of a self-inflicted wound. At least, it proves the gun was fired at close range."

"Of course it was fired at close range," Charles snapped. "I was damn near on top of the fellow when the bullet hit me. Everything they have is negative. There's no evidence at all pointing my way."

The case in the newspapers, though, began to appear more positive. Without taking a stand on Charles's guilt or innocence, the stories made it clear that there was only his unsupported word to indicate the existence of a prowler. Even the simple biographical details about him, it seemed to Charles, were slanted toward the worst possible interpretation.

"The jury's obliged to come to court without an opinion." He slammed the paper down in front of the lawyer. "But there won't be an unbiased juror in the state if they keep printing stuff like that."

"We can't stop them," the other returned, "unless they publish something that's not true."

"There are ways of twisting the truth, of making it seem worse than it is." Charles crumpled the sheet into a ball, flung it across the room. "I don't deny that Helen was rich and I was poor. I was a salesman for the Kent Company when I started taking her out and after the wedding I was vice-president. But that isn't why I married her. And even if it had been, it's a long jump from marrying for money to killing for it."

"A very long jump," the lawyer agreed.

"There was something between us in the beginning," Charles went on. "But it didn't last. How could it in that setup? I wasn't cut out to be a gigolo. I had ideas about the company, ways of improving distribution, reorganizing the sales force—but everything I suggested ran into Arthur's veto. He was willing to give me a fancy title, an upholstered office, and a generous drawing account. All he asked in return was that I keep my nose out of the business and make his sister happy. I scored high on the first requirement, but struck out on the second. Helen started drinking too much, and so did I. And sometimes we shouted at each other in public. But I'm sure you've heard all this from Arthur."

"He filled in some of the background, yes."

"There are plenty of witnesses to the failure of our marriage. They won't help my case, will they?"

"No," the lawyer said, "they won't. But none of that will matter if the real killer is found. And I've some good news for you there. Mr. Kent has engaged a private investigator to supplement the police search."

"That's decent of Arthur—and a little surprising. The way we've gotten along the last few years, I'd have expected him to dance at my hanging. I don't like taking favors from him either, but as things stand I don't have much choice. Justice has a high price tag. And I don't suppose there's much chance of my using any of Helen's money till I get out of here."

"No chance at all," the lawyer said. "So long as you're charged with her murder, you can't be her heir."

"Funny thing, once I'm acquitted, everything Helen owned will belong to me, including her half of the Kent Company. But if I should be convicted, it would all go to Arthur. Under the circumstances, I wonder if I'm being smart to let him pick my lawyer."

"Our firm has represented the Kent family for many years, Mr. Selden," the other said stiffly. "But of course if you feel that someone else could—"

"No offense," Charles said. "The thought just struck me. Arthur isn't going to like having me for a partner. But I don't really believe he'd try to frame me for murder. Not unless he thinks I did it. That's a possibility too."

"Mr. Kent is convinced of your innocence," the lawyer said. "We discussed the matter thoroughly before I accepted the case. As you say, he does not have a very high regard for you. But he has known you for a long time and he doesn't believe you capable of premeditated murder."

"Lack of brains?" Charles asked. "Or lack of guts?"

"I don't pretend—" The lawyer then ignored the question. "He is not chiefly motivated by concern for your welfare. Most of all, he wants his sister's murderer captured and brought to justice. He would also like to avoid the scandal that would inevitably result from your trial and conviction."

"That's a typically Arthurian motive," Charles said. "It's no disgrace to be shot by a stranger, but a murder within the family is a permanent blot. I'll concede that hard as it must be for him, Arthur's on my side. But what if the picture changes? If the evidence gets blacker against me, he may change his mind."

"Do you know of such evidence, Mr. Selden?"

"There's no evidence," Charles said firmly, "to support this charge of murder. Anything the police turn up has to confirm my story, help prove there was a robber in the house that night and that he shot Helen. But there are other facts—facts unrelated to the shooting—that might tip the scales for Arthur. Then what becomes of my defense?"

"Mr. Kent is paying my fee, Mr. Selden, but you are my client. My obligation to defend you is not subject to outside influences. I hope I may have your full confidence."

"I'm sure you'll do your best," Charles answered with perfunctory politeness.

He did not, even then, believe that the quality of his defense was of real importance. To cooperate with the attorney, to answer his questions, to go through the motions of preparing for the trial—this was a routine that must be followed until the burglar was found. If Charles's hopes had temporarily sagged in the bleak atmosphere of the jail, they were freshly buoyed by the knowledge that a private investigator had entered the case. Today, tomorrow—it was only a matter of time till the criminal was taken. Then Charles would be free.

But the private search was no more fruitful than the official.

Time ran out and suddenly it was the day of the trial. Charles was swept by a near numbness as he sat in court, his attorney by his side, the prosecution staff across the aisle. He looked up at the judge, over to the jury box, back to the crowded spectators' section.

It was like an old movie into which he had suddenly been thrust as the leading actor. It can't be happening, his mind throbbed the refrain. It can't be happening to me. Memory swerved back to the beginning, to that moment of sudden awakening, to the sight of the stranger in the bedroom, to the roar and flash of the intruder's gun.

It will be all right, Charles told himself as he fought his mounting tension. I'll tell my story to the jury and they'll believe me—they'll *have* to believe me. Yet he had told that story to the police and they had arrested him for murder; he'd told it to the press and their reports had insinuated his guilt.

"That man!" His control failed and he reached out to clutch his lawyer's arm. "Why can't they find him? They've got to find the man!"

They didn't find the man, but they found the woman.

On the third day after the jury was chosen, Diane took the stand as the prosecution's star witness and Charles watched his hopes dwindle to near zero.

She testified reluctantly, but the reluctance sprang from concern for her own reputation, not for his life. Once he caught her eye and she turned quickly away, but not before her glance had told him that she, like everyone else, believed he had killed his wife, believed he had done it for her—and feared and despised him for it. Yet looking at her in this courtroom he felt again the obsessive desire that had for so many months ruled his life.

Question by question, the prosecutor dragged from her the damning facts about their relationship. Her admission that she had been his mistress came in a voice that was barely audible, but Charles knew how loudly it must have sounded in the ears of the jurors.

"Did you have reason to believe," the questioning continued, "that the defendant intended to marry you?"

"Oh, yes." To this she could speak more firmly. "From the first he promised to get a divorce so that we could be married. He said it would take a little time to arrange, that I'd have to be patient. If I hadn't believed that, I would never have had anything to do with him."

"And when you found out that he wasn't going ahead with the divorce?"

"Then I told him that it had to be all over between us, that I wouldn't see him again, not ever."

The truth, Charles thought, but not the whole truth. That version left her with some shreds of respectability and he wouldn't strip them from her—wouldn't and couldn't, since to do so would establish even more strongly his reason for wishing his wife dead. He had a vivid recollection of that scene in Diane's apartment when she had at last forced a showdown.

"I'm not going on like this any longer, Charles." Her petulant little-girl voice had had an undertone of steel. "You still haven't said one word to your wife about a divorce and I don't believe you're ever going to. Are you, Charles?"

"It's not something to rush into, Diane." He had moved across the room to run his fingers through the soft fur of the scarf she had tossed on a chair. "Give me time."

"Time!" she had snapped. "For weeks and weeks you've made promises and done nothing. Does it take so much time to sit down with your wife and tell her you're through?"

"That could be done very quickly," he'd admitted. "What takes time is the financial settlement."

"Financial? You mean she'll hold you up for a lot of alimony?"

"Alimony?" He'd stared at her, startled. "Are you serious, Diane? Don't you understand how things are with me?"

"What is there to understand? You have plenty of money—haven't you?"

"I don't have a dime. All I have is a high-sounding job that I got by marrying the boss' sister." He'd found a grim satisfaction in pressing it home. "You were my secretary for three weeks. I thought my situation was the talk of the company."

"Nobody said a word. Somebody should have warned me. You should have told me."

"I'm telling you now." He'd picked up the fur, waved it at her. 'My wife's money paid for this. My wife's money pays for everything. And the day she agrees to a divorce, I'll be out on the street."

"You lied to me," she had said furiously. "You let me think you were rich and that we could be married. And all the time you were making a fool of me."

"That isn't what I had in mind." He'd gone back to the couch, put his hands on her shoulders, tried to pull her toward him. "Is that all it ever was, Diane? Just money? Haven't you any—"

"Don't touch me." She had given him a hard push. "Liar! Four-flusher!"

"Diane, please—"

"Get out!" She had sprung up, run to open the door to the hall. "Get out and don't come back. I never want to see you again, not ever."

It was that evening, in the finality of Diane's anger, that he agreed to go with Helen to the mountain cabin. But as the weeks passed he persuaded himself that the girl's decision was less than final, and he began to make allowances for her. Her rage, her disappointment were understandable. He had broken the news to her too abruptly. Naturally she felt herself deceived, ill-used. It wasn't true that she cared only for his money, and nothing for him. She had struck out only to hurt him.

He wrote her then and received no answer, and knew a growing anxiety to return to the city. He was sure that Helen sensed this and that it lay behind her insistence that they extend their stay in the cabin. Now in the courtroom he watched with horror as his letter to Diane was introduced as evidence.

What had he said? Desperately he tried to recall the phrases. I love you, I miss you, I need you. Certainly he had said that. But what more? "I promise you, my darling, that I will very soon make arrangements so that we can be together. Nothing else matters." He had written that and had meant simply the firm resolution to find a job, any job outside the Kent Company, so that he could divorce Helen and marry Diane. But read aloud here, with the prosecutor's special emphasis, the "arrangements" translated to coldly calculated murder.

Watching Diane leave the stand, he felt for the first time a sense of total hopelessness. To anyone who saw her as he did, she must supply a full and compelling motive. To the others—to the virtuous, to the women on the jury—he was branded an adulterer. What matter if they found "reasonable doubt" of his guilt of the lesser crime? There could be no doubt that this girl was both desirable and expensive. To keep her he had to rid himself of his wife and retain his wife's money. What else could the jury believe?

This blanket of despair covered him through the rest of the trial. When it was his turn on the stand, he told his story with a robot-like precision which he knew, without being able to do anything about it, must rob it of all conviction. The cross-examination was heavy with sarcasm. Taking him through the whole tale again, the prosecutor began almost every question with the phrase, "You ask us to believe," in a way that drove a wide gap between each detail and human credibility.

"You ask us to believe, Mr. Selden—" the fortieth repetition grated on all his nerve ends "—that this unknown man who was an expert marksman when he was aiming at your wife turned into a rank amateur when you were the target."

"I don't know what kind of a marksman he was."

"Then let me refresh your memory. There were three bullets fired. One killed your wife. One was found by the police in the wall between the beds. One scraped your shoulder. So you ask us to believe that this alleged prowler was able to send a bullet directly through your wife's heart and then missed you entirely at the same distance."

"I was moving when he shot at me."

"Ah, yes, you were moving. So his first shot went wild and he shot again. And you ask us to believe that this mysterious stranger, firing at a moving target, placed his next bullet in a spot where it could draw a little blood, leave a small wound for the police to see, but do you no lasting damage. Do you really expect anyone to *believe* that?"

"It's the truth," Charles said doggedly. "It's the way it happened."

"The truth is what we're seeking," the prosecutor assured him. "But I think we can come a little closer to it than you have so far. I suggest that after you killed your wife, you fired another bullet into the wall and then shot yourself in the shoulder to support your story of a prowler in the night."

"I didn't shoot myself," Charles said. "There was a prowler. That is the exact truth . . ."

By the time his testimony ended he felt a deadly certainty that, in the minds of judge, jury, and spectators, the prowler was a phantom, a man who never existed and could never be found. Almost with impatience he sat through his counsel's closing argument, seeing the weakness of his defense, its total dependence on his own word—in which no one now believed.

The prosecution's closing argument was circumstantial and convincing. If he was talking about someone else, Charles thought, I'd believe him—believe that this man, driven by desire, must have plotted the murder of his wife, broken into his neighbor's empty cabin to steal the gun he knew was there, and then, at his own convenience in the middle of the night, used it to kill his wife.

"But what a fool that makes me," he protested to his lawyer while they waited for the verdict. "I might have done all the things he said, but I'd know I couldn't get away with it, that I was putting my neck in a noose. To invent a robber who didn't exist would be too transparent, too stupid. But he did exist, he does exist, and somebody's got to find him."

"We're trying," the lawyer said. "We'll keep on trying."

The verdict was swift in coming and held no surprises. Guilty of murder in the first degree.

"We'll appeal, of course," the lawyer said. "And I've persuaded

Mr. Kent to offer a substantial reward for information leading to the real murderer. We're not finished."

Oh, yes, I'm finished, Charles thought. I'm through clinging to slim hopes. It's easier to face the worst and just drift toward the end. He took for granted the denial of his appeal, listened stoically to the pronouncement of the death sentence, and expected no more from Arthur's offer of a reward than the usual lineup of crackpots.

So complete was his resignation that when his lawyer, ten days before the date set for the execution, brought him a fresh strand of hope, Charles almost refused to accept it.

"I know we've had a string of cranks who were only after the money or the publicity," the lawyer admitted. "It's the reward that brought this man forward, too, and he's not a very savory character, but his story checks out. He was driving on the main highway that links with the road to your cabin about 3 a.m. on the night of the murder. The police got your call at 3:10. Assuming it took the killer half an hour to get down the mountain, that would allow less than an hour from the time he was in your house till you put in the call. That time fits pretty well, doesn't it?"

"I guess so. I wasn't watching the clock."

"This man's story is that a young chap hailed him and he stopped to pick him up. Said he looked about twenty or twenty-one, not tall, skinny, wearing jeans and a leather jacket. That matches your description, as much as you could give us."

"He was smaller than I," Charles agreed. "I remember at the time thinking that was good luck."

"Our witness says the young man was very nervous, talked about having to get out of town in a hurry. He also told us there was a long scratch down the left side of his face that looked as if it might have been made by a fingernail."

"A scratch? Yes, of course!" For the first time Charles felt a renewal of life. Remember carefully now, he told himself. Remember how it was. He had dived at the stranger, his fingers had clutched at his face. "I could have scratched him. I must have scratched him. And it was with my right hand, the side where I hadn't been shot, so it would be his left cheek. Your man's telling the truth. He saw the prowler, gave him a ride, he can prove my story. Oh, my God, it's going to be all right!"

"I think so," the lawyer said more temperately. "I think this is the link we need."

Charles had a week of soaring spirits. Their thudding drop on the seventh day was almost unendurable. The judge had appraised the new evidence, and decided it did not justify a new trial; the governor had also been unmoved by it.

"But that's impossible," Charles cried. "We've an eyewitness who backs up my story. They've got to believe him! Why would he lie to help me?"

"For the reward," the lawyer answered. "Unfortunately, our witness has a very bad record. He's served two terms for receiving stolen property, and been convicted once of perjury. The way the judge and governor see it, he'd swear to anything for a thousand dollars. Even if he had come forward before the trial, I don't think he'd have been much help to your case."

"But he saw the man," Charles insisted. "At least, he can furnish a lead on where he went."

"He dropped him at the railroad station. Nobody there remembers seeing him, which isn't surprising. He could have taken a train in either direction. Or he could have walked a few blocks to the bus depot and left town that way. There just aren't any more leads—not a single one."

"No," Charles said dully, "I guess I shouldn't have expected anything. But wouldn't you have thought that when a witness did turn up, he'd be a man whose word was worth something? Everything has gone wrong. I haven't had one good break, not one."

From then on it was a matter of marking time, of waiting for it to be over.

Constantly his mind went back to the beginning when it had all appeared so simple and so safe. He'd been standing at the window looking at the footprints in the snow, getting used to the idea of his wife's death. He'd turned back into the room and taken a few steps toward the phone.

"Is he gone?" Helen's voice had cut sharply through the dark. "Did you let him get away?"

"Yes, he's gone. I thought he'd killed you."

"I must have ducked just as he fired. It was close—but not close enough." She reached out to click on the bedside lamp. In its glow her smile taunted him. "Disappointed? Were you already counting your chickens, the ones you and that little tart could hatch? If only he'd been a better marksman, it would have made it so easy for you."

"Yes," he'd agreed quietly, "it would have made it so easy."

Somewhere out there, he'd thought, is a man who brought this gun here and fired it at Helen. When they find him and tell him she's dead, he won't be able to deny he killed her.

Slowly Charles had raised the gun and taken careful aim. He had watched her expression change from mockery to unbelief to fear. Then, as a scream formed on her lips, he had pulled the trigger.

THE GREAT GLOCKENSPIEL GIMMICK

by Arthur Moore

Here is an earlier report from the Runyon-like world of pros such as Faceless Robert, a minor employee on the payroll of your local God-father, who—and this with some justice—has yet to be accused of empathy for the erring.

Nobody embezzles from Faceless Robert's Horse Parlor. This is a rule which is never broke for reasons that are as durable as headstones. Except that Albert has got carried away and has come up short on the books. Tempted by a hot tip on a cool bangtail, he has dipped his hand into the till and the horse ran out. Not out of the till—out of the money.

Naturally, this is a calamity. Albert figures he has maybe twelve hours to make up the forty clamaroonies before Faceless notices the deficit and it is all over but the final posies and the slow music as the slab goes by.

I am sitting in Katzie's Saloon, nursing a small beer, when he shags in like a barnacle on payday. Only he is sad as a gee who has just been hung. He is walking like it is raining—on nobody but him.

He says to me, "H'lo, Dubois," and downs a straight shot that raises Jonesy's eyebrows, because it is before noon and a long way from the first race. Albert remarks like, "Jonesy, I have got to have the loan of forty frogskins or I am never gonna see another sunrise."

Jonesy blinks at him and his little moustache gets to wiggling. I can tell what he is thinking and I am thinking the same thing. Albert has never got up to see a sunrise in his life. I doubt if he would know what it is.

Jonesy apologises because, by an oversight, he has just laid out lucre for a few pressing saloon tabs. Albert looks at me, gives that up, and fills us in on the squeeze that he is the squeezee of.

Faceless Robert is not about to laugh off forty mintberries—or forty empty jars of moustache wax. Faceless has never been known to laugh about anything. One of his runners, in an attempt to improve the granite image, once spread the rumor that Faceless actually smiled. He admitted that this event took place at the time of the St. Valentine's Day Massacre, a natural thing for Faceless to enjoy.

After Albert swears us all to secrecy he sits down to get in some solid nail-chewing. He is squeezing his smarts very hard, and naturally there is nothing I can help him with in this line; so I bum a fresh beer from Jonesy who is so wrapped up in Albert's problem that he lets me put it on the cuff.

We will all be sorry that Albert is not around no more. Jonesy is getting sadder than Sitting Bull's Sioux when they run out of cavalrymen, because Albert is always good for a touch—when he is winning, which ain't often. And of course he is grouchy when he is studying the Form post facto—but it is easy to forget them things when a pal is about to take off for the Great Unknown and Heavenly Clambake.

I am busy reflecting that I can probably get cornflowers for the casket from Sidney's Flower Shop at half price, when Albert runs a finger around his collar and asks me to stop staring at him.

Just at that time a truck goes by on the street outside, and there is a brace of banjo players sitting in the back. Another guy is yelling through a loudspeaker that we should vote for some bazoo because he has a record of never doing nothing which proves that he never done nothing bad.

I notice Albert's eyes get wide all of a sudden, then he gulps. A thought has hit him like a missile.

"I got it!" he yells, and hops up knocking over the chair.

Jonesy jumps a foot and spills beer all over Left Foot Hamish who has just come in and ordered one. "You got what?"

"The glockenspheen!" he yells again, but now he is chasing out the front door like he is the Lone Ranger and the bad guy is grabbing at his mask.

Left Foot sops up the beer on his shirt as we explain the problem and he becomes sad like us. Left Foot is a wispy little creature with the eyes of a beagle and a brain like a bowl of noodles. He is famous as the Man with the Sock System. He owns three socks—not three pairs, just three socks. Every morning he washes one, then he puts the clean sock on the left foot, and moves the one he wore on the left foot yesterday to the right foot. Once he showed up wearing only one sock. He had bollixed up his system by washing two socks at once—and it took him three days to get straightened out.

Albert don't get back for a half hour, and then he is carrying a parcel which he unwraps and sets up on a table. We all gather round and stare at it.

Left Foot asks, "What is it?" A very reasonable question.

Albert is annoyed. "It's a glockenspiel. I got it in a trunk at an auction."

Jonesy says to me out of the corner of his mouth, "What the hell is a glockenspheen?"

"It's a musical instrument," says Albert like we are a bunch of round haircuts. He hits a couple of steel bars with a little hammer and the thing gives out a shrill squawk, till he stops it quick. "It's worth ninety simoleons if it's worth a dime. I will let it go at the bargain price of forty." He looks around at us and sighs. There are no takers.

"I never glocked much," says Jonesy, winking at me, "especially with a spheel."

"Ain't it hard to get parts?" Left Foot asks seriously.

"You don't get—" Albert starts shouting, then he takes a deep breath. "It's an antique from Europe." He gives us all a very hard look. "All right then, we will sell it to Goldberg."

I choke on my beer and Left Foot looks at Albert like he is missing some marbles, which is a very difficult thing for Left Foot to do.

"You mean pawn it?" Jonesy asks.

"I mean sell it. Goldberg would give nothin' on a loan. We have got to sell it outright."

"You are slippin' the strings on your dulcimer," I tell him. "Goldberg won't *buy* that object. He wouldn't buy the Holy Grail unless Galahad was standin' there with Limey scratch, waitin' to take it off his hands."

"Listen," Albert says, and he lowers his voice as we all lean toward him. "I know what I'm doin'. I got it all worked out." He holds up a paper that is covered with notations and scribbles. "Goldberg is a guy with an IQ like the fink that invented taxes. He is so sharp he has to wear iron underwear. Right?"

"He don't play the ponies," Jonesy mentions.

Albert ignores him. "Goldberg will not pass up a legit buck, right? We will use this failing to our advantage and force him to buy the glockenspiel."

"You're outa your bird," I say.

"You ain't heard the Plan—which you are in," Albert assures me. "He will fall for it like a brass nightingale. You, Dubois, will go along with Left Foot when he takes the glockenspiel to Goldberg."

I am astonished. "When *he* takes it?"

Albert looks at me like he has heard I am saving nuts for the winter. "Who else but Left Foot would own a glockenspiel? We got to make this look natural to Goldberg."

"I forgot," I tell him.

"Now," Albert looks at the paper. "We will hold a dry run." He points to me and Left Foot. "You two bring the glockenspiel to me —I'm Goldberg. You tell me you want to leave this rare musical thingamajig in my joint on consignment until some slob wanders in and buys it. You got that?"

Left Foot picks up the glockenspiel. We go through the motions of coming in the pawnshop. Left Foot stops in front of Albert and bangs on one of the steel bars till it makes a loud humming screech. "Mr. Goldbird," he says, "Albert wants you should—"

"Cut!" yells Albert, getting red in the face. "Don't tell him *I* want —you're the clown. *You* want to sell it!"

"Oh." Left Foot nods and starts again. "Mr. Goldberg, I have got here this swell glockentooter . . ."

"Glockenspiel."

"—Yeah, glockenspeel, and I want you should keep it in the window on account of I need forty clamoleons to pay back Faceless."

"No, no, no!" screams Albert. "You need the moo but you don't have to tell him why!"

Left Foot grits his teeth and starts again. "Mr. Golebird, I have got here this glockenwhatzit and I need one pair of Jacksons to—er— I just need 'em."

Albert says, "I don't want no dumb glockenspiel."

"Okey." Left Foot turns around and tramps away and Albert yells at him.

"I was just being Goldberg! That's what he'll say."

Left Foot looks doubtful. "You could be nicer," he pouts. "After all, this here's *your* glockenthing."

"It's just play-actin'," I tell him and he looks up at me with the beagle eyes till it sinks in. This is the knight on the white charger who Albert has picked to be his rescuer.

"I'll be nicer," Albert promises, soothing him. "I just want you should get used to what to expect."

Left Foot starts again. "I got this dumb glocken—"

"Respect!" shouts Albert. "You got to have respect for what you're toutin'. It's a rare antique gimmick which any hoi-polloi crumbum should be proud to shove in a corner of his pad. Now, try it again— and try to get it right this time."

Left Foot does it again—and again—and each time he does it Albert gives him a different answer and pretty soon it doesn't faze him. In about an hour Left Foot is able to go up to Albert without dropping the glockenspiel or forgetting his lines.

In the middle of all this, Alky comes stumbling in and leans on a beer to watch the show. He don't say much, but he is steadily going crazy with curiosity—and he is getting real annoyed with Albert.

Finally he can't hold it any longer. He yells, "Why don't you tell 'im NO, for Pete's sake?" He pounds on the bar and it and Jonesy both jump. "If you don't want the damn thing, why—?"

"We're play-acting!" Albert shouts, and it percolates through to Alky who opens his mouth at the wonder of it. Alky is a large lumpy individual, especially around the head; and he is constantly dusting off his baldish dome on account of the birds are flying over it very low. He is one of them old-timers who has come through the prohibition days with most everything intact but his teeth and his headbones. He is punchy as yesterday's bus transfers.

When he finds out what we are practicing about, he offers his services to Albert.

"All right," agrees Albert, "you can be the cinch man."

Albert explains that after Goldberg has put the glockenbox in the window, Alky is to go in and make a deposit on same. "This is important. We have got to do this by the numbers," he says. "Everybody set their watches."

Left Foot hasn't got a watch, but I set mine with Albert's and Alky does the same. It is becoming very serious with the watch setting—even Jonesy is looking impressed. This is like D-Day when we were all 4-F's waiting by the radio for the grim command to turn up the volume.

"At eleven-thirty," Albert says, trying to look Left Foot in the eye, "Dubois and Left Foot will go into the hockshop and plant the glockenspiel." He points to Alky. "At exactly one-fifteen, Alky will make the deposit."

Alky asks, "Why one-fifteen?"

Albert looks at him. "You're right. Okay, make it one-sixteen." Alky nods wisely and makes a note on the edge of his Racing Form.

Alky turns out to be a terrible ham. I have never realized this before, but then I have never seen Alky on the make-believe kick. If he ever played Shakespeare, he would do it with a real spear.

He pretends to walk in Goldberg's, and he stops very sudden and reacts. "Holy horrendous hominy grits!" he yells, which breaks up everybody. He points to the instrument. "That there's a honest to goodness glockenspoon! I gotta have it, Albert—I mean Goldberg. I gotta, I gotta—"

"Cut!" screams Albert. "You don't have to qualify for a Oscar Award."

Alky sticks out his lower lip. "I gotta feel it, don't I?"

Albert sighs, "All right, feel it, but don't wear it out. Now, do it again."

He tries it over and over, and finally he walks in and puts down the deposit without making it seem like he is buying Manhattan Island from a bunch of scheming redskins.

But Albert is looking less neat by the minute. I never see him work so hard. "Only one more thing," he says, and he comes over and pats me on the shoulder, so then I know this is the piece-of-resistance. "I have gotta depend on you, Dubois. This is where Left Foot has gotta hit the beanbag outa the park and touch all the bases like Seabiscuit in his prime. This is where I get the forty Irish flags or a plot in Evergreen Acres."

"Leave it to me," I say, and he bites his lip as he turns away with a great sigh—which makes me think of the cornflowers again. Albert takes a deep breath and stops in front of Left Foot.

"You have parked the glockenspiel at the hockshop and you have told Goldberg you gotta have forty clams for it, right?"

"Right," says Left Foot briskly. He has got that down pat.

"Now," says Albert, "Alky has come in and left a deposit on it, tellin' Goldberg he will be back right away with the rest of the dough. No matter how much Goldberg asks, Alky will agree. Right?"

Everybody, including Alky, nods. We are all with him so far.

"Fine. Then Dubois and Left Foot will go back to Goldberg at two-fifteen, and they will tell him they gotta have the glockenspiel because they got a hot customer who is going to shell out as soon as he gets his mitts on it."

"Hey!" Alky says suddenly. "I got a deposit on de t'ing." He is wrinkling his low forehead. Hollywood should hear about Alky.

"Good," beams Albert. "That's what Goldberg will say. He can't let you have the whozit because then he will have to give Alky his lettuce back and pass up the profit. Also, Alky could sue."

"I would, too," Alky says, glowering.

"So," Albert continues grandly, "Goldberg, knowing he can't stop Dubois and Left Foot from taking back their own property, will buy the glockenspiel from them."

Left Foot's mouth drops open. "Albert," he breathes, "you are a genius!"

Albert shrugs, but he is pleased. We rehearse the third act, where me and Left Foot get the scratch from Goldberg. We have to do it over and over again—because Left Foot is beginning to get over-organized and sometimes he adds things. He is so taken with the Plan that it is all we can do to keep him from offering Goldberg free glockenspiel lessons.

Finally Albert gets him cooled off. Jonesy closes the saloon, and all of us go together to the corner like we are going to watch a parade.

Then Left Foot goes to pieces. He sees the pawnshop just down the street and he forgets everything he has learned. He tries to get away and we all grab him. "I'll buy the thing myself," he yells.

Jonesy says, "He's got stage fright."

"A dollar a week!" Left Foot promises. "I allus wanted a—"

Albert saves the day. Grabbing Left Foot by the lapels, he stares into the watery, pink eyes. "Left Foot," he says with deep feeling, "I am dependin' on you—so I can see the sunrise tomorra. This here caper means life to me—more than anything—even more than a daily-double winner! You have just *got* to come through, like the true pal you has always been."

"Sunrise?" says Left Foot, astonished.

"It's an expression," Albert explains.

It seems to do the trick. Left Foot is so impressed by the idea that Albert would get up to see a sunrise that he forgets to be afraid. He takes the glockenbonger and the two of us shuffle off toward Goldberg's Put and Take.

Right then is where the whole Plan hits an unexpected snag.

Left Foot marches into the shop with me right behind him. Goldberg, who is a tall, black-haired type with horn-rimmed glasses and eyes four sizes too big, is having a cup of coffee at his desk in the back of the store.

I see his eyes fasten on the glockenspiel as soon as we get through the door. When Left Foot reaches him, Goldberg is standing up and his fingers are twitching. Left Foot don't get a chance to say anything. He opens his mouth and then just leaves it open.

"I'll be damned!" Goldberg says. "A glockenspiel! My old man had one in the ol' country. What you want for it, Left Foot?"

"Huh?" Left Foot says.

Goldberg does a magic trick and his wallet is open and I am instantly fascinated at how much cabbage can be packed into a small space lengthways. He riffles through it, then shakes Left Foot's shoulder to help his hearing. "I'll buy it. How much?"

"You ain't doin' this right," Left Foot mumbles.

"F-forty bucks," I manage to say, prying the glockenhummer from Left Foot. Goldberg counts out the sawbucks without a word and shoves them in Left Foot's fist. He grabs the glockenspiel and is as happy as a post office driver with a new corner to park on.

I am staggered, but I recover enough to steer Left Foot out of the store. He is clutching the forty flags in his fist and mumbling to himself.

As soon as we hit the sidewalk, Left Foot bumps into a phone pole; so I stop him, take the clamaroonies for safe keeping, and case the immediate area for a place to work off our numb. Left Foot says, very seriously, "Albert didn't do it that way. We gotta go back and do it right."

I grab him and hustle him across the street. I am only a pint size myself, but Left Foot could not fight his way out of a Caesar salad. I propel him into a saloon where we take a table and two beers.

We are on our fourth beer each before the shock begins to wear off. Left Foot is beginning to understand what has happened and how the Plan changed at the last second. It is clear to both of us that the rest of the Plan is not necessary. We finish another couple of brews and leave the establishment.

Then I spot Alky approaching the pawnshop. I inform Left Foot who is well ballasted with beer and has developed a heavy list to starboard. He nods and I run across the street.

"We did it!" I tell Alky triumphantly. "We got the moo, and the Plan is a success!"

But Alky is not listening to me. He is mumbling to himself, and I catch some of the words. He is still working on his lines.

"Alky!" I yell, "It's all over. We done it!"

He don't even focus on me. When I get in front of him, he just brushes me aside and enters the three balls.

I am afraid to go in. I can hear voices, which get louder and louder till finally I don't have to go in. I can hear them fine from a block away. Alky is yelling that he wants to buy the glockenspoon and Goldberg is yelling that it ain't for sale.

Alky wants to know what the hell kind of a hockshop Goldberg is running, and offers to call the mob. Goldberg tries to reason with him, gives it up, and goes back to yelling. Cops are mentioned and there are a few smashes, like Alky might be pounding on something —which is his wont when he becomes excited. They are standing nose to nose shouting at each other, and they are just beginning to get their second wind.

A big crowd gathers. Albert and Jonesy show up and Albert spots me and tries to talk but there is too much noise. I give him the greenies which pleases him, but he cannot understand what Alky is still doing in the pawnshop.

Then the cops arrive. As the wagon backs up, Left Foot comes to life and blows his beery breath in my face. "It's time to go back and get the glockenhorn," he announces.

He has reverted to being organized. I try to catch him but he is weighted funny and I cannot get a good clutch on him. He slips through the crowd and into the pawnshop and when I get there he is wrestling for the glockenspiel with a very perplexed and frantic Goldberg, and Alky is shouting that he will sue.

It costs Albert the forty skins to get us all out of the sneezer.

THE SMILER

by Charles Norman

The Smiler, and I hope this will not be misunderstood, may live down the street from some of you in one of those faceless buildings —which look so much like all the other faceless buildings put up by speculators a generation or two ago—behind the walls of which so many live and love and die, in the anonymity that is both the privilege and the curse, and the strength, of the majority of us.

There are sections of the city which seem to stretch interminably. Sheer facades of brick that does not look like brick, windows that look stamped out, turn what were streets into canyons. Sometimes there is sunlight on one side of these canyons, never on both; and despite overhanging street lamps, ever more of them, the fall of night brings a pervading gloom.

The people who live in such buildings resemble them in that they appear to be as alike in one building as another, one street as another, in those canyoned streets. But to the people themselves, there is sufficient awareness of one another. Everyone has been ticked off —docketed—by religion, it may be, or race; by occupation, mannerisms and peculiarities. To such general data are added, as they occur, specific events like deaths, marriages, births, communions and graduations. Newcomers, in particular, undergo this quiet surveillance, from the moment a van draws up and begins to unload. The extent and type of furniture, the size of the family, are noted, to be followed by piecemeal accumulation of other data. There are dossiers—mental ones—for all.

It was therefore surprising that the smiler with the knife passed among them unnoticed. The sheer horror of his deeds, the general fear, brought them, for once, closer together. They talked more, walked more together, and there were little knots of them in the canyoned street bounded by sharp corners where other streets, other avenues, stretched endlessly. The smiler, taking his place with them, did not smile, and his grim visage resembled theirs.

In that street, in one of those drab buildings, in an apartment on the third floor where there were four apartments with four facing doors, there lived a family named Dinkin. Mr. Dinkin, the father, went to work every morning, and was another of that automaton mass of humanity by whom clocks or watches could be set were they ever sufficiently noticed by anyone else. At 7:15 he was out of the apartment, at 7:16 on the sidewalk, at 7:20 in the subway, and he arrived at work promptly and precisely at 8. He was a tailor. Supper was always on the table when he returned, and his wife usually ate it with him; their daughter, who ate when it suited her, was often out.

Janet Dinkin was fourteen. She was very eager to look grown-up, although for a year she had looked merely bizarre in the kind of clothes she thought a budding young lady should wear who wished to appear older and wiser than she was. Make-up was confined to her eyes, lipstick having been forbidden; her eye make-up was a greenish blue, which she put on secretly before going out.

When the new style swept the world, Janet was eager to conform, even if it meant appearing less grown-up, the miniskirt being in effect a return to little girlhood. But she continued to wear eyeshadow. Having her back as a little girl would have contented her mother, were it not for the miniskirt which presented her, instead, with a daughter ripe for victimization or assault.

Mr. Dinkin did not know, and could have done little about it in any case, that there were often fierce quarrels between his wife and his daughter; the neighbors, however, knew because they could hear the shouting, even blows, screams, weeping, the sound of a door opening and the loud slam when it was shut as Janet rushed out. Whatever reasons Mrs. Dinkin gave in the past for trying to keep her daughter at home after dark, she now had a cogent one, for it was demonstrably unsafe for a young girl, or indeed anyone, to be out at night in the stricken street. Janet bided her time—she was as frightened as everyone else.

Slowly, almost imperceptibly, the canyon in which she lived settled back to its former calm, and its apparent anonymity. A month had passed since the last victim had been found. The slaughter appeared to be over.

One evening, a short time before Mr. Dinkin arrived home, neighbors heard the familiar clamor in his apartment. Mrs. Dinkin and her daughter were at it again. The door, as usual, opened with a bang and was banged shut; but this time it opened again. Janet's mother had followed her to the stair and was peering down into its gloom.

"I won't let you in," Mrs. Dinkin yelled. "Do you hear me? I won't let you in," she repeated with a sob.

Then she went back. She, too, slammed the door.

Promptly at 6:44 Mr. Dinkin entered the building. Had he entered the one to the left, or the one to the right, he would have found himself in the same rectangular maze; the vestibules were all alike, and for such large buildings incongruously small. It was as if the owners had asked the architects—builders, really—to provide the maximum amount of human density in the tight, available space, and the "architects" had complied. There were as many doors on the ground floor as on those above, although these were farther apart— two on the left, and the other two on the right. Straight ahead was the stair, of gray slate worn and washed to blackness, and rising in murky zigzags to the roof. It was steep, which conserved space, and lighted only where the lights in hallways reached the top or the bottom steps.

Mr. Dinkin turned the key in the lock and let himself in. It was 6:45. As was usual with him, he accepted the fact of his daughter's absence, a fact which belonged to a realm he little understood, although in his tired, groping way he hoped his wife did. He ate his meal in silence, not noticing that his wife ate hardly at all; later, when she emerged several times from the kitchen to gaze at the clock, he saw that its hands had moved hardly at all.

Mr. Dinkin was astonished to note that the hands had moved a great deal when he awoke. He had dozed off in his chair, and his eyes went to the clock as he started to rise in answer to the knock— Janet's knock—which he had heard on the border of waking. It was one minute to eleven. His wife was already on her way to the door, and he sank back into his chair.

But now a puzzled expression began to spread over his face. In the loud ticking of the clock he realized that the door had not been opened, that Janet was still outside, still in the hall, and that his wife was inside, standing by the locked door, waiting, listening. He joined her when the knock—Janet's knock—was repeated.

"Why don't you open it?" he asked, full of a strange agitation, but she merely gave him a look that frightened him more.

"Let her wait," she said to the door. "I warned her."

The second knock was followed by a pounding with both hands, and together they heard Janet's voice.

"Let me in," she pleaded. "Please!" There was an edge of hysteria to her words which struck terror to the tailor's heart.

"It's late!" he shouted. But when he tried to get past his wife, she barred the way.

"I'm going to teach her a lesson," she said, more to the door than to him.

Mr. Dinkin shrugged and went back to his chair, baffled and helpless before his wife's resolution and obstinacy.

"Let me in," Janet wailed on the other side of the door, and then she screamed. Mr. Dinkin jumped up and went to the door again. His wife's back was to him, but he could hear her breathing; he also heard a moan—Janet's moan.

"Let her in," he commanded his wife, and thought of striking her. His heart was pounding. He did not know what to do.

Mrs. Dinkin opened the door. Her eyes were red from weeping, and at first she thought it was an optical illusion, because the walls appeared to be splotched with red. But when she looked down there was red on the floor, too, a pool of it in which Janet lay, her long legs stretching to the stair. Her eyes were closed, and her mother stared down at the two spots of greenish blue eye-shadow on the blanched, little-girl face.

Far down the stair, in the enormous stillness of that moment, Mrs. Dinkin heard the flutter of fading footsteps, like leaves falling in a dark wood. Her neighbors were listening behind their doors, which opened together at her prolonged shriek.

Outside, some people had already gathered. They stood in a compact group, their eyes furtively probing the gloom. Few words were spoken, and these were hushed; but their mental processing of data continued. I was still smiling when I joined them.

THE WINEO MURDER

by Percy Spurlark Parker

By a coincidence, we have here, side by side, two reports on the deaths of relatively unimportant men. They may in their youths have been loved—in their deaths they are entries on file cards, the raw material for tomorrow's evasive pomposities on crime statistics in your and my town. Normally they will freeze to death on a cold winter night, or cough out their lives in a charity ward. If they are lucky, they die quickly. Like Pops.

A cloud drifted across the sun as Big Bull Benson stood at grave side, watching the polished mahogany casket lowered into the ground. Some of the winter's chill still hung in the early spring air. It got to him even though he wore a coat, or maybe it was the moment, the place.

Pops Smith had been a fixture in the neighborhood for so long, it was difficult for him to recall a time the old wineo was not around. The services were small, and Reverend James had rushed through it. There had not been many people there, some of the dudes from the street, a couple of Pops's drinking buddies.

Bull was the only one who made it to the cemetery. Reverend James had some pressing church business to take care of, and the others did not dig the scene. Standing there he began thinking of the same question that had been with him all week, since Pops's death, through the inquest, with him while he made arrangements for the funeral. Why had someone killed Pops?

It really did not make sense. Pops was a nobody, a nothing, an old black ghetto relic living from bottle to bottle, making it off his social security checks and what little side hustles he could turn. The idea that someone had taken the time to put a slug in him was difficult to believe even though it had happened. What could Pops have done to deserve that?

He turned away as the first shovel full of dirt was thrown onto the casket, heading back to the small path where his car sat behind the hearse. His ride was a two-year-old El Dorado, gold with a black vinyl top. It had a lot of style about it, and handled so smoothly that he had given up any thought of trading it in this year.

A dull Ford sedan now sat behind his caddy, and as he approached, detective Vernon Wonler got out.

"Little late for the party, but I guess Pops doesn't mind," Bull said, taking a cigar from his breast pocket.

"Lieutenant Hamilton sent me around to check on a couple of things," Vern said. He stayed on the driver's side of the car, leaning somewhat against the open door. A tall, slender dude, with a thin mustache and moderate Afro hairdo.

There were a lot of years he and Vern had shared. They ran the streets together when they were in their teens, hustling, busting heads. They were quite a pair. Then Vern did a tour in the Army, came out, and joined the force. Bull missed that scene, since there was no big rush with the draft in those days. But he had wakened to the fact that with his knowledge of cards and dice the odds were in his favor at this method of making a living, rather than some nine to five gig, or by putting a gun into somebody's gut. His decision had been the right one, he felt. It was in a poker game five years back where he had picked up the deed to his hotel. This had lifted him from the ranks of common gambler to property owner and prominent citizen.

"What's bugging the lieutenant," he asked, lighting his cigar.

"It's this whole deal with Pops," Vern said. "Where the body was found, you taking over the funeral arrangement. The lieutenant ain't so sure you're as clean in this as you say you are."

He shrugged. "Big deal."

Pops had been found at the back stairwell of his hotel. There was a trail of blood that proved that he had traveled at least a block and a half to get there. The question was, why had he come to the hotel? Was it to ask his help? Was Pops just looking for a place to hide? He did not know. He had told the police that already. As for the funeral arrangements, Pops did not have any folks, and no one else seemed to be interested enough to see that things were handled decently. He had rapped this to them before, but he went through the whole thing again.

"You know he wants to get something on you bad, Bull," Vern said.

"When I do something wrong, I'll start worrying," he answered, puffing on his cigar. It did not seem to taste as good as usual.

The sun peeped from behind a cloud, was covered again. Vern looked into the sky, then to him, "I'll tell the lieutenant I couldn't come to any more conclusions than what we already got, which ain't a hell of a lot. Be expecting to see me around though. I got a hunch he'll be wanting me to stick close to you."

He watched Vern get into the car, made a sweep with his open hand that served as a wave, and drove off.

He rolled the cigar between his fingers, started to throw it away, changed his mind and got into the caddy. So he was going to get some sweat from the cops. Well, he had taken pressure from them before. What bugged him though, was that the cops were going to start reading all kinds of things out of him arranging for Pops's funeral. What were they thinking, that he killed Pops and footed the bill for the funeral to ease his conscience? Fairy tales. Hell, no one else was breaking their neck to see to it that things were handled right. A man who survives the ghetto, lived as long as Pops had, at the very least deserved a decent funeral.

Most of the first floor of the hotel was taken up by the Bull Pen, a restaurant-lounge combo that he really enjoyed owning. It was a popular joint in the neighborhood, and it helped him keep in tune with what was happening with the people. He had finished his cigar by the time he arrived, parking the caddy at the back of the hotel. There were two entrances he could use, one leading onto the kitchen, the other onto the stairwell where Pops had been found.

He usually used the kitchen entrance. This time he did not. He stood just within the door, looking at the spot where Pops's body had lain. It was well scrubbed and disinfected. No traces of blood remained to hint at what had happened here. It was just an ordinary alcove, with a broom closet beneath the staircase, and another door which opened onto a hall giving access to the kitchen, his office, and the restaurant-lounge itself. Yet, a man had died here. Why?

He used the side door to his office, not expecting anything, going in too fast to retreat.

Some dude sat at his desk, a leg hanging over the arm of his swivel chair, a nickel-plated .38 in his hand.

"Play dead or be dead, Benson. Ya got a choice. Make it."

Split for the door, rush the dude, or play it cool was the alternatives, but he never got the chance to decide. He heard the door close behind him, the sound of another gun being cocked. Hell, he only had one way to go from the start.

He raised his hands, smiled at the dude at his desk. "It's your cards, baby."

"Ya got that right, big man," the dude said, making a motion with his gun.

From behind, Bull was frisked one handed. "He's clean," the cat said behind him.

"Good, good," the dude at the desk grinned. "I never trust a stud that carries a gun. Come and cop a squat over here." He indicated the chair by the desk with his gun. "Oh, and ugh, sit on your hands, Benson. We don't want things to get physical, do we?"

He complied. The position did not render him helpless, but it would slow him down enough to keep the advantage theirs.

The one that had frisked him stood before him now, six or seven feet away. The other one at the desk straightened his position on the swivel chair. They were both young, in their early twenties, probably. Both were dressed in dark double-breasted suits. The one at the desk was wearing a wide collar red shirt and no tie. He had a thick curly natural, bushy eyebrows, a narrow pointed nose with large nostrils, and a bottom lip that took up more room than it should. The other one was wearing a tie, but his natural was more unkempt than his partner's. He had thin eyebrows matching the slits he used for eyes, a wide nose, a mustache as shabby as his hairdo, and a large scar on his left cheek of a recent vintage with half a dozen or so smaller scars keeping it company. He also was carrying a snub nose .38.

"You going to run it down to me, or do I just sit here?" he asked, thinking how easy it would be to pick these punks out in a line-up.

"We want the package," Scars said.

Great, he thought, punks with guns and guessing games. "What damn package?"

"Playing dumb ain't the right move, big man. The package Pops had the night he went to that great wineo heaven," Curly said. "You got it, and we want it."

"How does that figure. I wasn't even the one that found the body."

"A broad that made the wrong turn coming from the washroom, the papers said. Yeah, we know about her. But you came out of this office when you heard her screaming and took charge of things until the cops arrived," Scars said.

"We checked her out," Curly said. "More tactful than we're doing now. But then, there's no need to front with us. Naw, you've got it, Benson, and ya gave Pops a nice send off as kind of a thank you. But it's not going to do you any good. We've been through too much for it, and we want it."

"You telling me you're the ones that killed Pops?" he asked.

Curly stood stepping behind him, letting the muzzle of the gun rest against the back of his head. "I'm telling you that you can get offed if we don't get our package. Think about it. We'll be back."

He knew what was coming, tried to brace himself for it. But how can you really brace against a sapping?

Something cold was being rubbed across his forehead. When he opened his eyes he saw Sam Devlin, one of his bartenders, bending over him administering the treatment.

"Okay, okay," he said, brushing the cold towel away. "I give up, you win."

"Wha' happen'?" Sam asked, as he helped him to his feet. He was a frail little guy nearing his sixties. The dark skin was drawn so tight about his small skull his eyes seemed to bulge.

"Just getting my exercises in for today, Sam, that's all."

He took the towel from Sam, mopped at the side of his head where he had been struck. The spot was tender as hell, and waves of pain vibrated throughout his head. He checked the towel for traces of blood but did not find any. The sapping had not broken the skin.

He started toward his desk, but his legs were not working right, and he might have fallen if Sam had not grabbed his arm, steadying him.

"How long have I been out?" he asked, after Sam helped him to the swivel chair.

"Few minutes is all," Sam said. "I saw a couple of young cats comin' from back here I hadn't seen come in. I comes back here and there you is, laid out like somebody's bear rug. Thought you had gone to join Pops at first."

"Naw, not yet, Sam. I'm putting that trip off as long as I can." From his desk drawer he got a bottle of aspirins, two glasses, and a fifth of hundred proof Grand-Dad. He filled both glasses pushing one toward Sam, then downing three aspirins with a hefty portion of the bourbon.

Sam took a swallow of his drink, cleared his throat. "Damn good alcohol," he said, looking at his glass. "You feelin' better?"

"Yeah," he nodded. The aspirins had not begun to work that fast, but the Grand-Dad was, and the pain in his head began to subside.

"I didn't get a chance ta tell'ya before, Bull. Ya know, 'bout me not makin' it ta Pops's funeral. Just that I, well, hell, man. I'm pretty old maself. And I keeps thinkin' maybe next time it'll be me in that damn box."

"Forget it, Sam. A lot more people didn't show for less reasons."

Sam shrugged. "Yeah, but it seems like I let Pops down. You know how I is 'bout drinkin' behind that bar. Well, I keeps a bottle in the broom closet out back. Pops knew it were there. Lots of times I've gone back there and found my bottle empty. I'd cuss the old fool plenty about it, but I never changed my hidin' place. Know what I mean? Hell, I ain't been back there since Pops died."

"I know what you mean, Sam," he said, raising his glass. "Let's make this one to Pops."

They finished their drinks, talked a little longer about the studs that had sapped him, without him giving Sam any more information than he had before.

With the assurance that he was feeling okay, Sam went back to the bar, and he reached for the phone. He wondered if those two had actually killed Pops. If they had, this had been a bold play they made exposing themselves to him. Either they were sure that he would not be able to do anything about them, or the risk was worth taking. That package they were looking for must be pretty valuable. He could call Vern and let the cops take care of the two punks if they were not hiding out. But he knew a surer method of locating them. He made three phone calls, one to Little Willie, Ears Jones, and Mama Street. He gave them the description of the two, told them to do it quiet, but that there was a hundred bucks for whoever came across with their names and whereabouts. It was an effective system that had worked well for him in the past. All he had to do now was wait.

He had lunch in his office, and was just finishing when the front door opened. Red Dobbs stood there with his hand buried beneath his coat. A young dude of tannish complexion and a mop of reddish-brown hair. He had come over from St. Louis three or four years back, working his way up the rungs of the Harry Harris mob.

Harris came in behind him, walking up to the desk, and Red closed the door positioning himself against it.

"We got some talking to do, Benson," Harris said. He wore a black car coat, opened, showing off a well tailored suit that must have set him back some heavy bread. He was a wide built man, with gray temples, and a well kept gray speckled mustache.

"What'd you want, Harry, a rematch?" he asked, referring to a poker game a month ago. Harris had dropped a couple of grand at that table and he had gotten most of it.

"Nothing that small time, Benson. I'm talking about Pops and the package he was carrying the night he was killed."

The package again, he thought. Now a heavyweight like Harris is on the scene. He had felt confident in being able to handle the other two when he caught up with them, but Harris was something else. He had been in the game a long time, and he did not stay there without running over a few people. Harris had only one method of taking care of people who got in his way.

"You want to clear that up for me, Harry. As far as I know, all Pops had on him when he was killed was thirty cents and a dirty handkerchief."

"That's not exactly true," Harris said. The Grand-Dad was still sitting on the desk. He picked it up along with the glass Sam had used.

"There's a clean glass in the drawer," Bull said, thinking of the gun that was also kept there.

Harris smiled at him. "This'll do," he said, pouring a drink. "Let's start it this way. I've put out twenty-five grand for a shipment of heroin from New York."

"Heroin," Bull repeated. "Stepping out of your field, aren't you, Harry. I thought you stuck to bookmaking."

Harris shrugged. "So I'm branching out. Twenty-five grand in pure heroin can bring back five times that much when it's cut right. Red, here, was my go between man when the stuff was brought in. He dropped off the bread, but the word was out that the cops were nosing around. He passed the package to Pops to make it to the next drop. Apparently someone else saw the switch. Pops never made it."

Bull leaned back in his chair, a lot of questions forming in his mind. "You got all this info from Red, ugh?"

Harris smiled again. "I know what ya thinking, Benson. Red's been with me too long to try anything. Besides the New York boys saw him pass the package to Pops. Red's not dumb enough to cross me."

Red was still by the door, maintaining his menacing poise, but not reacting to what was said.

"Why pick me?" he asked. "If it went down the way you said, what makes you think whoever killed Pops didn't get the stuff?"

"I'm covering the angles. No one can set up shop in this town without me getting wind of it. But I'm leaning more to the idea that you've got it, Bull. Pops came here for some reason I'm betting it was to give you the package. There'll be a lot of time and effort saved if you hand it over now, and we can go on being friends."

"You're dreaming, Harry."

"Maybe so, but I doubt it. Remember, ya can't start pushing the stuff without me knowing it. You had a chance to get out of this easy. Pity you didn't take it." He finished the Grand-Dad, sat the empty glass back on the desk. "Thanks for the drink," he said, and he and Red made their exit.

He got a cigar, lit it. A hundred and twenty-five thousand dollars worth of heroin on the retail market. Well, Pops had not been killed over peanuts. That kind of bread can make people do a lot of strange things, and murder was the least of them. He slowly blew the smoke toward the ceiling, watching it expand and dispense as it rose higher.

He thought about his own position, the three way squeeze being put upon him. There were the cops, the two punks earlier, and now Harris, all looking for answers. He would have to make the next move, and fast, or he probably would not get the chance. Curly and Scars most certainly were the ones who killed Pops, but they had not gotten the package. Harris did not have it either. If the cops had found it with Pops, then everyone would have known about it. Pops had come here for a reason. Why? Then he thought of something Sam had said. It was possible. It just could be.

He left his office, going to the stairwell where Pops was found, to the broom closet where Sam kept his bottle. It was there, wrapped in a brown paper bag, under some old rags next to a half-empty bottle of scotch. He did not have to taste the white powder in the package to assure himself this was it. There were enough blood stains on the bag to prove that it was the one Pops had been carrying.

Why the police had not found it when they checked out this area, he did not know. Maybe there was no reason that they should have searched the closet when it was evident that Pops had traveled here under his own momentum. Why did he hide it? Was he planning to get himself to a hospital, get well, then come back and peddle it himself? Or had he known he could not make it any farther, and stashed it there so if his killers were following him they would not get it. These were questions he could not answer. He would like to think that Pops was coming to him for help. Although he could not help him now he could see that his killers paid.

He put the package back in the closet. It had served as a good hiding place thus far.

He heard his phone from the hall, rushing into the office, catching it on its third ring.

"Bull, baby." It was Mama Street, a fat little gal who ran a bar on the West Side.

"Yeah, Mama, you got anything?"

"Don't I always, baby, just tell me when."

He laughed. "Later, Mama. This is for real."

"Okay, okay. I located those cats for ya. One of my girls was with them last night. They got a room at the Star Hotel on 18th. Cat with the curly hair name's Will Logan. His buddy's Bob Hamlers." She paused. "The only other thing my girl added was that they were from St. Louis, been here about a week, but wouldn't say what they were doing. Is that enough?"

"Better than what I expected, Mama. You'll be hearing from me."

He hung up, flipped cigar ashes into the tray on his desk. It was too much of a coincidence for it to be a coincidence. He got his phone book, found Harry Harris's number and dialed it. He went through three people before Harris came to the phone.

"I expected to hear from you, Benson, but not this quick, I just got back myself. What do ya want?"

"To do you a favor, Harry. I know where the punks are that blew Pops away."

"Good to see ya getting some smarts about yourself. Where are they?"

"Star Hotel on 18th, names Will Logan and Bob Hamlers."

"They got the stuff with them?"

"I guess so, they're the ones that got Pops."

"Okay, Benson, let's say you're not as high on my list as you were before."

"Well here's a little something else for you. Both Logan and Hamlers are St. Louis imports. Isn't that where Red came from."

There was silence for a moment at the other end of the phone. Then, "Yeah he does, Benson, thanks."

He reared back in the swivel chair. One more phone call and the whole thing would be wrapped up. He waited until he had finished his cigar first, smoking it down to an inch long nub. Then he dialed ———

"Hello, Vern."

"Bull, I was on my way over to see you. Hamilton wasn't too pleased with our talk this morning."

"Well, maybe this'll make him happy," he said, then told Vern what had been happening to him today. "I've got the stuff here waiting for you, Vern. But you'd better get over to the Star Hotel before they kill each other off."

"Will do, Bull. See ya later."

He had felt somewhat smug about his plan. Now that it was all in the works he was not sure if he had handled it right. Maybe it would have been best if the cops found the heroin with them. It was probably the only concrete way Harris could be tied into the deal. Well, he was really after the studs who killed Pops. If Harris took the fall along with the rest he could consider it a bonus.

He busied himself about the office for nearly an hour, waiting for Vern or word from him. He tried doing some book work, but it did not have his attention. He was wondering what was happening at the Star Hotel.

Red Dobbs came into his office so fast it was as though he had not opened and closed the door. He did not have his hand under his coat this time, but held a .45 cocked and aimed.

"Surprised, Benson? Did ya think Harry or the cops would've handled me by now?"

"Something like that," he admitted, looking at the .45 and the steadiness in which it was held.

"I was on the extension when you made that call to Harry. You blew my game, Benson, I didn't have any choice but to kill him."

"So you killed Harris," he said, wondering if he should make a play for the gun in the desk, try stalling until Vern showed, or what.

Red nodded, coming closer to the desk, keeping the gun pointed at his head. "I was going to pick my boys up, then swing back ta see you. But the cops beat me to them. You arranged that, I'm sure."

He shrugged. "I tried," he said. "But I should have guessed anyone with guts enough to cross Harris would take special handling. What were you going to do, peddle the stuff back in St. Louis?"

Red, whose complexion seemed to be darker than usual, smiled for the first time since entering the office. "You're on time there, Benson. It would have been sweet too. I had it all figured. I spread the word about the cops prowling around. Didn't tell Pops what was in the package, thinking he'd be easy to handle. Hell, the old dude slapped Bob with a wine bottle. That's how he got his face fouled up. Bob got off one shot, but the old man was down the alley and gone before they could catch him.

"So that brings it back to you, Benson. You've been through the routine before. Give me the package."

"Why should I?" he asked, thinking of no reason to deny having the package now.

"How about your life? They're going to be after me for Pops and Harry. Killing you ain't going to gain me anything. We'll make a trade, your life for the package."

He wondered what the hell was keeping Vern. "Okay, Red," he said, nodding. "I got it out back."

"Let's go get it, then," Red said, motioning with his gun. He stood, started for the side door. "Tell me, if I'd refused to give it to you, would you have used that gun in here? That big monster would've been heard through the whole building."

"I would have emptied the damn clip in ya," Red said, jamming the .45 into his back.

It was a mistake. Maybe Red realized it, but he realized it too late. Bull swung around, knocking the gun arm aside as the .45 discharged into the wall. He went for the gun arm, grabbing, twisting, forcing Red to drop the automatic. Then he swung backhandedly, smashing into the side of Red's face reeling him backward.

Red stood in the middle of the office, fists clenched, eyes watering, blood coming from the corner of his mouth. Without his gun he was no match for him, they both knew that. Bull started forward. Red turned, running for the front door. Three quick strides and Bull had caught him, swung him around and pinned him to the door.

He got his left around Red's neck, lifting him off the floor. Red gagged, fought, and pulled at his arm but it did no good. He swung his right fist smashing it into Red's stomach, Red went limp, and he swung again and again and again.

He stopped when he realized Red was too far gone to feel it any more.

Sam and some of the other help rushed into the office in response to the gun shot. They looked from the lump on the floor that was Red, back to him as he lit another cigar.

"Back to work, fellas," Sam said with a smile. "Boss just doin' his exercises again."

THE HOT TAMALES MURDER CASE

by J. F. Peirce

As was asked when this story was first published, "Was the crime committed by Juan Diego, or was it committed against him?" What *is* your reaction?

There was a lull in the trial. The prosecuting and defense attorneys had approached the bench and were discussing a point of law with the judge, speaking in low tones that reached me as a murmur. From my vantage point in the jury box I took the opportunity to study the defendant.

His name was Juan Diego. He was a Chicano, a Mexican-American, and from his appearance more Indian than Spanish. He sat, as he had throughout the trial, with his hands folded, with a quiet dignity that verged on the Stoic. He was a small, tightly knit man and wore an old-fashioned walrus mustache that accented the downcast expression of his mahogany face and his sad brown eyes.

He was dressed in an expensive banker's-gray suit, a reminder of the days when he was reputed to have been a multimillionaire. It was hard to believe that this soft-spoken, mild-mannered little man had once been a business tycoon. It was even harder to believe that he was now a murderer, that he had killed a man apparently without provocation, a man he had known less than fifteen minutes.

I remembered the first day of the trial, as he stood with his lawyer facing the judge, while the charge was read against him.

"How does the defendant plead?" the judge asked. "Guilty or not guilty?"

Juan Diego's lawyer answered for him. "Not guilty, your Honor, by reason of temporary insanity."

There was no sign of insanity in Juan Diego's eyes or face now. Certainly he was aware of everything that was going on. He had been an excellent, an intelligent witness in his own behalf, speaking simply, directly, answering all questions in a straightforward manner.

I tried to weave a pattern from the threads of testimony that had been given by the various witnesses.

The facts of the case were unchallenged. Juan Diego had killed a man. No one denied that, least of all Juan Diego. "I regret it very much," he said, "as Christ is my witness. May God forgive me. I cannot forgive myself."

The man, a stranger, had entered Juan Diego's small, cluttered, home-owned grocery store located beneath his family living quarters in the Mexican section of the town. The man had purchased a pack of cigarettes, eaten a homemade hot tamale, and exchanged a few words with Juan Diego, commenting on the tamale's excellent quality; whereupon Juan Diego had pulled a revolver from under the counter, where he kept it as "insurance against a possible holdup," and shot the man dead.

"He kept pulling the trigger even after the gun was emptied," a customer who had witnessed the murder testified. "It kept going click, click, click until I took it away from him."

Though I pride myself on my imagination, I could not "see" this humble little man standing over a bloody corpse, mechanically pulling the trigger of the pearl-handled revolver that had been introduced into evidence as "Exhibit A."

According to the testimony read into the record, the events of that fateful fifteen minutes had had their beginning some two years earlier. They had begun in a strangely similar fashion. A newspaper reporter named Eric Scott, unknown to Juan Diego, had stopped at this same little grocery. Scott had been covering a fire in the neighborhood, had phoned in his story, then stopped off at Juan Diego's, on impulse, to pick up a six-pack of beer to take home.

Juan Diego was eating his evening meal at the checkout counter when the reporter came in and sniffed the air in appreciation of the tantalizing odor of hot tamales that pervaded the store.

Instinctively Juan Diego held out a plate with half a dozen steaming tamales on it for Scott to take one. The reporter, once he finished eating, licked his fingers to capture the last lingering taste of the tamale.

"Homemade," he said.

Though it was a statement, not a question, Juan Diego nodded. "I make them from a recipe that has come down in my family from my great-great-grandmother. The secret is in adding a kiss of pork to sweeten the beef and grinding the meal just so, to give them the right texture."

"You have them for sale?" the reporter asked.

Again Juan Diego nodded, then led the way to a refrigerator at the back, where big fat tamales, wrapped in real corn shucks, were stacked in neat rows.

"I bought two dozen," Scott testified, "and in the excitement of finding real homemade tamales I forgot my original reason for stopping. I was halfway home before I remembered the beer. I shrugged and said aloud, 'What the hell, I can buy beer anywhere, anytime, but homemade tamales—' "

Two days later a feature story under Scott's byline appeared in the paper, a nostalgic piece about his childhood, the trips he had made downtown to buy homemade tamales from the old Mexican who sold them from a 10-gallon lard can on the bank corner. It was a story about a bygone America, and he had put his heart, his soul, and his taste buds into it. He ended it with "I bring you tidings of great joy. This day, in a little grocery store in the Mexican section of our fair city, hot tamales—real honest-to-goodness homemade hot tamales swaddled in corn shucks—are being made and sold. Enjoy! Enjoy!"

Legend has it that if you build a better mousetrap, the world will beat a path to your door. This may or may not be true. It *is* true if you make a better tamale. Juan Diego was living proof of that. The world beat a path to *his* door.

The very night that Scott's story appeared in the paper a dozen people roused Juan Diego out of his living quarters above the store and pleaded with him to open up and sell them tamales. Each time, though with increasing reluctance, Juan Diego complied.

All the next day Anglos appeared at the grocery, trying to recapture a taste of their past, seeking the hot tamales that they remembered from their youth, hot tamales steaming with flavor—not the paper-wrapped canned variety that they bought infrequently at their neighborhood supermarkets.

Those who were fortunate enough to get some found them to be even better than the tamales of their memories. But most who came were turned away in disappointment, as Juan Diego's small supply was quickly depleted. But he took their orders and promised to fill them as soon as possible: "*Sí*. Perhaps *mañana*. Who can say?"

At first Juan Diego was happy over the sudden increase in his business. It came at a good time. Family illnesses had caused his bills to mount up. He needed the money. And he and his wife, Consuelo, worked diligently making the tamales with loving care to fill the orders. The finest ingredients were used, the proportions measured precisely, the meal ground to the mystical moment of perfection, the tamales rolled, wrapped in corn shucks, and tied just so before being put in the cooker to steam. After all, it was only a temporary thing surely, he thought. He and Consuelo should make the most of this opportunity while they could. The lost sleep could be made up later—when business was slow or when there was no business.

But business did not slow. It increased. Word of mouth proved once again to be the best form of advertising. People came from all over the city to the store, as to a shrine, and Juan Diego pressed first his daughter María, next his son José, and then his married daughters and their families into making tamales to supply the ever-increasing demand.

Fortunately, he had a large supply of shucks on hand, and it was the right time of the year to get more. He sent neighborhood boys out to the farms for miles around to gather corn shucks. And when these proved not to be enough, he wrote to his brothers in the Midwest to ship him more.

Soon people from neighboring towns found their way to Juan Diego's grocery. They could be seen cruising slowly along the street searching for the tiny sign that proclaimed: Juan Diego—Grocery & Meat Market.

The other merchants began to complain. They were jealous of Juan Diego, and their customers were having a difficult time finding places to park.

Juan Diego's regular customers also complained. They resented having to wait for service and being shoved aside by pushy Anglos.

Before long the tail began to wag the dog. The tamales became Juan Diego's main source of income, and after a time, reluctantly, he closed his grocery business and turned the store into a tamale factory.

Then, at the suggestion of one of his customers, a banker named Hunter, he began marketing his tamales through other stores throughout the city. " 'After all,' I told him," Hunter testified, " 'the majority of your customers are Anglos who live in other parts of the city. It would be a convenience for them. If they could buy tamales more easily, they'd buy them more often.' "

Shortly thereafter Hunter made a gift of two dozen of Juan Diego's tamales to the then President of the United States. And two weeks later an order for fifty dozen came from the White House, where they were served at a state dinner.

As a result Juan Diego's tamales were written up in all of the media, but the sight of the President on a TV news report, eating one of Juan Diego's tamales with obvious gusto, was the ultimate advertisement.

The next day a national grocery chain ordered five thousand dozen tamales.

"Juan Diego was overwhelmed," Hunter went on in his testimony.

"He wanted to refuse the order, but I persuaded him to take it and secured a warehouse for him on which our bank happened to have a lien. I also suggested that he hire some of the city's hard-core unemployed to help make the tamales, which he did, putting the members of his family to supervising them.

"Of course there was a slight loss of quality in the mass-produced tamales. They weren't made so precisely or with the same loving care as when Juan Diego and Consuelo themselves made them. But to people who had never eaten the originals they seemed like heaven —at least, no one complained."

The five thousand dozen tamales were sold out the same day they were put in the chain stores' refrigerated display cases. The next order was for ten thousand dozen, and then the chain contracted for one-hundred-thousand-dozen lots.

"I was able to find another warehouse for him," Hunter continued, "and the State Employment Agency produced hundreds more employables."

At the behest of the City Council, the mayor proclaimed "Juan Diego Appreciation Day" for his "having hired so many of the city's unemployed, for his having brought honor to the city, and for his et cetera, et cetera, et cetera." But the proclamation made no mention of Juan Diego's ballooning taxes.

Juan Diego and his family began to be recognized in other ways. They were invited out more and more often by members of both the Anglo and Chicano communities: by realtors, car salesmen, furniture store owners; by anyone and everyone who had something to sell. And María began to date an Anglo boy whom she had mooned over in school for years but who never before had appeared to know she existed.

"The business continued to grow dramatically," Hunter replied in response to a question. "Then it peaked, suffered a slight decline, but quickly leveled off, stabilizing on a high plateau of production."

Though at first distrustful of his success—not believing it could happen to someone like him, let alone to him—Juan Diego slowly began to believe in his prosperity and to enjoy it. At the urging of his family and his many new friends he began to spend money—he bought a new home "in a better section of the city," he bought cars, jewelry, clothes, anything and everything his family wanted. All his new friends turned out to be very helpful, aiding him in getting "some really good buys." After all, "the best only *seems* to cost more —it has a longer life, needs less repairs, stays in style longer."

"María had a coming-out party," Scott recalled. "It was attended by most of the prominent business and social leaders of the community. As a climax to the party Juan Diego announced María's engagement. The wedding was set for the following summer. And from all reports it was to be *the* social event of the season."

Everything was turning up roses. Nothing Juan Diego tried could go wrong.

Then everything did.

"Without Juan Diego knowing it," Scott testified, "union organizers had infiltrated the tamale factories, organizing the workers, persuading them that Juan Diego was a vampire getting fat on their blood, that he owed them more, that they owed him less. Blinded by greed, envy, jealousy, the workers believed it, forgot that they had been jobless when Diego had hired them, that they had been hungry when he had fed them, that he had enabled them to pay the rent, put a down payment on a car or TV set. They forgot that they had been on welfare and he had given them dignity and pride."

When the union representatives came to Juan Diego with their demands Juan Diego exploded. "Not on the surface," he testified, "but inside. Outwardly I remained calm, polite. The demands were not impossible. If the workers had come to me directly, if one of them had said, 'Juan, you have so much, we have so little,' I might have agreed to their *requests* without argument. But not to their *demands* made through a third party. My own pride, my own dignity were hurt. So I refused."

The workers went on strike.

"Even then," Juan Diego admitted, "it might not have been too late for a meeting of the minds, but José reminded me that there was a sizable inventory of tamales in the huge walk-in freezers. It would be good to let the workers miss a paycheck or two. Let them remember what I had done for them. Besides, Mr. Hunter happened to know where I could get some tamale machines quickly.

" 'You don't even have to buy them,' he told me. 'You can rent them for as long as you like. And if you do decide to buy them the rent will apply to the purchase price.'

" 'No,' I said. 'I'll rent them, but only for the duration of of the strike,' and Mr. Hunter agreed."

The machines were duly installed. The strike floundered, almost collapsed. The machines were doing the workmen's job. The tamales were not so fat as before, the quality not quite so good, but the strike resulted in only a small decline in production and sales.

Juan Diego waited for his friends among the workers to come to talk to him. They in turn waited for him to approach them.

"Some of the strikers grew angry and impatient," Scott testified. "A fire broke out at one of the factories, three of Juan Diego's refrigerated trucks were run off the road and overturned, a bomb explosion shattered the windows and one wall of his new home, José was waylaid and beaten. There were bitter words, recriminations, open threats."

Juan Diego's heart hardened, his resistance stiffened.

"The supply of corn shucks began to dwindle," Hunter testified, "and I persuaded Juan to substitute paper. 'After all,' I told him, 'shucks don't work as well in the machines—they require too much preparation; and they're much too expensive. Besides, it's the meat and meal, not the shucks, that give the flavor.'"

"I knew that was not completely true," Juan Diego conceded. "The steam penetrates the shucks more easily than it does paper. Still the question was—how do you say?—academic. No shucks were available.

"The paper wrapping caused another slight loss of quality, another small loss in sales; but it speeded up production, increased inventories."

The sabotage continued.

"I had to hire guards to protect my factories, my drivers, my family. Once there was an exchange of gunfire. One of the strikers was killed, one of the guards wounded.

"Mr. Hunter suggested setting up factories in other parts of the country, closer to the chief markets—shutting down locally until things cooled off.

"'If you think it best,' I said.

"'The thing to do is to incorporate,' Mr. Hunter said, 'and build new plants from scratch, factories specially designed to produce nothing but tamales.'

"I shook my head. 'Where could I get so much money?' I asked.

"'Leave it to me,' he answered. 'We'll get it from the government. Show the government boys that you can give jobs to thousands of hard-core unemployed, and they'll gladly lend you the money, and at a low rate of interest.'"

Sites were selected, factories were designed, machinery was purchased, loans were floated. Overnight Juan Diego became a multimillion-dollar corporation, a financial power.

"When I suggested putting the tamales in cans, the better to store and protect them, since his inventories were getting out of hand,"

Hunter went on, "Juan hardly protested. Of course he had been renting the freezer space for storage, and the cost had been prohibitive. That may have helped to reconcile him to the decision."

The truth was that the heart had gone out of Juan Diego. Perhaps as a result of "the hatred I saw in the eyes of pickets who had been, not just my workers, but my friends; they stood silently as I drove through the picket lines in my big limousine, and I could feel their hatred like a cold lump in my stomach."

Scott's testimony was often interpretative. "Because of the strike," he explained, "María's wedding was quietly postponed—perhaps for fear of what some of the more fanatical strikers might do at the sight of so much pomp and luxury. By then most of them were back on relief—their cars and washing machines and TV sets repossessed for failure to make payments.

"At about the same time the bottom dropped out of everything. When the canned tamales hit the market they sold almost as well as they had in frozen form and in bulk. But people bought them only once, discovering that somewhere along the line the product had changed. The ingredients had lost some of their quality, some of their unique flavor. Even the texture was no longer the same. Now they were not any better than the other canned brands on the market. And when the housewives of America went back to the supermarkets to buy tamales, they also went back to their old brands."

Scott hesitated, then looked away from Juan Diego before he continued: "I don't know when Juan Diego learned that his son had sold him out along with the rest. At first Juan had mixed the ingredients for the hot tamales in secret. Then, when the business expanded, he had José help him. Finally, in the press of setting up the new factories, he turned the complete responsibility for mixing the ingredients over to his son.

"José didn't see the need to buy expensive cuts of meat. He didn't see the need to add pork or grind the meal as fine. So he substituted inferior meat and meal, then had the suppliers bill his father as before, with José pocketing the kickbacks."

Much of Hunter's testimony had to be pried from him by persistent questioning. Only when the answers reflected credit to him did he speak freely. "The factories continued under construction. The machines that Juan Diego had ordered piled up in warehouses. The inventories grew and grew until there was no more space to store them. Then everything ground to a halt. Reluctantly I advised bankruptcy."

Scott talked as if he were writing a news story. "When it was over and done," he reported, "Juan Diego lay buried under his paper empire. All that he possessed in his own name was his original little grocery store, which out of sentiment he had never sold and which still remained in the records as his home, instead of the half-million-dollar estate in the exclusive country-club district to which he had moved his family at the height of his success."

Juan Diego's own testimony was painfully honest. "Without ever quite knowing how or why it had happened," he said, "I found myself back in the grocery business—at the same old stand, as they say, but not as before. Too many things had changed. My friends, both old and new, had turned against me. I was a laughing-stock throughout the city. My son had disappeared with the funds he had skimmed from the dregs of my failure. But the wound that ached most of all was the one caused by the death of my daughter.

"The collapse of my business brought the collapse of her hopes for marriage. Her young man broke their engagement and María's heart. And almost immediately he married another girl.

"The day her young man married I found her 'sleeping' and could not wake her.

"After that I went through the motions of running the grocery store. And in time the pain lost a little of its bitter sting. People began to forget. Old customers returned, drifting back gradually in ones and twos. After all, my grocery *was* convenient and my prices *were* right.

"Then one day Consuelo suggested that we make some tamales. Not to sell, you understand, but just for ourselves. I shrugged and said, 'Sí. Why not?'

"Late in the afternoon, several days later, a young man entered the grocery and bought a pack of cigarettes. I had never seen him before.

"I was eating my supper at the checkout counter as usual at that time of day and the young man sniffed the air appreciatively.

" 'Hot tamales!' he said. 'Homemade hot tamales!'

"Instinctively I held out the plate with the tamales on it and he took one, wolfed it down, and licked his fingers. Then the thought evidently hit him.

" 'You know what?' he said. 'A fellow could make a mint of money with tamales like these. I bet they'd be almost as good if *we* mass-produced them. The main thing is to get them before the public— let them know what we've got to sell.

" 'I've got a friend, a newspaperman. I'll get him to write a story saying, "There's this little Chicano down in Mexican Town who makes the best damned tamales ev—"'

"Something went *click* in my mind. I knew what I was doing—but couldn't stop myself. It was as if I was standing off watching myself from one side, as if my hand acted independent of my brain. I saw it reach out, take the revolver from under the counter, and begin shooting.

"I'd be pulling the trigger still if someone hadn't taken the gun from me."

As he spoke, I felt *my* finger tighten, and I knew I could cast my ballot only one way.

DEATH OF A NOBODY

by Bill Pronzini

As we've seen, all men are not always equal in the face of death. Far from it. There is a tendency to dismiss as unimportant the deaths of those who either have "no fixed address" or who obviously neither share our mores nor understand our ways. Thus a murder can become a suicide—or an accident. It simplifies things. . . .

His name was Nello. Whether this was his given name, or his surname, or simply a sobriquet he had picked up sometime during the span of his fifty-odd years—I never found out. I doubt if even Nello himself knew any longer.

He was what sociologists call "an addictive drinker who has lost all semblance of faith in God, humanity, or himself."

And what the average citizen dismisses unconcernedly as "a Skid Row wino."

He came into my office just before ten o'clock on one of San Francisco's bitter cold autumn mornings. He had been a lawyer once —in a small town in Northern California—and there were still signs of intelligence, of manners and education in his gaunt face. I had first encountered him more than twelve years ago, when a police lieutenant named Eberhardt and I had been rookie patrolmen working the South of Market area. I didn't know—and had never asked— what private hell had led him from small town respectability to the oblivion of Skid Row.

He stood just inside the door, his small hands nervously rolling and unrolling the brim of a shapeless brown fedora. His thin, almost emaciated body was encased in a pair of once-brown slacks and a tweed jacket which had worn through at both elbows, and his faded blue eyes had that tangible filminess about them that comes from too many nights with too many bottles of cheap sweet wine. But he was sober on this morning—cold and painfully sober.

I said, "It's been a long time, Nello."

"A long time," he agreed vaguely.

"Some coffee?"

"No. No, thanks."

I finished pouring myself a cup from the pot I keep on an old two-burner on top of one of my filing cabinets. I took it to my desk and set it down on the blotter there. "What can I do for you?"

He cleared his throat, his lips moving as if he were tasting something by memory. But then he seemed to change his mind. He took a step toward the door. "Maybe I shouldn't have come," he said to the floor. "Maybe I'd better go."

"Wait, now. What is it, Nello?"

"Chaucer," he said. "It's Chaucer."

I frowned a little. Chaucer was another habitue of the Row, like Nello an educated man who had lost part of himself sometime, somewhere, somehow; he had once taught English Literature at a high school in Kansas or Nebraska, and that was where his nickname had come from. He and Nello had been companions on the Row for a long time.

I said, "What about him?"

"He's dead," Nello said tonelessly. "I heard it on the grapevine just a little while ago. The police found him in an alley on Hubbell Street, near the railroad yards, early this morning. He was beaten to death."

"Do they know who did it?"

Nello shook his head. "But I think I might know the reason for it; why he was killed."

"Have you gone to the police?"

"No."

I didn't need to ask why not; non-involvement with the law was a code by which the Row people lived—even when one of their own died violently. But I said, "If you have some information that might help find Chaucer's killer, you'd better take it to them, Nello."

His lips curved into a sad, fleeting smile. "What good would it do?" he asked. "They don't care about a man like Chaucer—a wino, a bum, a nobody. Why should they bother when one of us dies?"

"Do you really believe that?"

"Yes, I believe it."

"Well, you're wrong," I said. "When someone is murdered—no matter who he is—the police do everything in their power to find the party or parties responsible. I know that for a fact, Nello; I was a cop once, remember?"

"I remember."

"Then why did you come to me?" I asked quietly. "In a way, I'm still a cop. If you don't believe the police will care, what made you think I would?"

"I don't know," he said. "You were always fair and decent to me, you and your friend. I thought . . . Look, maybe I just better go."

"It's up to you."

He hesitated. There was a struggle going on inside him between an almost forgotten sense of duty and the unwritten decree of the Row. Finally, he moved forward in a ponderous way and sat in the modernistic office chair across from me. He put the fedora on his knee and looked at the veined backs of his hands.

I said, "Do you want to tell me about it now?"

"I can't pay you anything, you know."

"Never mind that," I said. "About the only thing I can do is take whatever you give me to the police, and see that it gets into the proper hands. Communication with me isn't privileged; that's the law."

"I know the law," Nello said. "Or I knew it once."

"Okay, then."

He took a long breath, coughed, and wiped at his mouth with the palm of one hand. When he began talking, his voice was low, almost monotonous. "About three weeks ago, Chaucer and I were sharing a bottle of muskie in a doorway on Sixth, just off Howard. It was after midnight, and the streets were empty. Old Jenny—she was one of us, a nice old lady—was standing on the corner across the street, waiting for the light to change. When it did, she started across the intersection. There were headlights approaching along Sixth, coming very fast, but I thought the car would stop at the red light. Only it didn't. It came straight on through. There was no time for Chaucer or me to call out a warning. The car hit Old Jenny, slowed for a moment, and then kept on going. It disappeared around the corner, left on Mission. Chaucer and I ran over to where Old Jenny was lying in the street, but there was nothing we could do for her; she was dead. We left, then, before the police came."

Again, the code of non-involvement. Nello passed a hand over his face, as if the length of his explanation had left him momentarily drained. I waited silently, and after a moment he went on, "Last weekend, Chaucer was panhandling in Union Square. He saw the hit-and-run car parked on the street near there. It had been repaired, he said, and had a fresh coat of paint."

"How did he know it was the same car?" I put in.

"He had gotten the license number that night on Sixth."

"Did he tell you what it was?"

"No," Nello said. "I think he found out the name of the car's owner on Union Square, from the registration, but he didn't tell me who it was. I saw him yesterday afternoon, around three, and he was in high spirits. He said he had to take care of some business, and that if it panned out he was going to be in the chips for the first time in a long while."

I began to get it, then. "You think he went out to see the owner of his car and tried to shake him down, is that it? And got himself killed for the effort."

"Yes," Nello said.

"Is there anything else you can tell me? Anything that might lead to the owner?"

He moved his head from side to side.

"Chaucer didn't mention the make and model?"

"No."

"Or where the owner lived?"

"No, nothing at all."

I got a cigarette lighted and looked at the end of it and thought over in my mind what he had told me. After a time I said, "All right, Nello. I'll see what I can do. As soon as anything turns up, I'll let you know."

He nodded listlessly and got to his feet. I had the feeling, watching him shuffle toward the door, that he didn't really believe anything would turn up at all.

Eberhardt had some people in his office when I got down to the Hall of Justice a half hour later, and I had to wait in the Detective Squad Room until he finished his business with them. I smoked a couple of cigarettes and discussed the political situation with an Inspector named Branislaus whom I knew slightly, and after half an hour three men in business suits came out of Eberhardt's cubicle. They marched out of the Squad Room in single file cadence, like Army recruits on a parade field.

I sat there for another five minutes, and then the intercom on Branislaus's desk sounded and Eberhardt's voice said it was all right for me to come in. He was cleaning out the bowl of his pipe with a penknife when I entered, and not being particularly careful about it; there were bits of dottle scattered across the paper-littered surface of his desk. He said without looking up, "So what the hell do *you* want?"

"How about a kind word?"

"Did you see those three men who just left?"

"I saw them, sure."

"They're with the State Attorney General's Office," Eberhardt said, "and they've been giving me a hard time for a week on a certain matter. As a result, I haven't seen my wife in two days and I haven't eaten since eleven o'clock yesterday morning. On top of all that, I think I've got an abscessed tooth. So whatever it is you've come for, the answer is no. Call me Sunday afternoon, and if I've made it home by then we'll have a beer together."

I said, "Okay, Eb. But it has to do with the murder last night of a Skid Row type named Chaucer."

He frowned. "What do you know about that?"

"I can tell it to whichever homicide team is handling it, if you want."

"You can tell it to me," Eberhardt said. "Sit down."

I took his hat off one of the straight-backed chairs and put it on a corner of his desk and then sat down. I lit another cigarette.

Eberhardt said, "You smoke too damned much, you know that?"

"Sure," I said. "Do you remember a guy named Nello? A companion of Chaucer's? They were both on the Row when we were patrolmen."

"I remember him."

"He came to see me this morning," I said, and outlined for him what Nello had told me.

Eberhardt put the cold pipe between his teeth, took it out again, scowled at it, and set it in the ashtray on his desk. "There might be a connection, all right," he said. "Why didn't Nello come down himself with this?"

"You know the answer to that."

"Yeah, I guess I do." He sighed softly, tiredly. "Well, I was reading the preliminary report a little while ago, before those state clowns came in; I recognized Chaucer's name. There's not much in it."

"Nello said he was beaten to death."

"Not exactly. There were some marks on him, but that wasn't the cause of death."

"What was?"

"Brain hemorrhage," Eberhardt said. "Caused by a sharp blow. The investigating officers found blood on the wall of one of the buildings in the alley, and the way it looks, his head was batted against there."

"What about the time of death?"

"The Medical Examiner fixes it at between midnight and 2 A.M."

"Was there anything in the alley?"

"You mean like fingerprints or shoeprints or missing buttons?"

"Like that."

"No," Eberhardt said. "And nobody saw or heard anything, of course; that area around the railroad yards is like a mausoleum after midnight."

"You really don't have much, do you?"

He shook his head. "There is one other thing, though. Chaucer had thirty-eight dollars and some change in his pockets when he was found."

"That's a lot of money for one of the Row people to be carrying around."

"Uh-huh."

"It sort of substantiates Nello's story, wouldn't you say?"

"Maybe. But if this hit-and-run guy killed Chaucer, why would he give him the money first?"

"It could be that Chaucer asked for a hell of a lot more than what he had in his pockets," I said. "The guy could have given him that as a down payment, and then arranged to meet him last night with the rest."

"And killed him instead," Eberhardt said. "Well, it could have happened like that."

"Look, Eb, I'd like to poke into this thing myself if I've got your permission."

"I was wondering when you'd get around to that. What's your big interest in Chaucer's death?"

"I told you, Nello came to see me this morning."

"But not to hire you."

"No," I admitted.

"Then who's going to pay your fee?"

"Maybe I'll do it gratis. I don't have anything else right now."

"You doing charity work these days?"

"Come on, Eb, knock it off."

"You feel sorry for Nello, is that it?"

"In a way, yes. You know what he thinks? He thinks the cops don't give a damn about finding Chaucer's killer."

"Why would he think that?"

"Chaucer was a nobody, just another wino. Who cares, Nello said, if some wino is murdered."

"Yeah, well, that's a crock."

"Sure, it's a crock," I said. "But Nello believes it. I wouldn't be surprised if the whole Row believed it."

Eberhardt got wearily to his feet. "I think I can spare a couple of minutes," he said. "You want to come with me down to Traffic? We'll see what Hit-and-Run has on Old Jenny."

"All right."

We walked out through the Squad Room and rode the elevator down to the Traffic Bureau on the main floor. We went into the office of an Inspector named Aldrich, who was in charge of the Hit-and-Run Detail. He was a big, red-haired guy with a lot of freckles on his face and hands. Eberhardt told him what we wanted, and Aldrich dug around in one of his file cabinets and came up with a thin cardboard folder. He spread it open on his desk and squinted at the contents; I had the impression that he needed glasses, but that he was too stubborn or too proud to admit the fact. He said at length, "Woman named Jenny Einers, sixty-three years old, hit-and-run at the intersection of Sixth and Howard streets three weeks ago. That the one?"

"That's the one," Eberhardt said.

"We've got damned little on it," Aldrich told him. "It happened at approximately 12:50 A.M. and there were no witnesses."

"There was one witness," I said. "Two, actually."

"Oh?"

I filled him in on what Nello had told me. When I was finished, he said, "Well, that's more than we were able to come up with."

Eberhardt asked, "Any broken glass on the scene?"

"Several shards of it, yes. One of the headlights. Nothing identifiable, though."

"What about paint scrapings?"

"Uh-huh. Forest green. General Motors color, 1966 to 1969."

"Were you able to identify the make and model?"

"No," Aldrich said. "It could have come off any one of several GM cars."

"Was there any fender or grille dirt?"

Aldrich nodded. "We put it through chemical analysis, of course. Common ground dirt, a little sand, and some gravel chips. Nothing unusual that we could work with."

"Anything else?"

"One thing. I don't know what it means, if anything."

"Yes?"

"Sawdust," Aldrich said.

"How's that?"

"Sawdust. We found several particles of it on the street near the point of impact."

"What kind of wood?"

"White pine," Aldrich said.

Eberhardt's forehead wrinkled. "What do you make of it?" he asked me.

I shook my head. "I don't know."

Aldrich said, "We sent out word to all the body shops in the Bay Area the morning after. That's standard procedure. There were a couple of late model GM's with forest green paint jobs brought in for body work, but one was a rear-ender and the other had the right front door banged up. We checked the accident reports on both, and they were clear. There was nothing else."

"Dead end," Eberhardt said.

"Yeah," I said.

He thanked Aldrich for his time and we went out to the elevator bank. Eberhardt pushed the UP button and then said, "I just can't take any more time on this right now, so you can poke around if you want. But make sure you call me if you turn up anything."

"You know I will."

"Sure," he said. "But it doesn't hurt to remind you."

The elevator doors slid open and I watched him get inside and press 4 on the panel. When the doors had closed again, I crossed the lobby and went out to Bryant Street. Fog banks sat off to the west in great folding billows, like carnival cotton candy. The wind was up, carrying the first trailing vapors over the city. I walked rapidly to where I had parked my car.

I sat inside for a time with the windows rolled up and the heater on, wondering where I would go from there. Nello had said he had last seen Chaucer around three the previous afternoon, apparently just before he left the Row; and Eberhardt had said that the Medical Examiner had fixed the time of death at between midnight and 2 A.M. That left approximately nine to eleven hours of Chaucer's time unaccounted for. Assuming that Chaucer had had the money which had been found on him prior to his death, and knowing the type of individual he had been, it seemed logical that he would have circulated along the Row—even though Nello hadn't encountered him. If that were the case, then somebody there had to have seen him or spoken with him or possibly even spent some time with him.

I drove the six blocks to Mission Street and found a parking place just off Fifth. I made my way over to Seventh and began to canvass the Row from Market to Harrison north-south, and from Seventh to Third west-east.

During the next two and a half hours, I walked streets littered with debris and wind-swept papers and hundreds of empty wine bottles, even though the City Sanitation Department works the area every morning. I talked to stoic bartenders with flat eyes in cheerless saloons; to dowdy waitresses with faces the color of yeast in cafes that sold hash and onions for thirty-five cents; to tired, aging hookers with names like Hey Hattie and Annie Orphan and Miss Lucinda; to liquor store clerks who counted each nickel and each dime with open contempt before serving their customers; to knots of men huddled together in doorways or on street corners, panhandling indifferent passers-by and drinking from paper-bag-wrapped bottles with only the neck showing—men called Monkey-face and Zingo and Yahoo and Bud-Bud and dozens of other names.

I learned nothing.

I was on Third and Harrison then, and my feet had begun playing hell with me; but I decided to try the area around South Park before giving it up. I walked down toward Brannan and went into a place called Packy's. One of the men sitting at the bar there was a study in varying shades of gray—iron-gray hair, washed gray eyes, red-veined gray skin, gray pinstripe suit, white-gray undershirt. He was Freddy the Dreamer, an old-timer on the Row. I went up to him and told him why I was there and asked my questions again for the hundredth or thousandth time.

And he said in the dreamy voice that had given him his nickname, "Sure, I seen Chaucer yesterday. Hell of a thing, what happened to him."

"What time, Freddy?"

"Around six," he answered. "He was just getting off a bus up on Mission."

"Which line?"

He shrugged. "Who knows?"

"Did you talk to him?"

"Sure," Freddy said. "We had us a party. Scotch whisky, can you believe? Old Freddy with his very own jug of Scotch whisky."

"Chaucer paid for it?"

"He was carrying a roll like you never seen. We got a flop down by the Embarcadero and went to work on that Scotch."

"Where did he get the roll, Freddy?"

"Chaucer was a kidder, you know? Him with his fancy education, a great kidder. I asked him where he picked it up, who did he mug, and he just laughed kind of secretive. 'Robin Hood,' he says. 'I got it from Robin Hood.' "

"Robin Hood?"

"That's it."

"Are you sure?"

"Yeah, I'm sure."

"Okay. What time did Chaucer leave this flop last night?"

"Who knows?" Freddy said dreamily. "With a jug of real Scotch whisky, who knows?"

"Do you have any idea where he went when he left?"

"To see Robin Hood."

"Is that what he said?"

"He was a kidder, you know?" Freddy said. "A great kidder."

"Yeah."

"Listen, I hope you find whoever done it to him. I sure hope you do. I can still taste that Scotch whisky."

I got out of there. Robin Hood, I thought as I walked up to Fifth to where I had left my car. It could have meant something—or nothing at all. The same way the sawdust Aldrich had mentioned could have meant something or nothing at all.

I decided to go back by the Hall of Justice and talk to Eberhardt again. But when I got there, he was out on something; one of the cops in the Squad Room said that he was expected back around 4:30. The clock on the wall read just a little after three, and I didn't feel much like waiting there for him.

I drove over to a restaurant on Van Ness and had something to eat; the food, through no fault of the management, was tasteless. I felt a little depressed, the way I used to feel when I was working the Row as a patrolman. My office seemed as good a place as any to go right then, and I paid my tab and went over there.

A single piece of mail had been shoved through the slot in the door, and I picked it up off the floor and put it on the desk. As usual, it was very cold in there. I turned on the valve on the steam radiator and then sat down and opened the letter.

It was a bill from a magazine readership club. In a weak moment some time back I had succumbed to the sales pitch of a doe-eyed college girl; but I had never received any of the magazines to which I had subscribed. Across the bottom of the bill, in ball point, was written: *Your continued indifference to this matter will leave us no alternative but to turn collection over to our legal department. This could seriously damage your credit rating. To avoid such action, and the resultant embarrassment to you, remit the above amount today!*

I folded the bill and the envelope and put them into my waste-basket. Then I sat there and lit a cigarette and looked at the wall and listened to the ringing knock of the radiator as it warmed up.

Robin Hood, I thought.

Sawdust.

I stood up after a time and crossed to the file cabinet-breakfast bar and took down the metal pot. It was half-full with my morning coffee. There was a thin sheen of oil on the surface, but I replaced it on the two-burner anyway. I turned on the gas and got the thing lighted.

I returned to the desk and sat down again and looked at the top for a while. There was nothing much on it save for the telephone and a desk calendar and an empty wire basket. I lit another cigarette.

Sawdust, I thought.

Robin Hood.

To hell with it, I thought. Let Eberhardt handle it; maybe he could make a connection. I looked at my watch. It was twenty past four. When 4:30 came, I would call him and put it in his lap. I had done all I could for Nello.

The coffee began to boil. I stood up again and walked over there and poured some of the black liquid into a cup. I carried it to the window behind my desk. The city of San Francisco looked cold and lonely and hoary-old through the ebbing steel-wool banks of fog. I glanced down at Taylor Street three floors below; rush hour was fast approaching, and there were a lot of cars jammed up down there. A small flatbed truck was blocking two lanes of traffic trying to back into a narrow alley across the way. It was carrying a wide load of ply-wood sheeting, and the driver was having difficulty jockeying the truck into the mall's slender mouth.

I watched him for a time, listening to the angry horn blasts of the blocked cars drift up from the street, and then the answer came drifting up, too, and hit me square in the face. I spilled some of the coffee getting the cup down on the desk. I pulled open the bottom drawer and dragged out the San Francisco Telephone Directory and got it open to the Yellow Pages. Half a minute later, my finger came to rest on a boxed, single-column advertisement at the bottom of one of the pages under *Lumber—Retail*. Freddy the Dreamer had been right; Chaucer, the former teacher of English Literature, had been a great kidder.

I caught up the telephone and dialed the Hall of Justice. It was 4:30 now, and maybe Eberhardt had come back.

He had.

"Sherwood," I said when they got him on the line. "Sherwood Forest Products."

"It was the owner's son—Ted Sherwood," Eberhardt said. "We saw the car—one of those El Camino pick-ups, actually, a jazzed up 1968 model with mag wheels and chrome exhausts and the like—parked in the company lot in Daly City when we drove up. I checked the registration and found out it belonged to the Sherwood kid. He was still there, he and his old man, supervising the unloading of a shipment of pine boards. We put it to him the first thing, and he lost his head and tried to run for it. He should have known better."

I nodded and drank a little of my beer. We were sitting in a small tavern on Boardman Place, near the Hall of Justice. It was after eight o'clock, and Eberhardt had just come off duty. He had called me forty minutes ago, and I had been waiting for him for about fifteen.

I said, "Did he confess?"

"Not right away," Eberhardt said. "The old man insisted he have his lawyer present, so we took him down to the Hall. When the lawyer showed, he and the old man went into a huddle. When they came out, the lawyer advised the kid to tell it straight."

"Did he?"

"He did," Eberhardt said. "He'd been out joyriding with his girl friend and a case of beer that night three weeks ago. He'd just taken the girl home, out on Potrero Hill. I guess he must have been pretty tanked up, though he won't admit it; he says he thought the light was green at the intersection. Anyway, when he hit the old lady he panicked and kept right on going."

"The impact must have jarred those particles of sawdust loose from the bed of the pick-up," I said.

"Apparently," Eberhardt agreed. "The kid told us he made small deliveries—plywood sections, mostly—from time to time."

"How did he get the dents ironed out?"

"Some friend of his works in a body shop, and the two of them did the job at night; that's why Hit-and-Run didn't get a report from any of the garages. With the new paint job, and the fact that nothing had happened for three weeks, he figured he was home free."

"And then Chaucer showed up," I said.

Eberhardt inclined his head. "He wanted five hundred dollars to keep what he'd seen quiet, the damned fool. The Sherwood kid put him off with fifty, and arranged to meet him down on the Embarcadero last night with the rest. He picked Chaucer up there and took him out to that alley on Hubbell Street. Sherwood swears he didn't mean to kill him; thought all he was going to do, he said, was rough Chaucer up a little to get him to lay off. But he's a pretty big kid, and he waded in a little too heavy. Chaucer hit his head on the building wall, and when Sherwood saw that he was dead, he panicked and beat it out of there."

"Which explains why Chaucer still had the rest of the fifty dollars on him when he was found."

"Yeah."

I finished the last of my beer. Eberhardt said, "One thing. How did you finally make the connection?"

"I'd seen this Sherwood Forest Products place once, when I was in Daly City on a skip-trace," I said. "Watching that truck loaded with plywood maneuver on Taylor Street brought it back to mind."

We sat there for a time, and then Eberhardt said, "Listen, I called my wife before I left the Hall and told her to put on some steaks. You want to come out for supper?"

"Rain check," I said. "I've got something to do."

"What's that?"

"Look up Nello. I promised him I'd let him know if anything turned up."

"Uh-huh."

"Maybe it'll restore some of his faith in humanity. Or at least in the minions of the law."

"After fifteen years on the Row?" Eberhardt said. "I doubt it."

"So do I. But there's always the chance."

Eberhardt nodded, staring into his beer glass. "So long, social worker," he said.

"So long, cop."

I went out into the cold, damp night.

OBJECT LESSON

by Ellery Queen

Ellery returned to school that morning, determined to cope with a problem which even then, in those more innocent days, was a fact of life in the neighborhood. Ellery's problem was not to catch a murderer, but rather to forestall what could happen to these boys . . .

Ellery hurried down West 92nd Street toward the main entrance of Henry Hudson High School stealing guilty glances at his watch. Miss Carpenter had been crisply specific about place, date, and time: her home room, 109; Friday morning, April 22nd; first period ("Bell *at 8:40*, Mr. Queen"). Miss Carpenter, who had come to him with an unusual request, had struck him as the sort of dedicated young person who would not take kindly to a hitch in her crusade.

Ellery broke into an undignified lope.

The project for which she had enlisted his aid was formidable even for a crusading young teacher of Social Studies on the 9th Grade Junior High level. For two months merchants of the neighborhood had been reporting stores broken into by a teen-age gang. Beyond establishing that the crimes were the work of the same boys, who were probably students at Henry Hudson High School, the police had got nowhere.

Miss Carpenter, walking home from a movie late the previous Monday night, had seen three boys dive out of a smashed bakery window and vanish into an alley. She had recognized them as Howard Ruffo, David Strager, and Joey Buell, all 15-year-old home-room students of hers. The juvenile crime problem was solved.

But not for Miss Carpenter. Instead of going to the police, Miss Carpenter had gone to Ellery, who lived on West 87th Street and was a hero to the youth of the neighborhood. Howard, David, and Joey were *not* hardened delinquents, she had told him, and she could *not* see their arrest, trial, and imprisonment as a solution to anything. True, they had substituted gang loyalty for the love and security they were denied in their unhappy slum homes, but boys who worked at after-school jobs and turned every cent in at home were hardly beyond recall, were they? And she had told him just where each boy worked, and at what.

"They're only patterning their behavior after criminals because they think criminals are strong, successful, and glamorous," Miss Carpenter had said; and what she would like him to do was visit her class and, under the pretext of giving a talk on the subject of

Notorious Criminals I Have Known, paint such a picture of weak, rat-
ting, empty, and violently ending criminality that David and Joey
and Howard would see the error of their ways.

It had seemed to Ellery that this placed a rather hefty burden on
his oratorical powers. Did Miss Carpenter have her principal's permission for this project?

No, Miss Carpenter had replied bravely, she did *not* have Mr.
Hinsdale's permission, and she might very well lose her job when he
heard about it. "But I'm *not* going to be the one who gives those
boys the first shove toward reform school and maybe eventually a
life sentence!" And besides, what did Mr. Queen have to lose but an
hour of his time?

So Mr. Queen had feebly said yes, he would come; and here he
was, at the door of the determined young woman's classroom . . .
seven minutes *late*.

Ellery braced himself and opened the door.

The moment he set foot in the room he knew he had walked in
on a catastrophe.

Louise Carpenter stood tensely straight at her desk, her pretty
face almost as white as the envelope she was clutching. And she was
glaring at a mass of boy and girl faces so blankly, so furtively quiet
that the silence sizzled.

The first thing she said to him was, "I've been robbed."

The terrible mass of boy and girl eyes followed him to her desk.
In his nose was the pungent smell of ink, glue, paper, chalk, musty
wardrobe closets; surrounding him were discolored walls, peeling
paint, tarnished fixtures, warped window poles and mutilated desks.

"Robbed in my own classroom," Miss Carpenter choked.

He laid his coat and hat gently on her desk. "A practical joke?" He
smiled at the class.

"Hardly. They didn't know you were coming." They had betrayed
her, the sick shock in her voice said. "Class, this is Ellery Queen. I
don't have to tell you who Mr. Queen is, and how honored we are
to have him visit us." There was a gasp, a buzz, a spatter of applause.
"Mr. Queen was kind enough to come here today as a special treat to
give us a talk on crime. I didn't know he was going to walk in on
one."

The spatter stopped dead.

"You're sure there has been a crime, Miss Carpenter?"

"An envelope with seven one-dollar bills in it was stolen, and from the way it happened the thief can only be someone in this room."

"I'm sorry to hear that."

He deliberately looked them over, wondering which of the forty-one pairs of eyes staring back at his belonged to Joey Buell, Howard Ruffo, and David Strager. He should have asked Louise Carpenter to describe them. Now it was too late.

Or was it?

It seemed to Ellery that three of the twenty-odd boy faces were rather too elaborately blank. One of them was set on husky shoulders; this boy was blond, handsome, and dead-white about the nostrils. The second was a sharp-nosed, jet-haired boy with Mediterranean coloring who was perfectly still except for his fingers, and they kept turning a pencil over and over almost ritually. The third, thin and red-haired, showed no life anywhere except in a frightened artery in his temple.

Ellery made up his mind.

"Well, if it's a real live crime," he said, turning to Louise, "I don't imagine anyone wants to hear me ramble on about crimes that are dead and buried. In fact, I think it would more interesting if I gave the class a demonstration of how a crime is actually solved. What do you think, Miss Carpenter?"

Understanding leaped into her eyes, along with hope.

"I think," she said grimly, "it would be *lots* more interesting."

"Suppose we begin by finding out about the seven dollars. They were yours, Miss Carpenter?"

"One dollar was mine. Miss McDoud, an English teacher, is being married next month. A group of us are chipping in to buy her a wedding present, with me as banker. All this week teachers have been dropping in to leave their dollars in an envelope I've had on my desk. This morning—"

"That's fine for background, Miss Carpenter. Suppose we hear testimony from the class." Ellery surveyed them, and there was a ripple of tittering. Suddenly he pointed to a little lipsticked girl with an Italian haircut. "Would you like to tell us what happened this morning?"

"I don't know anything about the money!"

"Chicken." A boy's jeering voice.

"The boy who said that," Ellery kept his tone friendly. It was one of the three he had spotted, the husky blond one. "What's your name?"

"David Strager." His sneer said, *You don't scare me.* But his nostrils remained dead-white. He was the boy Miss Carpenter had said worked after school as a stock boy at the Hi-Kwality Supermarket on Amsterdam Avenue.

"All right, Dave. You tell us about this morning."

The boy glanced scornfully at the girl with the Italian haircut. "We all knew the money was in the envelope. This morning before the bell rings Mrs. Morrell comes in with her buck and Miss Carpenter puts it with the other money and lays the envelope on her desk. So afterward the bell rings, Mrs. Morrell splits, Miss Carpenter picks up the envelope and takes a look inside, and she hollers, 'I been robbed.'"

The thin boy with the red hair called out, "So what are we supposed to do, drop dead?" and winked at David Strager, who had already sat down. The big blond boy winked back.

"And your name?" Ellery asked the redhead.

"Joseph Buell," the boy answered defiantly. He was the one who worked at Kaplan's, the big cigar, candy, and stationery store on 89th Street. "Who wants their old seven bucks?"

"Somebody not only wants it, Joey, somebody's got it."

"Aaa, for all we know she took it herself." And this was the third of the trio, the sharp-faced dark boy. If Ellery was right, he was the one who delivered part-time for O'Donnel's Dry Cleaning on Columbus Avenue.

"And you are—?"

"Howard Ruffo."

The Three Musketeers, rushing to one another's support.

"You mean, Howard, you're charging Miss Carpenter with having stolen the teachers' money?" Ellery asked with a smile.

The boy's dark glance wavered. "I mean maybe she took it like by mistake. Mislaid it or somepin'."

"As a matter of fact," came Louise's quiet voice, "when I saw the money wasn't in the envelope, my first thought was exactly that, Mr. Queen. So I searched myself thoroughly."

"May I see the envelope?"

"This isn't the one I was keeping the seven dollars in"—she handed him the envelope—"though it looks the same. I have a box of them in my locker there. The lock hasn't worked for ages. This one must have been stolen from my locker yesterday, or earlier this week."

"It's a blank envelope, Miss Carpenter. How do you know it isn't the one that contained the money?"

"Because the original had a notation in ink on the flap—*Gift Fund for Helen McDoud.*" She looked about and glances fell in windrows. "So this theft was planned, Mr. Queen. Someone came to class this morning armed with this duplicate envelope, previously stolen and filled with worthless paper, prepared to make a quick exchange if the opportunity arose. And it did. The class was milling around while Mrs. Morrell and I chatted."

The paper in the substitute envelope consisted of a sheaf of rectangular strips cut to the size of dollar bills.

"At the time you placed Mrs. Morrell's dollar among the others in the original envelope, was everybody here?"

"Yes. The door opened and closed only once after that—when Mrs. Morrell left. I was facing the door the whole time."

"Could Mrs. Morrell, as a practical joke, have made the switch?"

"She wasn't anywhere near my desk after I laid the envelope on it."

"Then you're right, Miss Carpenter. The theft was planned in advance by one of the boys or girls in this room, and the thief—and money—are both still here."

The tension was building beautifully. The boy must be in a sweat. He hadn't expected his theft to be found out so soon, before he got a chance to sneak the money out of the room.

"What time does the first period end, Miss Carpenter?"

"At 9:35."

Every head turned toward the clock on the wall.

"And it's only 8:56," Ellery said cheerfully. "That gives us thirty-nine minutes—more than enough time. Unless the boy or girl who planned this crime wants to return the loot to Miss Carpenter here and now?"

This time he stared directly from David to Howard to Joey. His stare said, *I hate to do this, boys, but of course I'll have to if you think you can get away with it.*

The Strager boy's full lips were twisted. The skinny redhead, Joey Buell, stared back sullenly. Howard Ruffo's pencil twirled faster.

It's one of those three, all right.

"I see we'll have to do it the hard way," Ellery said. "Sorry I can't produce the thief with a flick of my wrist, the way it's done in books, but in real life detection—like crime—is pretty unexciting stuff. We'll begin with a body search. It's voluntary, by the way. Anybody rather not chance a search? Raise your hand."

Not a muscle moved.

"I'll search the boys, Miss Carpenter. You roll those two bulletin boards over to that corner and search the girls."

The next few minutes were noisy. As each boy was searched and released he was sent to the blackboard at the front of the room. The girls were sent to the rear.

"Find anything, Miss Carpenter?"

"Rose Perez has a single dollar bill. The other girls either have small change or no money at all."

"No sign of the original envelope?"

"No."

"I found two boys with bills—in each case a single, too. David Strager and Joey Buell. No envelope."

Louise's brows met.

Ellery glanced up at the clock. 9:07.

He strolled over to her. "Don't show them you're worried. There's nothing to worry about. We have twenty-eight minutes." He raised his voice, smiling. "Naturally the thief has ditched the money, hoping to recover it when the coast is clear. It's therefore hidden somewhere in the classroom. All right, Miss Carpenter, we'll take the desks and seats first. Look under them too—chewing gum makes a handy adhesive. Eh, class?"

Four minutes later they looked at each other, then up at the clock. 9:11.

Exactly twenty-four minutes remaining.

"Well," said Ellery.

He began to ransack the room. Books, radiators, closets, supplies, lunchbags, schoolbags. Bulletin boards, wall maps, the terrestrial globe. The UN poster, the steel engravings of Washington and Lincoln. He even emptied Louise's three pots of geraniums and sifted the earth.

His eyes kept returning to the clock more and more often.

Ellery searched everything in the room, from the socket of the American flag to the insect-filled bowls of the old light fixtures, reached by standing on desks.

Everything.

"It's not here!" whispered Louise in his ear.

The Buell, Ruffo, and Strager boys were nudging one another, grinning.

"Well, well," Ellery said.

Interesting. Something of a problem at that.

Of course! He got up and checked two things he had missed—the cup of the pencil sharpener and the grid covering the loudspeaker of the PA system. No envelope. No money.

He took out a handkerchief and wiped his neck.

Really it's a little silly. A schoolboy!

Ellery glanced at the clock.

9:29.

Six minutes left in which not only to find the money but identify the thief!

He leaned against Louise's desk, forcing himself to relax.

It was these "simple" problems. Nothing big and important, like murder, blackmail, bank robbery. A miserable seven dollars lifted by a teen-age delinquent in an overcrowded classroom . . .

He thought furiously.

Let the bell ring at 9:35 and the boy strut out of Miss Carpenter's room undetected, with his loot, and he would send up a howl like a wolf cub over his first kill. *Who says these big-shot law jerks ain't monkeys? The biggest! He's a lot of nothin'. Wind. See me stand him on his ear? And this is just for openers. Wait till I get goin' for real, not any of this kid stuff* . . .

No, nothing big and important like murder. Just seven dollars, and a big shot to laugh at. Not important? Ellery nibbled his lip. It was probably the most important case of his career.

9:30:30.

Only four and a half minutes left!

Louise Carpenter was gripping a desk, her knuckles white. Waiting to be let down.

Ellery pushed away from the desk and reached into the patch pocket of his tweed jacket for his pipe and tobacco, thinking harder about Helen McDoud's seven-dollar gift fund than he had ever thought about anything in his life.

And as he thought . . .

At 9:32 he was intently examining the rectangles of paper the thief had put into the substitute envelope. The paper was ordinary cheap newsprint, scissored to dollar-bill size out of a colored comics section. He shuffled through the dummy dollars one by one, hunting for something. Anything!

The forty-one boys and girls were buzzing and giggling now.

Ellery pounced. Clinging to one of the rectangles was a needle-thin sliver of paper about an inch long, a sort of paper shaving. He fingered it, held it up to the light. It was not newsprint. Too full-bodied, too tough-textured . . .

Then he knew what it must be.

Less than two minutes left.

Feverishly he went through the remaining dollar-sized strips of comic paper.

And there it was. There it was!

This strip had been cut from the top of the comic sheet. On the margin appeared the name of a New York newspaper and the date *April 24, 1955.*

Think it over. Take your time. Lots of seconds in a minute.

The buzzing and giggling had died. Louise Carpenter was on her feet, looking at him imploringly.

A bell began clanging in the corridor.

First period over.

9:35.

Ellery rose and said solemnly, "The case is solved."

With the room cleared and the door locked, the three boys stood backed against the blackboard as if facing a firing squad. The bloom was gone from David Strager's cheeks. The blood vessel in Joey Buell's temple was trying to wriggle into his red hair. And Howard Ruffo's eyes were liquid with panic.

It's hard to be fifteen years old and trapped.

But harder not to be.

"Wha'd I do?" whimpered Howard Ruffo. "I didn't do nothin'."

"We didn't take Miss Carpenter's seven dollars," said David Strager, stiff-lipped.

"Can you say the same about Mr. Mueller's baked goods last Monday night, Dave?" Ellery paused gently. "Or any of the other things you boys have been making love to in the past two months?"

He thought they were going to faint.

"But this morning's little job," Ellery turned suddenly to the red-haired boy, "you pulled by yourself, Joey."

The thin body quivered. "Who, me?"

"Yes, Joey, you."

"You got rocks in your skull," Joey whispered. "Not me!"

"I'll prove it, Joey. Hand me the dollar bill I found in your jeans when I searched you."

"That's my dollar!"

"I know it, Joey. I'll give you another for it. Hand it over . . . Miss Carpenter."

"Yes, Mr. Queen!"

"To cut these strips of newspaper to the same size as dollar bills, the thief must have used a real bill as a pattern. If he cut too close, the scissors would shave off a sliver of the bill." Ellery handed her Joey's dollar. "See if this bill shows a slight indentation along one edge."

"It does!"

"And I found this sliver clinging to one of the dummies. Fit the sliver to the indented edge of Joey's bill. If Joey is guilty, it should fit exactly. Does it?"

Louise looked at the boy. "Joey, it does fit."

David and Howard were gaping at Ellery.

"What a break," Joey choked.

"Criminals make their own bad breaks, Joey. The thing inside you that told you you were doing wrong made your hand shake as you cut. But even if your hand hadn't slipped, I'd have known you were the one who substituted the strips of paper for the money."

"How? How could you?" It was a cry of bewilderment.

Ellery showed him the rectangular strip with the white margin. "See this, Joey? Here's the name of the newspaper, and the date is *April 24, 1955*. What date is today?"

"Friday the 22nd . . ."

"Friday, April 22nd. But these strips of colored comics come from the newspaper of April 24th, Joey—*this coming Sunday's paper*. Who gets advance copies of the Sunday comics? Stores that sell newspapers in quantity. Getting the bulldog editions in advance gives them a jump on the Sunday morning rush, when they have to insert the news sections.

"Nothing to it, Joey. Which of you three boys had access before this morning to next Sunday's bulldog editions? Not David—he works in a supermarket. Not Howard—he works for a dry cleaner. But you work in a big cigar and stationery store, Joey, where newspapers must be one of the stock items."

Joey Buell's eyes glassed over.

"We think we're strong, Joey, and then we run into somebody stronger," Ellery said. "We think we're the smartest, and someone comes along to outsmart us. We beat the rap a dozen times, but the thirteenth time the rap beats us. You can't win, Joey."

Joey burst into tears.

Louise Carpenter made an instinctive gesture toward him. Ellery's head-shake warned her back. He went close to the boy and tousled the red head, murmuring something the others could not hear. And after a while Joey's tears sniffled to an end and he wiped his eyes on his sleeve in a puzzled way.

"Because I think this is going to work out all right, Joey," Ellery said, continuing their curious colloquy aloud. "We'll have a session with Mr. Hinsdale, and then with some pretty right guys I happen to know at Police Headquarters. After that it will be up to you."

Joey Buell gulped. "Okay, Mr. Queen." He did not look at his two friends.

David and Howard communicated silently. Then David turned to Ellery. "Where do we stand, Mr. Queen?"

"You and Howard are coming along."

The blond boy bit his lip. Then he nodded, and after a moment the dark boy nodded, too.

"Oh, I almost forgot." Ellery dipped briskly into the jacket pocket that held his pipe and tobacco. His hand reappeared with a wrinkled envelope, its flap written over. From the envelope protruded the corners of some one-dollar bills. "Your Helen McDoud wedding gift fund, Miss Carpenter. With Joey's compliments."

"I did forget!" gasped Louise. "Where did you find it?"

"Where Joey in desperation slipped it as I was frisking the other boys. The only thing in the room I didn't think of searching—my own pocket." Ellery winked at the three boys. "Coming, fellas?"

LETTER FROM A VERY WORRIED MAN

by Henry Slesar

Here, within a thousand words, is a vignette—a portrait of our disturbing times . . .

Abby had spent the past four days with her parents in Springfield. So as soon as she got back to Chicago, she anxiously examined the accumulated mail in her mailbox. She shuffled hurriedly through the envelopes, magazines, and leaflets until she saw the familiar scrawl of Richard's handwriting. She wanted this letter above all, because it was from her fiance, all the way from New York where he was attending a physicists' conference.

She waited until she was settled in a lounge chair, with a fresh cigarette between her lips. Then she tore open the envelope and extracted the folded sheet.

Dear Abby,

I love you. We're in the fourth day of the Conference now, and nobody's gotten drunk yet. What a convention! You'll be happy to hear that there are only four women physicists in the crowd, and they're all strictly from Lower Slobbovia, so you can stop worrying about my dubious virtue. Did I mention that I love you?

There was a seminar yesterday on the Physicist's Responsibility in the Modern World, or some such jawbreaking title. The yawn might have come up like thunder in the audience, except that there were some pretty scary headlines on the hotel newsstand that morning, so everybody was a bit edgy. I got up and did some talking myself, but maybe I should have kept my mouth shut. You know how I am when I get started on Topic A.

I know what you're thinking now: old guilt-ridden Richard's off the deep end again, blaming himself for helping to make the H-bomb. Well, I've been thinking about it, sure. How can you help it in this atmosphere? And when I look at the headlines, and remember that we're getting married in two weeks—how can you blame me for a slight case of jitters? We're walking down the aisle under the most menacing shadow that ever fell across this cockeyed world. We're going to have children (in due course, or didn't you know?) that will have to live, and maybe die, with the H-bomb in their backyard. You can't stop these thoughts, Abby, not even by trying.

I thought about it all last night, and not sleeping much, if you want the truth. Wondering how a guy like me, a guy who helped put the thing together, who feels like a criminal, has a right to such happy prospects. Marrying you, settling down, raising kids, just like everybody else, just like Joe Normal. But then I think, well, I'm Joe Normal, too, and if the bomb hits, I go to pieces like everyone else; if the Strontium 90 starts filling up the water, and the milk, and the green vegetables, well, I'll get just as sick and dead as the next man. I'm not so special, honey. I don't feel guilty any more; just scared.

But you know something? I learned something out here. Sitting around with the guys, meeting up with the science boys from England, and France, and Yugoslavia (yep, they're here, too) I began to realize something. I began to think that maybe the problems of getting along with each other aren't much worse than math problems. Even the big political problems, the ones which end up Bang! if the answers come out wrong, they can be licked, too. Sure, we'll be depending on a lot of people whose actions we can't predict or control—but we put our trust in strangers every day. The guy who drives the bus. The airline pilot. The elevator operator. The short-order cook. One wrong step, and these guys could end our short, worried lives, too. So why not have faith? Why not trust a little bit? Maybe there won't be any big boom to put an end to our plans. Maybe there'll be sweetness and light for a change. Peace on Earth, good will to men, and all that jazz.

I don't know what started me feeling this way. (No, I haven't touched a drop.) But all of a sudden, I'm hopeful. I feel good about you, and about us, and about our wedding day. I feel good about how we're going to live, and how the kids are going to grow up, and how we're going to sit in front of the fireplace for the next fifty years until we run out of things to say. The truth is, honey, all of a sudden I'm an optimist. I think we're going to lick our problems, all of them. I think the patient's really and truly going to live.

Well, that's all the ink in this pen. I'm going to take a walk around this town now, and see how it looks for a honeymoon. I'll let you know if it measures up to our high standards.

I love you, by the way.

Yours,
Richard.

Abby sighed happily at the conclusion of the letter, and ground out her cigarette in an ash tray. Then she looked at the next envelope in the pile of mail. It appeared to be official and had a local postmark, so she opened it curiously.

The contents were brief.

Dear Miss Butler:

We have been unable to reach you for the past few days, to inform you that the New York Police Department has contacted us regarding a man identified as Mr. Richard Cole. Mr. Cole was killed on the night of September 4 by a street gang of young hoodlums, and your name and address were discovered among his effects. We would appreciate it if you would contact Lieutenant Frank Kowlanski, Precinct 63, Chicago Police Department.

M AS IN MUGGED

by Lawrence Treat

In the original call for material, we asked for both police procedurals and other stories reflecting these days. On his sixtieth birthday, Homicide Chief Lieutenant Decker, "something of a character even to himself," has reason to discover that neither he nor the world have changed since his rookie days.

Lieutenant William Decker, Chief of Homicide and something of a character even to himself, woke up at six a.m. and remembered that this was his birthday. The idea annoyed the hell out of him.

He sat up and glanced at his wife, Martha, sleeping alongside him. He slipped out of bed as quietly as he could, went into the bathroom, and peeled off his pajama top. In the mirror he saw a tall straight figure. His stomach was lean and flat, his gray eyes were somber, and the amount of his hair was moderate. Just moderate.

He slapped his chest hard, and laughed. "Brother!" he said aloud. "*You* ain't sixty!"

But he was.

He might have accepted the fact and survived the day without incident if it hadn't been for Martha's birthday present. It was wrapped in fancy paper and propped up in front of his plate at the breakfast table. After he'd started the coffee, he picked up the package and untied the ribbon. Inside was a framed photograph of himself, in uniform, at the age of 28. Underneath the picture was the printed caption, PATROLMAN WILLIAM DECKER.

He remembered that picture. He'd been a rookie then, and the police were looking for a man named McGovern who'd held up a filling station and killed the attendant. McGovern came from what was called Tough Town in those days, and you didn't go down there unless you belonged. But Patrolman Bill Decker went anyhow—to a big wake they were holding for somebody whose name he'd forgotten long ago. Young Patrolman Decker figured that McGovern might show up there, and he did.

Thinking back, Decker realized that he owed that first triumph to a kind of cockeyed daring, along with more luck than any man had a right to expect. He'd drifted around the crowded hall until he'd spotted McGovern. The killer was standing near a door, and Decker grabbed him and hustled him out to a waiting car. Everybody who saw the scuffle assumed it was a private fight—just a couple of brawlers feeling their oats, the way it sometimes happens at a wake. Consequently nobody interfered.

As a result of the arrest Decker had got a citation and a promo-
tion, and his picture in the newspaper. This one. And Martha must
have gone over to the *Chronicle* offices, borrowed the negative, and
had it reproduced, framed, and touched up. Because even Bill
Decker himself didn't think he'd ever looked *that* handsome.

On his 60th birthday he was at his desk at nine, in the tiny cubicle
crammed with filing cabinets and stacks of technical magazines he
had kept to read and had never managed to. Nobody, including the
stuffed crocodile on the bookcase, gave him flowers or a medal or
even sang *Happy Birthday* to him—for all of which he was deeply
grateful.

Out of the morning's batch of reports that had reached his desk
for initialing, he selected two for the Homicide Squad's attention.
One was an assault case that he put Bankhart on; the other was a
burglary that he assigned to Mitch Taylor—actually, it was a stolen
car case and not the responsibility of the Homicide Squad. They
handled crimes against the person, but they were notified of all
larcenies, and when Decker thought it worthwhile, he ran an independent investigation.

The stolen car was a green Chevy, 1965 model, out-of-state license
plates, 649T87. Owner, Harold Waverly, dress salesman. He'd been
traveling with his wife and he'd stopped at an antique shop. Since
he'd neglected to lock the car and take the key out of the ignition,
he was practically asking for somebody to get behind the wheel and
drive off; and somebody obliged.

The report listed the loss, in addition to the car and the Waverlys'
personal belongings, as 20 dresses valued at fifty dollars apiece, plus
another thousand dollars worth of expensive accessories. Which made
quite a haul for the obliger.

So—had Waverly been inexcusably careless, or had he set up the
crime and collaborated in it? The answer could be either way, and
Lieutenant Decker told Taylor to send for the Waverlys and see
what cooked.

With that off his chest, Decker picked up the latest issue of *Law
& Order* and started reading. But his mind kept wandering, and after
a few minutes he got up and went down the hall. He spent the
better part of an hour in the Records Room, going over some new
procedures that had just been set up.

When he returned, Mitch Taylor was in the outer office with a
young couple who Decker assumed were the Waverlys. She was a
slender willowy brunette with adoration in her eyes, and she was

saying, "It was such a beautiful day. We stopped on the road to pick some flowers and—"

Decker marched past and closed the door to his office, but the image of the girl stayed with him as if it had been stamped on his retina. Still, because he always noticed people and had developed the habit of filing faces and remembering details, he had a picture of the husband, too. He had dark hair and an Irish-looking face, and he was well-built.

Later on, Taylor came in and reported. "The guy's up on Cloud Nine," he said. "He says he feels like a jackass, leaving the car unlocked, but they were on their honeymoon and business trip, both. And with a dame like this Brenda—well, you saw her."

Decker had, and he thought of Martha and himself more than 30 years ago. She'd looked like this girl—they could have been sisters. But where did Taylor come off reminding Decker of things like that?

"Apart from the nuances of burgeoning love and its impact on an ignition key," Decker said coldly, "what did you find out?"

Taylor looked hurt, as he usually did when Decker threw his vocabulary around. But that was one of the ways Decker maintained his authority. He could sling vernacular with the best of them, but none of his boys could hit hyperbole at the Decker level. He assumed the squad repeated some of his soaring poetical flights. In any case, they were supposed to. His rhetoric kept him a cut above their level.

Taylor put some style sheets, with the dresses reproduced in full color, on the desk. "This is the line he was carrying. High-class stuff." Taylor, an authority on whatever happened to be the subject, pointed to one of the pictures. "Brenda was wearing this one. You know, Chief, they stopped off to look at the view at High Point, and later on they parked along the road and went out into a field. She picked flowers, a whole bunch of them. She's a city gal and doesn't get the chance often, and then they—" Taylor broke off and studied the ceiling.

Decker, thinking of his own honeymoon with Martha and of the time *she'd* picked flowers, jerked back to attention. "Brother!" he said. "That was some investigation you made. Got the wedding pictures to go with it?"

Taylor pushed the style sheets aside. "Well," he said, "I guess that's all there is to it."

Decker had his usual lunch across the street, with some of the bureau heads, but after returning to his office he couldn't get down to work. He kept thinking of Patrolman Decker and how he'd collared McGovern 30 years ago. No gun—just man to man, with an armlock and with hard fists to back him up. He kept wondering how 60-year-old Lieutenant Decker would stack up alongside that rookie patrolman.

Suddenly tired of sitting and moping, Decker slapped his desk drawer shut, got up, and stepped outside. He said he had an errand, would take his car, and they could call him if anything turned up. He strode out, muttering to himself. What would anybody need him for? An old man of 60—

He drove down to the river to Tough Town. It wasn't called that any more. It was still a reasonably tough district, but the Irish had moved on to other places; they'd given up their political control and let the Italians and Puerto Ricans take over. The tight cohesiveness of a single ethnic group was broken.

Decker parked in front of a small supermarket, buzzed the despatcher, and said he was leaving his car and would be back in an hour or two. Then he locked the car and started walking. For some obscure reason he wanted to find the hall where that wake had taken place 30 years ago. It was near here, somewhere. Down an alley, as he remembered it. But the buildings had changed, and that new supermarket had him all mixed up. He tried an alley but wasn't sure whether it was the right one.

It was bounded on one side by the brick wall of a warehouse, and on the other by a high wooden fence. The fence was broken in several places, and you could step through to an empty lot where, judging by the rubble and the charred beams, there had recently been a fire. Farther on there was a broad gap in the fence. A couple of jalopies were parked in the lot, together with a brand new Thunderbird and a green Chevy. The Chevy had out-of-state plates, 649T87. Decker walked over to the car and opened the door.

The key was in the ignition. A metal bar had been fitted across the rear to hold a rack of dresses, and a couple of hangers and the remains of a bouquet of wild flowers were strewn across the back seat. He noticed daisies and buttercups, a few weeds, and to his surprise some shiny green leaves that he recognized as poison ivy. If Brenda had picked those, she certainly was a city girl. And a damn lucky one, too, not to be all blistered up today and having one hell of a honeymoon.

Decker locked the car, put the key in his pocket, and started to retrace his steps, to report what he'd found. As he emerged from the lot, he noticed a girl at the other end of the alley. She was wearing a bright, yellow dress—one of the models Taylor had shown him in Waverly's style sheets.

Decker switched directions and followed the girl.

She had dark hair and she walked with a light, springy step, and she was young. She had no idea anyone was behind her, so she was easy to follow. She swung left at the end of the alley, floated along for a couple of blocks, then entered a tavern. The neon sign read *Gino's*.

The Lieutenant, marching along in no particular hurry, reached the tavern door, opened it, and went inside. The girl wasn't there.

A quick look told him all he needed to know. There was a curtained doorway at the rear. The girl had gone either to a back room or upstairs, or else had slipped out through a side exit.

The bartender was squat, partly bald, and had tired, worried eyes. A broken-down rummy, sitting on a stool at the far end, was draped over the bar. He lifted his head to see who had come in, then let it drop back. The juke box, going full blast, was playing rock-and-roll, and seven boys in their late teens were bunched around a rear table.

At Lieutenant Decker's appearance they seemed to react to some unspoken signal; they swung around and stood clear of the table.

Decker had seen enough. All he had to do was say, "Sorry, I guess this is the wrong place." Then he could have turned around and left, as any sensible cop would do when he walked in on a gang of young punks who were obviously spoiling for a fight. He has nothing to gain and everything to lose. But Decker was 60 today, and he was out to prove something—at least, to himself.

He sat down at the bar. "Make it a beer," he said.

The rummy, lost in his alcoholic daze, grunted. The bartender merely frowned, looked even unhappier than before, and drew a beer. In the mirror Decker saw six of the gang deploy to cut him off.

They wore the uniform of delinquency—black boots, tight trousers, and zipper jackets with their names lettered across the back. The boy who went to the front door had *Joe* written on the back of his jacket, and the one who covered the rear was *Pete*.

The four others fanned out in a rough semicircle, three of them behind their leader who, according to his jacket, was *Duke*. There was only one boy who seemed not to be a member of the gang, and he was sitting at the table around which the others had been grouped.

The non-participant had a Coke bottle in front of him, and judging by his neck and the oversized Adam's apple that bobbed up and down inside his throat, he was tall and gawky and on the scraggly side. Can't count on much help from him, Decker decided.

Duke came over and straddled the stool next to Decker. He made a clucking sound to attract attention. "Hi, Grampa," he said. "You come from around here?"

Decker turned slowly. Duke was about 19, dark-haired, slightly chubby of face, heavily built. His eyes and manner were insolent, as if he intended to have some fun at the expense of an old man.

"More or less," Decker said.

"That's a hell of an answer, from an old geezer like you."

The bartender put down the glass he was polishing and moved to Decker's end of the bar. "Not in here, Duke," he said. "I don't want any trouble."

Duke laughed. "Who's making trouble? I just thought I'd let Grampa stand us a round. You need the business, don't you?"

The bartender, evidently Gino the owner, scowled. Decker heard a sound at the rear of the room and looked past Duke. Duke turned, too.

The girl Decker had followed in here had just parted the curtains at the rear. Instead of the yellow dress, she was now wearing a skirt and a blouse, and her body seemed to flow inside it. The gawky boy stood up, and she stopped next to him. They said something to each other and they both smiled; but her smile froze as she became aware of the menace from Duke and his gang. As if seeking support from the gawky boy, she reached out for his hand, but he yanked it back with a wince.

She drew in her breath and gave him a questioning look. He whispered something that apparently satisfied her, and she took his other hand. Then the pair of them came over to the bar.

She spoke to Gino. "Dad," she said, "we're going over to Alma's. I'll be back for supper."

Gino nodded. "Fine. See you later." He was obviously relieved to see her go, but he tensed up as she reached the door and Joe grabbed her companion by the shoulder.

"Take it easy, Benjy," Joe said. "Little boys shouldn't run after girls."

The girl faced Joe angrily. "He's coming with me and you have no right to stop him."

Benjy touched her shoulder. "Go ahead, Louise, I'll make out. Just go ahead—*go!*"

She hesitated and looked at her father for support, but he shook his head and repeated Benjy's words. "Go ahead." She seemed to sag for a moment, then she went out swiftly.

Benjy stepped back. There was a rash on his hand, covered with the kind of white lotion used for poison ivy. Decker picked up his beer glass, took a leisurely sip, and gave Duke his full attention. "If you want me to buy you a round," he said, "maybe you'd better tell me who you are."

Duke, still straddling the stool, bent forward and bowed in mockery. "Duke the Fluke," he said. "And who the hell are you?"

"Got a last name?" Decker asked. Duke didn't bother answering, and Decker went on. "How about your friends—who are they?"

"You're a nosey old guy, Grampa," Duke said, and he reached out to tweak Decker's nose. Decker jerked back, and Duke let out a roar of laughter. "How about those beers, huh?" he said.

Gino, inching over, said in a low voice, "Better do what he says, Mister. You're in trouble."

And that, Decker reflected, was the understatement of the year. He was in the wrong place, under the wrong circumstances, and he was trapped. If he tried to walk out now, they'd block him off or trip him up or slug him. He was up against a nasty situation, and he had to face it.

Staring at Duke and holding him with his eyes, Decker casually pulled back the flap of his jacket. His badge showed briefly as he took his gun out of its holster and leveled it.

"Copper!" Duke exclaimed, jerking backward.

Decker nodded. "That's right. So why don't you boys just run along and forget all about this?"

Duke, gazing at the gun, licked his lips and blinked. Then he raised his hand, and the gang tightened the circle, surrounding Decker. For a moment the idea flashed across his mind that the rookie patrolman of 30 years ago would have handled this with his fists. Maybe. And got the living daylights beaten out of him.

"You going to shoot all six of us?" Duke asked, grinning confidently.

The punk knew his way around. He knew that the last thing any cop wants to do is use his gun before he's actually attacked and before his life is in danger. In a way, pulling the gun had put Decker on the defensive and placed him in the wrong.

Then he did a crazy thing. It was a violation of every basic rule of police work, and specifically of Section 48-a of Department regulations. If Mitch Taylor or anyone else on the Homicide Squad had pulled a fool trick like this, Decker would have given him a lecture that would have made his hair curl, and stay curled. But what was the use of being a Lieutenant if you had to stick to the book?

So what Decker did was to shift his grip on the gun, take it in both hands, and break it open. He removed five of the six bullets and held them out. "For souvenirs," he said amiably. "One apiece."

His action, calm, friendly, and completely unexpected, threw them off balance. With no idea of how to handle the new situation, they automatically accepted Decker's invitation and reached out greedily. "Gimme—gimme!"

Pete, coming from the rear of the room, called out, "Hey, how about me? I want one, too."

"Sorry, Pete," Decker remarked. Addressing the boy by name split him off from the gang and helped break up their solid front. "None left," Decker said, "except the one I'm keeping for myself." He pulled his jacket open so that they could see he had no cartridge belt. Then, snapping his gun shut and holstering it, he slid off the stool.

"Come on, Benjy," he said to the gawky lad. "We're leaving."

Again the gang, uncertain of themselves now and wondering whether this was an arrest or a rescue, accepted Decker's authority and just watched uneasily as he took Benjy by the arm and led him outside. Benjy came along docilely.

They'd gone almost a block before the boy spoke up, with a slight, nervous stutter. "M-mister," he said, "they'll beat me up after this. They'll half kill me."

"What for?"

"For siding with a copper."

Decker made no comment. He kept on walking, turned into the alley, and headed for the empty lot where the cars were parked. He strode over to the green Chevy and unlocked the door. "Get in," he said.

Benjy hung back. "W-what—"

"Get in."

Nervously, Benjy obeyed, and Decker sat down next to him. "Why did you take it?" he asked.

Benjy gave Decker a pleading look.

Decker said, "You got poison ivy from handling the flowers back there, and your girl was wearing one of the stolen dresses. So I know you took the car."

"Louise had nothing to do with it. Are you going to arrest me?"

"Just tell me what happened."

"Please, I—"

"Better tell me, Benjy."

"That gang—I want them to lay off me." Benjy compressed his lips and stared at the dashboard. His fists clenched and unclenched as he tried to make up his mind.

"I took the car," he said suddenly. "I saw it there, nobody was around, and the key was in the ignition. If I drove it over here and let them have the dresses—all except one, that was for Louise—well, I thought they'd stop riding me. I never did anything like it before and I never will again, and I didn't keep anything, except that yellow dress for Louise."

"And after you brought the car here, what then?"

"The flowers were on the front seat. I moved them out of the way, and I went riding with Louise. When we got back, the gang was waiting and they said they wanted to see me this afternoon, at that bar. I think they wanted to sell the car and make sure I wouldn't talk about it or about the dresses or anything else. Then you came in and —well, that's all."

A cop is no social service worker. He's neither judge nor D.A., and he doesn't decide whom to arrest and whom to let go. A cop enforces the law and lets others wrestle with social and moral questions. Even a rookie like young Decker had known that much.

And therein lay the difference. Lieutenant Decker, 60 years old, listened, asked questions, and heard a long story of Benjy's background and struggles. When the boy had finished talking, Decker made his decision.

"Benjy," he said, "move over to the other side of town and never show up around here. If you do that, I'll see that you get a job. But stay away from this neighborhood."

"And Louise?"

"You'll have to work that out with her."

"And you're not going to arrest me?"

"What for?" Decker asked.

You get sentimental on your 60th birthday. You do things that make no sense and can kick back at you later. You violate rules and take a chance on nobody's finding out.

A few minutes later, when Decker and Benjy climbed out of the Chevy and the Lieutenant headed back for his own car, he didn't feel particularly young, but he had a heady feeling that exhilarated him. It lasted until he'd gone part way down the alley and saw an old man who was trying to crawl to the protection of a doorway; the going was rough.

Decker ran over, bent down, and supported him. "What happened?" Decker asked.

"They hurt me," the man said, gasping. "They took my money."

"Who?" Decker demanded.

"They came from behind. I couldn't see."

Decker called to Benjy. "Get to a phone and send for the police and an ambulance. Tell them Lieutenant Decker, signal eight, and tell them how to get here."

"Sure," Benjy said. He went off quickly.

Decker removed his coat, folded it for a pillow, and made the old man as comfortable as possible. "What's your name?" Decker asked.

"Slater. Walt Slater."

"How much money did they get?"

"Fifteen bucks. I just won it. Pool game. I—"

Decker noticed Slater's fingers, smeared with blue cue-chalk. "Take it easy," Decker said. "I'll take care of you."

He could see the spot where Slater must have been mugged, next to a break in the fence. You could hide behind the fence, step out, and grab a man from behind. The victim would never see who hit him, and if you beat him up the way this old guy had been beaten, he'd be in no condition to identify you when you ran off. For that matter, you didn't have to run—you could just walk.

Decker, scanning the ground and wondering if there'd been other muggings here, saw the cartridge. He picked it up. It was the same make and caliber as those from his own gun, and it was a fair guess that this was one of the five souvenirs he'd handed out a little while ago. One of the punks must have dropped it accidentally during the mugging.

The cartridge wasn't proof positive, and Duke and his gang would certainly alibi each other; but the cartridge was enough to make Decker sure in his own mind. He fingered the piece of ammunition for a moment, then he broke open his gun and inserted the cartridge. He slipped it in the chamber next to the one that was still filled, then he lined up the cylinders so that, if he pulled the trigger, he'd fire those two bullets and not just lick away on empties.

The job took him only a few seconds, then he put the gun back in its holster and returned to the old man. After about five minutes

Decker began to wonder why a patrol car hadn't arrived. At the least, he ought to be hearing the sound of a siren.

He looked to the far end of the alley and saw Duke come sauntering toward him. Three of the gang were following him and the other two brought up the rear, with Benjy in tow. They'd intercepted him, and now Duke had come to finish the episode in the bar. He'd lost face and he had to re-establish himself, regardless of risks. If a cop had made a monkey out of him, he had to make a monkey out of the cop.

Decker backed against the wall and waited for Duke to reach him. Duke stopped a few feet away, three of the gang next to him.

"Some trouble?" Duke asked sarcastically.

"Phone the police," Decker said crisply.

Duke's grin was insolent. "Who, me?"

"I gave you an order," Decker said.

Duke shrugged. "Did you beat him up?" he asked with a smirk.

Decker, staring, noticed the streak of blue chalk on Duke's cheek. Slater, in the struggle, must have clawed at Duke and left the mark. It could be analyzed and shown to match the chalk on Slater's fingers.

If Decker could grab Duke now and keep that smear of chalk intact, the kid was a dead duck; but if Decker waited, if the chalk rubbed off, the case would depend on Duke's alibi and probably collapse.

So how do you immobilize a cruel and ruthless punk and keep him from running away if you get help, or from assaulting you if the help doesn't come in time?

Decker took out his gun. "I gave you an order," he said again.

Duke laughed, and Decker raised his gun and fired a shot in the air. "Help—police!" he yelled.

Duke motioned to Joe and Pete, who were standing beside him. "Let's take him," he said. "He fired at me, I got a right to defend myself. You saw him fire, and it's his last bullet!"

"Stand back," Decker said quietly. "Stand back, or I'll shoot."

"With what?" Duke said. He laughed contemptuously. "Put that toy down. Copper, I could take you with my left arm in a sling and my right one tied up. Want to see?"

He lunged, and Decker fired his second bullet. Duke fell, clutched his leg, and lay there writhing.

"Anybody else?" Decker asked, pointing the gun.

The trio who'd been backing up Duke turned and started to run. The pair holding Benjy released him and followed.

When the patrol car came, in response to somebody who had heard Decker's shots, the two uniformed policemen found a mugging victim lying on the ground, and Decker holding Duke in his arms and, almost tenderly, mopping the sweat from his forehead before it trickled down to a bluish mark on his face.

Decker's first question was a strange one. "Got some scotch tape?" he asked. "I want to lift off some chalk."

It came off nicely, too.

After dinner that evening, Decker hung the picture. The rookie who stared at him from the frame had his points, but he could never have pulled off what Decker had done today. Too young. Too inexperienced.

CIRCLES IN THE SKY

by Daoma Winston

This is not the West of the cigarette advertisements. One day the sun will own the land again, and there'll be nothing to show for the sweat and the blood and the tears—and the prayers—of the generations who've lived and died there. Not even the memory of Death.

For three days Jim Conrad slumped on the up-ended keg and watched the buzzards make lazy black circles over the cottonwood trees. The dusty limbs tipping the red slope were the only green visible for miles around.

Over it, the buzzards swooped. It would take them a good while, he knew, to finish their pickings. They wouldn't leave until the bones were white and dry in the hot New Mexican sun.

A man could say it started a month ago when Kelsy came by and asked if Jim were going to town. Jim was surprised. He hadn't seen his brother for five weeks, even though they lived so close that only the slope and a bit of barbed wire separated them.

But Jim understood when Kelsy said, "I want to leave the car for a tune-up. Figured I'd ride back with you."

That was Kelsy. When he wanted something, he didn't mind asking for it. Otherwise he'd hide away for a month of Sundays.

And all the better, Jim thought. A man couldn't choose his kin. But that didn't mean he had to love Kelsy Conrad.

Still, he said, "You can ride back with me if you've a mind to."

"Meet at the post office?" Kelsy asked.

Jim thought it over. "No. Make it the Two Corners Bar. In case I got to wait for you, like I probably will."

"Two o'clock?"

"Three," Jim corrected. "If that's no good, get another ride."

Kelsy grinned like three o'clock was what he'd wanted all along, and Jim was tempted to change it back to two. But then he decided to let it go.

In town, Jim took his time picking up a sack of potatoes, sausage, and flour. He wouldn't hurry for Kelsy. Then, having killed an extra half an hour, as much as he had patience for, he dropped his groceries off at the car. It was so old and dusty it didn't have a color. The steering had gone bad, making it ride hard to the left, like a horse blind on one side.

It wasn't like in the old days when the Conrad spread had five strings of horses with the little "c" brand on them, and enough head of cattle to keep twelve hands busy throughout the whole year.

Jim and Kelsy had come too late. They got what was left by their mother. Two parcels of land good for nothing but soaking up a man's sweat, and burning the seed he put into it.

Even in that Kelsy somehow came out top dog. *His* land had two cottonwood trees and a thin stream.

But they'd both hit natural gas under the mean earth. Not enough, maybe, to set a man up in style. Yet the small check that came in every month was something to count on when you had to buy your grub.

Jim liked to tell himself that if the lease had come through in time, Nellie would have stayed on with him. That all she cared about was a roof over her head, and three squares a day. But he knew better, and he didn't blame her for pulling out. He heard the whine of the windmill the same as she did. In his bones, he, too, knew that one day the sun would own the land again. With nothing of the Conrads left to show for three generations' sweat.

Besides, he wasn't much of a bargain. Stoop-shouldered, and weathered dry. But Nellie hadn't been a whole lot either, with her three-colored hair and raw hands.

He met her in the diner. He was two years back from the war then, and still wearing the old fatigues and boots. He kidded with Nellie over three cups of coffee, and when she went off, he picked her up.

They drove around for a while, then parked. She was soft and warm as a lamb. He took her on the front seat without promises or love words. But afterwards, he asked, "You like it so much in that diner? Or you want to come stay with me. Not that I got anything. But if you should want to . . ."

She flipped a hand at him. "I got nothing myself. I don't mind. If you really want me to."

He didn't ask for her reasons, nor even wonder why she'd have him. The next afternoon, he stopped at her rooming house. She carried the one bag to the car and got in. Back at the place, she smiled wryly, looking at the windmill. "Looks like I'm back where I started from."

He pulled her down on the bed that had been his mother's. It was the only piece of the old furniture that he'd gotten. Kelsy hadn't wanted a broken bedstead. Later, Jim went out to do the chores.

Having Nellie with him hardly made a change in his life. Sometimes he would think of things to say to her, but by the time he got around to it, he felt foolish and held his tongue.

He considered her as a person only once. The day Kelsy came to borrow the grindstone. Nellie was washing clothes in a tub out back, and Kelsy kept staring at her. When he left, Jim heard him mutter to himself, "For crying out loud!"

Jim turned to look at Nellie. Her face was beet-red and her mouth was as tight as an Indian's. The liver-raw hands clenched tight around a pair of jeans. He had in mind to tell her to pay no attention to Kelsy. But he didn't, mostly because he couldn't think on Kelsy too long without getting mad.

One day when he got back from fence riding, Nellie was gone. He thought of looking for her but figured it wasn't worth the gas. If she'd had enough, he couldn't talk her into coming back. Saturday night, when he was in town to do some beering, Kelsy made sure Jim heard how Nellie had gotten a bus for Santa Fe.

Gradually the blankets she'd scrubbed went back to gray, and the kitchen became the mess she'd found it, and there was nothing to show she'd lived three months with Jim.

The only time he thought of her was when something reminded him that it was over a year since he'd had a woman.

As he loaded the groceries in the car, the *something* was the sight of two girls crossing the road to go into the Two Corners Bar. Jim dropped the flour sack on the floor and turned to watch.

They were a picture, all color and brightness in skin-snug frontier pants and shirts. The swagger, as nice a roll as a man ever whistled at, came from Western boots that hadn't yet been broken in, and probably never would be. The girls disappeared into the bar. To Jim, it seemed as if the sun had been turned off.

He hesitated. By now, Kelsy would be in there waiting for him. But to go in, walk past those pretty fillies . . . He shook his head. He'd feel like a fool.

Then he got mad. It was *his* town. If they didn't like it, they could have stayed at home. Wherever that was. Automatically, he checked the plates on the new Chevrolet they'd parked across the road. He stumbled on the curb, looking back at the familiar color. Funny. He'd never have guessed those girls as coming from Albuquerque.

Watching for them out of the corner of his eyes, at first he didn't see the hand Kelsy held up to him.

They sat in a booth, laughing between themselves, and staring around so boldly that Jim felt as if he and the few others there were on display, like prize bulls at the state fair.

The thought brought a flush to his cheeks, and he swung up to sit beside Kelsy, thinking all could see it, and read his mind. A good look at his brother made it worse. Kelsy had his stool half-turned, his eyes glued on the girls. Watching with the secret, anticipating stare Kelsy always had before he got something he'd set his heart on.

Jim was about to nudge him to quit being a fool when Kelsy spoke up. "You girls just passing through?" he asked.

Jim's body went still, ready to dive behind the bar for cover, or to hang one on Kelsy. Girls like that could cut a man to ribbons with a look. Jim wasn't sure which way he'd fall if pushed by that shame. He never found out. One of the girls answered, proving she wasn't Albuquerque-bred, car or not.

"Yes, we are," she said in the flat Eastern tone that didn't sound snotty coming from her. "Beautiful country you have here."

"It sure is," Kelsy agreed. He leaned toward them. "I hope you won't think I was forward asking if we could buy you girls a drink."

"If you want to," the same girl answered.

Kelsy got up, shoved at Jim with a bony elbow. In front of the booth, he introduced himself and Jim, and pulled off his black Stetson with a flourish.

Watching him, Jim grinned. That Kelsy, playing at being a big Texas rancher, drawling soft and slow, smooth back iron-gray hair.

Jim meant to do like Kelsy and raise his hat and shake hands. But the thinking slowed him until too late, so he jammed his fists in his pockets, said, "How do?" dryly and distantly, and sank in relief next to the girl who made room for him in the booth.

It turned out they were cousins, Leila and Mary Danner, from Philadelphia. Jim couldn't tell which was which until they'd traded sharp cracks back and forth. Then he knew the blonde one was Leila. The girl beside him was Mary.

He slid a quick look at her, and found she was watching him. She was a pretty little thing. Small enough so he could lean his chin on the top of her head. It would feel good. Her hair was black, and shiny as satin. She was filled out solid even for being so small, and her cheeks were smooth. Eastern cheeks. He looked down at his sandpaper hands.

"Your cousin, she do all the driving?" Kelsy asked Leila.

Jim watched her lips move in answer. They were bright and full. The paint was left off part of the lower one. Like she'd tried to hide the natural pout in it. Always, as she talked, her eyes moved, going back and forth over the table, then shifting to search the room.

Jim felt the old familiar heat stir in him. He glanced at Mary. That didn't help. Either one of them fit too good into a man's body.

He was glad when Shorty came up to get the order. The way his mind was going on both sides, he needed the drink bad. He needed it so bad he felt like smacking Kelsy for deliberating over what he wanted as if he wasn't going to end up with bourbon and branch water, no matter what.

Jim's judgment was right. He sat back, grinning again, when it was bourbon and water all around. He was doubly proud he'd hidden the double-take when the girls made it four a go. Maybe he was wrong, but they didn't look like bourbon girls to him.

He let the words wash over him without listening. It would add up to the same lie-swapping that always went on between men and women who met in a bar.

But then he found Mary looking at him, knew she'd asked a question. He glanced helplessly at Kelsy.

Kelsy grinned and took care of it. "No. Jim's got his own place. Down a ways from mine."

"What's it like?" Mary asked.

He understood that she was trying to draw him into the talking. But he didn't know how to help her out. Finally, he shrugged. "You seen plenty like it, driving on the road."

"All I saw was barbed wire and a lot of land."

He stared at the table edge where her soft white fingers played with a dead match. Shorty turned up with refills and saved Jim from having to answer her. It was the third round, and the table already looked like a hard night had been put in. Bits of paper napkin drowned in puddles of glass sweat, and dunes of cigarette ash. Shorty went at it all with a half-hearted swipe that landed much of the debris on Jim's thighs. He didn't mind. The jeans were already shot. Had been, now that he thought of it, for a month.

"What do you do, back in Philadelphia?" he asked finally.

They were secretaries. They'd saved for three years to take their trip West. It took a while for Jim to think that over. In the end, it didn't tell him anything. But he stopped listening when Kelsy's soft voice took over. If a couple of girls wanted to ride around New Mexico to see what was what, that seemed all right. A waste of time maybe, when you knew there wasn't anything to see. But nothing wrong with it either.

Kelsy was talking about the land. It caught Jim's attention because he sounded as if he meant it. Yet Jim knew he didn't. Kelsy was like a two-headed coin. Both sides looked good, but all together, it was nothing.

"A man gets to feel his own size out here. With nothing between him and the horizon." Kelsy shot the girls an embarrassed look. Like he was saying too much.

Jim agreed. Saying too much of nothing. A man got to feel his own size all right, listening for the creak of the windmill, and hanging around General Delivery for the gas company check. More than anything, he felt how he was nothing, and wouldn't ever be anything either.

But it went over big with the girls. Jim could see that. And in a minute, he got what Kelsy was driving at. For once he gave his brother whole-hearted admiration. Between the two of them even, they surely didn't have money to sit drinking in the bar the rest of the day. But Kelsy knew what he was about.

He was saying, "I'd like for you girls to see our places. If you want to know what living is, that's how to do it. It's a whole lot different from what the tourists get at the rodeos."

That Leila, Jim thought. She's got a wooden leg or two under those pants. All that bourbon and the lipstick isn't even smeared. He glanced sideways at Mary. And the little one, too. They were a pair all right.

He made himself listen to Kelsy although the sound of the smooth voice going on in that fake drawl made his hackles rise. Turned out it was worth it.

"Why don't we ride out and show you?" Kelsy demanded, being the hospitable Westerner wanting to share God's country.

Still, Jim was surprised when the girls agreed. He caught the look that passed between them. They were older, wiser, than they seemed. The look fit in with the bourbon. They knew how to take care of themselves. He wondered if they were sharp enough to outwit Kelsy, though. Jim hadn't ever seen anyone do that. It would be a treat.

Kelsy settled up with Shorty, and they started for Kelsy's place. Jim felt good, warmed through with liquor and the soft laughter of the girls. He was so relaxed he handled the wheel like reins, and gave the fool car her head. She didn't pull sideways near as much as usual. That bewildered him, but it was nice, too.

Mary had sat up front without his having to ask. She stared out the window at the fields. In back, Kelsy kept talking. Jim caught a couple of words about the Conrad spread, and stopped listening. He didn't want to hear any more about that. It was one thing for Kelsy, who'd managed to graduate from high school, to talk about that. But Jim knew better. The only Conrad spread there'd ever be again was when both the Conrad boys were spread in the earth.

Kelsy yelled, "Hey! Whoa a minute, Jim," and Jim slowed down, his mouth going dry. But the scare was for nothing. The fifth of whiskey hovered over the seat.

Mary grinned, "Don't you want refreshment?"

He dared a smile, keeping his lips closed to hide his broken front tooth. "Sure I do." He took a long pull at the bottle, and barely kept from choking. Then he passed the bottle to her.

Her hand went over the top of the neck as if she didn't notice that she was wiping it. Jim thought to tell her that hooch murdered germs. But he didn't. When she held the bottle to her mouth, her red lips puckered like they were kissing the cool glass. Her throat didn't move. He knew she was fooling. She hadn't swallowed any.

He was wondering about that when he paused at Kelsy's gate. Kelsy hopped out to open it, then rode the cracked running board up to the house.

Jim thought wryly that it was a good thing there wasn't a bronc around. Kelsy would sure of tried to break it, and broke his back instead.

The cottonwoods threw a nice blanket of shade over the house and yard. Jim got out of the car, and felt the breeze. It had been a long while since he'd been to Kelsy's. He looked at the place through the girls' eyes. Listening to their compliments. Not that sweet-talk ever paid for potatoes.

He followed them inside, stiff-legged as a colt under the rope for the first time. It was cooler, and neat as if a woman lived there. His mother's rocking chair was shining. Like when she used to sit in it. Jim wondered contemptuously how often Kelsy got down to polish it.

The girls made much over the old junk. Jim took another couple of pulls at the bottle that Kelsy offered him. He shoved back his hat, and leaned against the wall, waiting while Kelsy took the girls back to the chicken yard, and down to the stream.

Jim watched the lace curtains blow at the window. Even the dust was on Kelsy's side. It sifted against the outer walls, instead of creeping in. The dust knew Kelsy was boss, too. Jim wondered how it was that Kelsy should always be boss. It didn't seem right. Yet it was true. A man couldn't argue with what was true, could he?

When he led the girls in again, Kelsy was talking about Indian mustangs, and wagon trains. By God, Jim thought, in a minute he's going to fly the old cavalry flag. Maybe it was that. Maybe it was the drink. But Jim needed air.

He walked out as Kelsy was saying something about arrow heads. The sun was dropping fast. By dark it would be so cold a man would forget the sun's terrible heat, and wish for sunrise, and then be sorry and curse it when it came.

Jim swallowed hard on the sickness in his throat, and tried to smile as Kelsy and the girls came out, talking about hunting up flint stones.

"Not me," Jim said. "I want some supper. I'm not going any place but home."

Kelsy grinned at him. "You got something there, Jim. And the girls ought to see your place, too. What say you go on and get the potatoes started. The girls and me will go down to the flats."

"I start supper alone? Why should I?" Listening to the quietness that fell, Jim knew his power. The truth had a way of cutting deep.

Then Mary offered, "I could help you, Jim."

He still thought going to the flats was crazy. But Mary and him fixing supper, that would be nice. Maybe he could think of something to say to her.

"The only thing is," Mary was saying. "We have to get an early start tomorrow."

Kelsy said, "Now wait a minute, Mary. You getting skittish about us?" And Jim held his breath.

But she smiled. "I know I'm safe, Kelsy."

"You'll be in town plenty early," Kelsy assured her.

Jim grinned to himself. When he wanted to, Kelsy sure sounded convincing. But Jim would do the carrying through on Kelsy's promises. Just like he'd been doing ever since they were kids.

When he and Mary got out of the car at his place, he saw through her eyes again. She looked over the littered yard, across the dry, cracked fields, to the blackening silhouette of the windmill, and the hellfire of sunset behind it. She blinked at the shack, the paper-covered windows, the broken front step. "It's like Kelsy said," she whispered. "This country does something to you inside."

The sickness came back on Jim so full and fast that he had to stop and lean against the car. But finally he dragged the groceries out. If he thought of fixing supper, he'd keep his mind off the flicker he caught in the girl's eyes. Comparing Kelsy's place to his.

She offered to help him, but she didn't know how to do anything. She felt his resentment at that, and turned for a quick uncertain glance at him. So he pointed to the jug in the corner. "Get us drinks. We need something to go on."

He got the sausage rolled into patties, trying to hold back for himself to finish the week on. But saw what he made wasn't going to be enough, so he gave in and used it all. Peeled and sliced, the potatoes went into the big frying pan. He mixed up batter fast, and gave Mary a glass to cut the biscuits with. In no time, coffee was smelling up the untidy kitchen.

Kelsy and Leila still hadn't come back. All the while, Mary talked to Jim about Philadelphia, or asked him questions about where he'd been. He answered as well as he could, and felt proud at how he managed.

He poured himself another drink, though she wouldn't have one. Then he sat down in the rickety chair. "Nothing to do but wait."

She moved her head in agreement, went to look out the door. "It's beautiful."

He wanted to ask her what was, and why it was. To him it was just as natural as his own breathing. If it was beautiful, then he didn't know what beauty was.

Banked fury built up in him. She tried to act like she understood. But he was sure she didn't. Besides, he knew how different Kelsy's place was from his. There she'd exclaimed about the house and the furniture and the chicken yard. Here she brushed at the flour on her frontier pants, and went on about the sunset.

She went out for a last look, and when he followed her, she was staring at the windmill. It moaned on the night breeze just starting to come in, and he saw how she shivered.

"You cold?"

Though her arms hugged her small waist, he knew it wasn't that when she looked at him. Her eyes were scared. He put a hand on her shoulder. She didn't pull away from him. But after the first tingling touch, she just wasn't there.

He didn't let himself look down at his fingers the way he wanted to. He couldn't give himself away like that.

"It's lonesome," she said softly. "I don't know if I'd really like it."

His arms went around her, palms flat on her back, his elbows tight, so she was circled. He nuzzled her cheek and throat, trying to find her lips.

She didn't struggle, but her head kept turning, and he let his arms drop when he heard the sputter of Kelsy's old jeep. She started ahead of him, but swung around when Kelsy drove up to the house.

It was a sight then to see her face, the wide smile, the glowing unafraid eyes.

They were at the table. Leila showing off a pile of arrow heads. But Jim saw the secret separate look that passed between her and Mary. He opened his mouth to ask, "What?" But Kelsy cut in, "Butter?" stirring Jim's anger again.

"Sorghum," he grunted. He got the jug and while he was doing it, he caught up the whiskey.

Everybody fell to, Mary exclaiming how good the food tasted, Leila agreeing. Kelsy bragged on the cook Jim was. But Jim let the talk and laughter swirl past him, trying to keep it from pricking his skin.

The softness of Mary still touched him. He sneered to himself. The fright in her eyes was just to throw him off. One or the other of them he would have. Even if Kelsy took first choice. Jim promised himself that as he refilled his glass.

Kelsy offered him the dented coffee pot, but Jim shook his head. "That's for women and children," he muttered. "This," he tipped the jug, "is for men."

He promised himself. But some time during the meal, he knew he was wrong. Leila and Mary, they were different. You couldn't go by the bourbon, nor the taking up with strangers. They could be scared. But they never had sense enough to be afraid. Nothing would happen to them.

When Kelsy and the girls left the table a week's provisions had been eaten under the mask of laughter. Suddenly it was all over.

Jim sat, staring, while Leila picked up her bulging pocketbook, and Mary looked around the kitchen, eyes hidden to shutter her thoughts.

He lolled back in the chair, gazing stupidly at her and the others. Why, they'd as good as promised he'd have one of them. Kelsy and his drawl, the girls and their bright looks. The curves under the frontier shirts. The red lips that were like store-bought fruit.

Something in Mary's glance peeped knowingly at him.

"We'd better move," Leila said briskly.

But for a quiet minute, they watched him. When he pulled out cigarette paper, began, deliberately, to roll a cigarette, it was Kelsy that moved. He opened the door, herded the girls ahead of him.

From outside, Jim heard Mary, "What about him though?"

A blur of words, whispered but deep, answered. Kelsy. Jim snorted. Let Kelsy explain it. Let him try. Why, nobody could. Even Jim didn't know how to put it into words. They'd as good as promised, that's all. He meant to have his way. But he sucked on the cigarette.

There was a stumble on the broken step, a curse. Kelsy came in. "Driving us to town, Jim?"

"Hell, no. They can walk back, and you, too, for all I care." Jim rose. "Praise your house, and eat my food, and turn and run. What do I want to take them in for?"

"Now don't be like that, Jim."

"I'm like that," he snarled.

Kelsy stared at him, blue eyes flat. Then he agreed softly. "Yeah, you sure are."

"You're not taking them either," Jim offered.

"In the jeep, I will. She ran once today. She'll do it again." Kelsy grinned. "But come on, Jim. Forget it and drive the girls back and say goodbye and good trip."

Jim dragged on the cigarette, spat smoke at Kelsy. "You never had guts."

The door moved softly. Jim heard Mary again. "What's wrong, Kelsy? Isn't he coming?" Her voice going up on a strange note of regret.

"Let's go then." That was Leila. Jim could almost see her eyes moving back and forth, searching the horizon.

Kelsy rumbled something. Footsteps scuffed the dust. Jim grimaced as the jeep's motor protested but caught. Frantically he dug in his pockets, hunting for his keys. A moment later, he sprinted to his car. The mean red eye of the jeep bounced and wavered tantalizing him from the distance.

But at the gate, when Kelsy had to stop, Jim caught up. He leaped from the car, ready with his apology, with his goodbye. But Kelsy got in the way.

"Don't be a fool," Kelsy said loudly. "It's all right. Just sleep it off, Jim. I'll run the girls back."

The apology, the goodbye, was gone then. Jim yelled, "Just because you're not man enough to finish what you started . . ."

Mary peered out at him blankly. Now she was afraid. The very blankness of her face gave her away. She whispered, "What's wrong?" knowing, but pretending not to, because that was easier for everybody.

Leila looked away, across the dark fields toward town. It was as if Jim were not there, leaning at the window, yelling, "You promised . . ."

But Kelsy grabbed his arm, drew him off. The words came at Jim like the crest of a flash flood, drowning him. He didn't know what Kelsy was saying. It didn't matter. He was beaten again. Beaten, and put in the wrong. The girls would never know different. Mary would always be afraid.

When the jeep sped through the gate, Jim was standing at the edge of the road. "Don't come back," he yelled. "Don't never put your foot on my land again."

After a while, he drove back to the house, and threw himself on the grimy sheets. The jug was under his hand. Now and again, he took a long pull at it.

The month passed slowly. He spent the days looking across the fields, and listening to the occasional creak of the windmill. For hours, he stared toward the slope where the tips of Kelsy's cottonwoods showed.

He didn't see Kelsy. He figured that Kelsy drove to town in the jeep, and got somebody to ride his car out for him. It didn't matter.

Often Jim stood in the kitchen doorway. The dishes were on the table just as they'd been left the night Kelsy had taken the girls away, not even giving him a chance to say a polite goodbye.

Flour from the biscuit dough had blown across the floor. A little high-heeled boot print cut a pattern in it. He thought about the shape of the girls, their flower mouths juicy as southern fruit, their bright clothes.

He thought of Nellie, too. How she'd warmed him in the mornings, given him a reason for hurrying his chores. The way her raw hands had gone still on the jeans, listening to Kelsy, feeling his look on her.

One afternoon, Jim caught up his shotgun. He drove over to Kelsy's place. Kelsy was working in the yard under the cottonwood when Jim got out, his fingers wet, squeezing the stock of the gun.

Kelsy looked deep into him, said quietly, "How do, Jim?"

He raised the gun, sighting with slow pleasure. Then he fired.

Kelsy wavered and fell. The red of his blood, and the red of the earth was the same.

Jim climbed into his car and drove home. Whistling, he scrubbed the stale grease from the dishes and pans. He took a broom to the flour on the floor.

Now and again, he tipped the dirty jug of whiskey to his lips. Later, he went to stand outside in the dying afternoon. In three or four days, they'd find Kelsy. Both he and Jim had to sign papers at the bank come the middle of the week. If they didn't show up, somebody would come out.

He could run away. But in running a man lost his free and easy feeling. And where was there to go? He'd rather stay and think on how Kelsy's sweet smile was a liar, and the drawl false. How they'd praised Kelsy's house and Kelsy's trees, though they'd eaten Jim's own week's provisions and laughed on his drink.

Now Kelsy's empty blue eyes looked up at the empty blue sky, maybe still making promises he'd never keep. At the thought, Jim threw back his head and laughed.

When everything was ready, he sat down to wait.

After three days, he saw the first cloud of dust, and he nodded. Soon then.

He glanced at the shotgun that leaned against the shack. He'd unloaded it the day before, and carried the last cartridges down to the cold house and drowned them in the tiny pond. He wanted to be sure he didn't give trouble. It would be a shame to put up a fight at the last minute. A man's business ought to stay his own to the end.

The cloud sped away, back to town. Again, Jim nodded. Yes, soon indeed.

Forty minutes later, a new red cloud drifted over the road. It moved fast, and broke up on the limbs of the cottonwoods. In a few minutes, it gathered again, moved on to hover at the gate. Under it, the state police car rumbled up and stopped. The two troopers got out and hailed him.

He slumped against the wall, sucking on his cigarette as they walked up, hands uneasy at their holsters.

"Howdy, Jim," one of them offered. But both eyed the empty gun. "It's not loaded," Jim said. "You want it, take it."

The big dark one, his name was Bill Mayo, Jim suddenly remembered, caught up the gun and checked it.

"We got to take you in," the other, Cookie Rayburn, told Jim regretfully. "Kelsy mentioned in town there was bad blood between you two."

"No blood. Not kin blood," Jim told him absently.

He flipped his cigarette to the ground. Funny how he couldn't remember if they gassed a man or hung him. Hung him, Jim finally decided. It was cheapest that way. And only right, too. No need to waste money killing a man.

The three of them got in the scout car and Jim leaned back, eyes closed.

But at the slope, he turned to look.

The windmill was moving slowly on a hot breeze.

Over the tips of Kelsy's cottonwoods, the buzzards made easy black circles in the sky.